KNOCKOFF

KNOCKOFF

A NOVEL

by
Bill Levy

SILK PURSE PRESS

For reproduction rights,
please contact the publisher:

SILK PURSE PRESS
201 ANN STREET, 5TH FLOOR
HARTFORD, CT 06103
(203) 525-6341

Published in association with
Joel Friedlander, Publisher
P.O. Box 3330
San Rafael, CA 94912

This book is available at a special discount for bulk purchases.
Please contact the publisher for more information.

Design and typography by Joel Friedlander

First Edition
ISBN 0-936385-22-7

Library of Congress Catalog Card Number: 94-69936
Manufactured in the United States

To Jody, Michael and the little ones

Acknowledgements

The characters and events in *Knock-Off* are fictitious, but the information concerning domestic and international counterfeiting of domestic and international products and intellectual property is largely based on fact. Counterfeiting is an enormous business amounting to more than $200 billion a year worldwide. Despite the efforts of its corporate victims, a legion of attorneys specializing in copyright infringement and trademark counterfeiting, and law enforcement officers around the globe, this economic nightmare continues unchecked.

But the cost to consumers is much higher. Counterfeiting kills and maims. Automotive experts have no idea how many people are killed or injured as a result of bogus auto parts, but the figure is surely significant.

Assembling the facts has been an eight-year task and includes the help of dozens of people inside and outside of government. The author would like to thank officers of the U.S. Customs Service, the Federal Bureau of Investigation, the Justice Department and all others who provided information for their invaluable assistance. Thanks also goes to the International Anti-Counterfeiting Coalition in Washington, D.C., which continually provided updates as the global counterfeiting story continued to unfold.

I also owe a special thanks to Sandi Gelles-Cole of Pearl River, New York, who served as editorial consultant on *Knock-Off* and to Carole J. Nadeau and Nancy McCrone who provided constant encouragement and feedback.

KNOCKOFF

Prologue

As he had been doing frequently during the long drive, Dr. Robert Freeman allowed himself a brief moment to look up from the flashing ribbons of highway and see the two smiling faces in his rearview mirror. Then he glanced at his wife who was seated beside him in the front seat—a trim-figured thirty-year-old, and a physician like himself. How blessed they were, he thought, to have such beautiful children. And, with the recent promise of a shared career in medicine stretching in front of them, how happy they would be in their new home in Boston.

He glanced down at the speedometer of the Ford Taurus. The cruise control was fixed at sixty-five miles an hour, a shade over the speed limit on Interstate 90 near Erie, Pennsylvania, but allowable, he felt, given the sunny skies and perfect road conditions.

His left hand automatically flicked down the directional signal lever as he approached a red tractor-trailer transporting large coils of steel. He swung the vehicle into the left lane and, after easing past the fully-loaded flatbed, he flicked on the right-hand signal and turned the steering wheel, expecting a smooth response . . . and was stunned when nothing happened.

Then he realized to his sudden horror that the car, as if on its own blind initiative, was hurtling uncontrollably toward a long steel guardrail that framed the edge of the highway.

Freeman's first instinct was to step on the brakes, but he was stopped by the sight of the tractor-trailer bearing down on him from the rear. Better to take a chance with the guardrail and whatever was on the other side of it than risk being rammed from behind by a truck bearing tons of steel.

As the car slewed sideways across the graveled berm Freeman opened his mouth to shout a warning, but the words froze in his throat as he felt the large car slam through the guardrail. An instant later, with the screams of his wife and daughters filling his ears, he was aware that he was rising and then, almost leisurely, turning in the air . . .

It took only seconds for the white Taurus to tumble a half dozen times down the embankment and finally come to rest at the bottom of the slope, roof down, compressed to less than half of its original size.

State Patrolman Steve Stafford was traveling east on I-90, just south of Erie when the dispatch desk relayed a call from a motorist with a cellular telephone who had reported seeing a car suddenly, and quite unexpectedly, veer off the highway and crash.

"The guy said it's bad," the dispatcher said. "We're sending two EMS vehicles."

"I should be there in five minutes, maybe less," Stafford answered. He activated the siren and flashing roof lights and put the Ford cruiser into overdrive.

His stomach began to churn as it always did when he responded to an accident report. It was a reaction that embarrassed him. You would think, he often reprimanded himself, that a cop with your experience would get used to this kind of thing. But he had never gotten used to it. Nothing illustrated the swift, final moment that divided life from death more graphically than death at high speed on the highway. He had seen a lot during his twelve years on patrol . . . the twisted metal, the shattered bones, the broken dreams.

But nothing would prepare him for what he would find a few minutes later at the bottom of a grassy culvert just off the busy lanes of Interstate 90.

Chapter One

After more than twenty-five years of hard-earned experience (and he would proudly display his battle scars to anyone who asked), Barry Warner knew that the discount retailing business was nothing more nor less than a killing-field where the weapons of choice were chutzpah, nerves of steel and a silver tongue. He also knew one unimpeachable fact: The numbers never lied. Today the numbers were telling him there was virtually no way that Upscale, one of America's premier discount chains, could survive without a massive infusion of cash.

As he did every morning in the pre-dawn quiet of his sprawling home in Hunting Valley, Warner had risen, thrown on a white terrycloth robe, poured a glass of fresh squeezed orange juice and seated himself at an IBM PC in his cherry-paneled office. The PS2/Model 70 was networked to Upscale's computer network at corporate headquarters seven miles west in Beachwood. For Barry, this was, and forever would be, the moment of ultimate truth.

He had always been convinced, and it was a conviction that in a few short years had made him a very rich man, that the only way to beat the competition was to have the right merchandise in the right quantity at the right place at the right time.

And to do this he had to have more information than anyone else. Barry demanded and got access to the numbers and trends. What was selling and what was not. Which stores were performing well and which were not.

This morning's foray through a myriad of computer files had confirmed with unequivocal finality the chain's faltering cash position, its dwindling inventories and the enormous splash of red ink that covered Upscale's current balance sheet...and there wasn't a glint of good news anywhere on the computer's blue screen. He turned it off, took a long sip of chilled orange juice and wished there were more in it...three ounces of vodka. Then he quickly dismissed the thought as he recalled the amount of Absolut he'd consumed the previous evening while squiring his live-in, Jennifer Brooks, on a tour of his favorite watering holes.

Sometimes he wished he didn't have so much information. Life would certainly be simpler and there might even be some upside surprises. But, in the final analysis, it was information and the innovative use of computers, combined with a high level of merchandising and customer service, that had once made Upscale the envy of retailers around the world. Information had made Upscale a discounting powerhouse. It had given the hard-driving Warner the reputation as a ruthless retail genius and had put him on the covers of *Business Week, Fortune* and *Forbes*.

It had also provided him with enough money to engage in one of the midwest's most talked about bachelor lifestyles.

Warner walked out of the office and down the hall to the large bedroom where a network of electronic devices controlled everything from the tilt of the bed to the five-foot diagonal TV screen hidden behind sheer silk drapes. The sight of Jennifer Brooks lying nude on top of a red down comforter tugged at his groin. She had spurned his drunken advances hours earlier and he was angry. He was ready again.

But that could come later. He opened a closet door, pulled on a white Fila tennis outfit, laced on a pair of tennis shoes, grabbed two racquets from the top of a dresser and strode out into the sultry morning air.

Tony Hartley, Warner's tall, lanky and perennially suntanned employee, drinking companion, best friend and, when the occasion demanded, procurer of beautiful young women, was already on the meticulously groomed clay court, practicing the booming service that had once made him good enough to perform with marginal success on the professional tennis circuit.

"Hey, Barry, why so glum?" Hartley shouted when he saw the grim-faced Warner striding across the court.

"I'm in deep shit, buddy," Warner answered. "This morning's numbers are awful. We're headed for Chapter 11, or even worse, if I don't get some funding to shore up our cash flow position. Otherwise, Upscale will be out of cash in thirty days. And out of cash means out of business."

"This won't make you any happier," Hartley said as he walked over to a green wooden bench at mid-court and handed Warner a copy of the *Financial Chronicle* he had picked up that morning along with a cup of coffee at 7-Eleven. "It's all there on page one."

The banner headline at the top left little to the imagination.

Bankruptcy Court May Be Only Answer
for Retail Whiz Warner

CLEVELAND, OH—The once dynamic Upscale Discount Department Store Chain may be headed for Chapter 11 bankruptcy reorganization or, even worse, liquidation.

The Beachwood, Ohio-based firm, reacquired by founder Barry Warner in a leveraged buy-out 16 months ago, is months late in meeting its principal and interest payments. Banking sources say that lenders are prepared to pull the plug on the 52-year-old Warner, once the golden boy of retailing who built the chain into a nationwide powerhouse from a single store in a strip shopping center 25 years ago.

Upscale, which recently closed 150 unprofitable stores, still has 650 locations and revenues in excess of $3 billion a year. It reportedly lost more than $300 million in the first six months of the year.

A number of suppliers reportedly have stopped shipping merchandise on credit and, pending a bail-out of some kind, are demanding cash with shipments. The chain's cash position is said to be eroding quickly.

On the basis of chainwide losses of almost $3 million a day, Upscale's current bankroll of $100 million will be exhausted within less than a month.

Bankers in New York and Cleveland who put together financing for the LBO are said to be furious with Warner for refusing to ante-up a sizeable amount of his own fortune to help shore up the floundering chain.

Warner's personal wealth is reported to be in excess of $500 million. Banking sources say Warner's adamant about not risking any more of his private fortune.

Those same sources say that a showdown meeting is planned for a week from today, by which time Upscale's bank balance will have shrunk another $20 million. "If Warner doesn't come up with some of his own money to make this thing float, he's dead in the water," said one banker who declined to be identified.

Warner flung the newspaper into a green trash hamper. "This is a lot of bullshit. I don't know what we're going to do, but I know one thing for certain, I'm not putting one more dime of my own into this. Not one more dime! And if we can get those bankers to bail us out, you and I are going to be playing a lot more tennis."

There was the customary hiss of escaping air as Hartley ripped off the lid of a new can of tennis balls. He poured the three balls out of the can and handed them to Warner.

"Serve 'em up," Hartley said with a grin. "The life of a tennis bum wouldn't be all that hard to take."

Barry walked slowly across the court, musing to himself that there might be more than one way to skin a cat—that the banks might not be his only salvation.

Carole Nordstrom knew precisely the kind of information Barry Warner would want at the Upscale executive council meeting at ten o'clock that morning and she was determined to provide it. The one thing she did not need was one of Barry's tirades. It did not take much to get him started these days, given the state of the company.

It was seven in the morning and the Upscale executive vice president for merchandising had already been in front of her cream-colored computer terminal for an hour, preparing a report on the chain's out-of-stock condition and the growing list of vendors who were demanding cash with the order.

9

She was a lonely looking figure in the large square office, her shimmering blonde hair and beautiful round face, accented by a near-perfect nose, illuminated only by an antique lamp on the credenza and the blue glow from the computer screen. Her elegant French provincial desk was covered with dozens of pages churned from the HP laser printer and there was still more to come. The meeting with Barry and other top managers was still three hours away.

At thirty-eight, Carole Nordstrom was considered one of the top minds in retailing and the lavish $500,000-a-year salary offered her by Warner when he recruited her the year before was testimony to what he thought both of her ability and, she would quickly discover, her physical beauty.

But nothing in her sixteen-year career had prepared Carole for what was currently going on at Upscale, nor how to deal with her abusive boss.

Warner charmed her into joining Upscale with the assurance that her main task would be restructuring the look of Upscale's fashion merchandising image, and this was the final stroke that convinced her to leave Bloomingdale's where she had been a group merchandising vice president.

But the cordial professional relationship between Barry Warner and the soft-spoken native of Wisconsin had lasted only a few short months. It was not that Barry was unattractive. In fact, Carole thought his sharp angular features, perpetual tan and sand-colored hair, which dropped boyishly over his forehead, gave him a rugged outdoor look. She was also impressed by his superb physical condition. But what started out as convivial camaraderie was shattered by incessant sexual advances, which ended one evening over cocktails when she uncharacteristically and quite coldly told him to "fuck off." From that day on, their relationship had been icy and Carole sensed that Warner would dump her in a minute if he could generate sufficient reasons to abrogate her contract. She knew that in another era, when sexual harassment was not an issue, he would have fired her in a minute, cause or no cause, and let her sue to settle her contract.

Carole had decided months ago to make the best of the situation and do her job in a highly professional manner, maximize her creativity and work whatever hours it took to help the company survive. Right now, she was uncertain about Upscale's ability to weather the financial storm. The reports she was preparing for the mid-morning meeting underscored her feelings that the company might not even make it if Barry relented and put up a large portion of his personal wealth as the banks were demanding.

It took another ninety minutes for Carole to complete the confidential reports and collate them into sets for the meeting participants. She piled them neatly on the desk, locked the door to her office and headed home to shower and change for the rest of the day. On the way out she picked up a copy of the *Financial Chronicle*, which had been left outside the door. One look at the headline told her it would not be a pleasant meeting.

The sun was just breaking through the early morning clouds in New York when the stretched Cadillac limousine pulled in front of the four-story brownstone near the corner of East 57th Street and Third Avenue. The digital clock on the dashboard tripped to 8:00 A.M. as Ramon Cardiz opened the right door and stepped out.

"Stay in touch with Louise about the rest of the day," he said to the driver, gently closed the door and walked briskly to the double entrance doors to Commonwealth Investment Services. A security guard in a business suit, stationed just inside the lobby, activated the door release. Cardiz moved quickly inside and waved a greeting to the guard as he entered the elevator.

Cardiz slipped a green plastic card out of his lapel pocket and shoved it into a narrow slot on the elevator control panel. When he removed the card, the cab began to move upward, finally stopping on the fourth floor.

A red magnetic card gave him access to his office, a sprawling layout with six windows stretching along the 57th Street side. Cardiz flipped a switch near the door and the drapes covering the windows parted. A gush of light filled the office.

There was no mistaking Ramon Cardiz's Latin heritage. His face was handsomely sculptured and framed by coal black hair. His body was slender and tight, and to many he always looked as if he had walked off the pages of an advertisement in *GQ*. He removed the gray suit jacket, carefully hung it over the back of a hunter green armchair, and glanced at the paperwork on top of the large desk with mahogany legs and a brushed stainless steel top. Louise, his secretary, had already arranged the day's correspondence and files in neat little piles.

In the center of the desk she had placed the day's *Financial Chronicle*. The page-one story on Upscale had been carefully outlined with a red magic marker.

Cardiz moved behind the desk, picked up the paper and began reading it. Nothing in the story surprised him. Commonwealth's research department and investigators had already presented him with much of the same information the day before. The *Chronicle* article just confirmed the effectiveness of his intelligence-gathering organization.

"Louise, have Pedro come in here as soon as possible," Cardiz said softly into the intercom.

A moment later, Pedro Cardiz, almost a carbon copy of his older brother, stepped into the office and took a seat in front of the desk. Ramon handed him a copy of the *Chronicle*.

"I think we are ready to meet with Barry Warner," Ramon said.

Pedro silently digested the contents of the article, stood up and walked to the window.

"Most of this is old stuff," he said. "Our informants told us yesterday that the bankers will present Warner with an ultimatum: Come up with $150 to $200 million of his own money as a price for renegotiating the loans and some breathing room in operating capital, or lose control of the company. They'll put someone else in there to run it or take their chances in bankruptcy court.

"They are squeezing his nuts and I'm sure they are starting to hurt."

"We don't have a lot of time to waste, but I think we might just strike a mutually beneficial deal with Warner," Ramon said with a slight smile.

"I'll get in touch with Chip Holloway and have him arrange a meeting as soon as possible," Pedro said. "When we get Barry Warner in here, we'll find out what he has in mind."

Chapter Two

Shortly after ten in the morning Warner pulled his white Mercedes two-seat convertible into the parking lot at Upscale's spacious corporate headquarters off Enterprise Parkway in Beachwood. As always, the man who created this 200,000-square-foot architectural masterpiece was touched by the beauty of the surrounding trees reflecting on the mirrored surfaces of the five-sided building.

Warner had not spared a dime of the shareholders' money when the headquarters was built for $325 million when Upscale was still a publicly-held company. The 30 acres of wooded grounds that surrounded the main building included a large man-made lake, jogging paths, a picnic area and tennis courts. The interior decor of the building was a tasteful blend of pastel hues and natural cherry wood, accentuated by an array of paintings and sculpture—more than $10 million worth—donated by Warner from his own collection.

Upscale's executive committee was already in session in the third floor chairman's conference room when Warner, unsmiling as usual, entered from his office door, blue blazer in one hand and a copy of the *Financial Chronicle* in the other.

"I assume that you've all seen this," he said, tossing the newspaper onto the center of the oval-shaped conference table that stretched diagonally across the forty-foot room. "I'm sure this isn't the last of it, but we'll have to live with it."

He walked to the front of the room, pulled up the louvered doors covering a green blackboard and scratched the words "No Comment" across it. The screeching of the chalk sent a shiver up Carole Nordstrom's spine.

"You know that I've rarely been one to shy away from publicity, but from this point on we will not give aid and comfort to those who are trying to discredit us and make it difficult for us to regain our profitability. There will be *no* interviews with me or any executive of this company," he said, punctuating the words with short finger jabs. "Any employee divulging any information to any member of the media during this crisis is subject to instant dismissal—and that goes for everyone in this room. We'll make the same thing clear to all of our store executives during the noon satellite feed from our TV studio. Do I make myself clear?"

There was a mumbling of yes's from the table.

Warner nodded and took a seat at the head of the table.

"As to the status of our negotiations with the banks, my position has been and will continue to be that dipping into my own pocket again is an unacceptable condition, regardless of the consequences. As far as I'm concerned, the banks are going to make their decision on the basis of Upscale's track record over the years and whether they think this will be a viable business in the future."

He turned to Carole Nordstrom, seated next to him.

"What's happening with our suppliers? Who's shipping, who's not? Who wants payment up front?"

"It's all here, up to date as of eight-thirty this morning," she said quietly and handed him a copy of the report prepared earlier.

"I don't have time to read this shit," Warner responded with irritation and shoved the papers back to her. "Give me the high spots."

Carole looked coldly into his eyes and quickly ticked off a list of major suppliers who had demanded cash as a condition of shipment.

"I want to remember those bastards when we get out of this mess," Warner said. "They'll kiss my ass before they get another order." Then he turned to the man on his left. "What's the cash flow situation, Jeff?"

"We're continuing to bleed like hell," responded Jeff Weinstein, the company's chief financial officer. "The *Chronicle* was right. The losses are running about three million a day. And remember, we're not even making interest payments."

"And the traffic in the stores?"

"Traffic counts are up, but customers are just not buying the way they should," answered Walter Hood, whose department was responsible for day-to-day management of Upscale's stores. "Some of this is probably due to the fact we're short of merchandise in some of the basic categories because of our inability to get shipments."

Warner looked toward the end of the table.

"Mark?"

"It's not a pretty picture, Barry," said Mark Spencer, the company's president and chief operating officer.

Warner had heard enough, He stood up abruptly and pushed the chair out of the way. "Goddammit, we're going to lick this thing! If any of you have any operational problems direct them to Mark." And with that he turned and walked into his office, slamming the door behind.

A stack of telephone messages was on his desk. The top one, from Chip Holloway, who marketed himself as a "retail consultant," was marked urgent. Warner dialed the number himself and waited for what seemed like an eternity for his one-time employee to answer.

Holloway could tell Warner was irritated, but the retailer's mood changed when the moon-faced, gravily-voiced deal-maker told him he had made arrangements for a meeting that might solve Warner's immediate problem—finding the cash to save Upscale. If Warner's schedule could accommodate it, the meeting could be held in New York City as early as two the next afternoon.

"I thought you'd never get back to me," Warner said.

"Hey, man, these things take time," Holloway answered. "I'll get back to you with the details."

Warner thumbed through the remainder of the pink phone messages and pushed them aside. He brushed back a lock of sandy hair from his forehead and slumped back in the chair. He felt drained and knew he needed to reflect. "No more phone calls and no visitors until I let you know," he announced over the intercom to his secretary.

He swirled his chair around and stared out the window. The picture was serene. The careful landscaping and surrounding trees blocked out the vision of the Chagrin Boulevard commercial strip less than a half mile away, with its helter-skelter collection of office buildings, hotels, retail establishments, service stations and restaurants.

Warner suddenly experienced a mild sense of panic. For the first time in his life, his love affair with retailing was hanging in the balance and soon, very soon, might come to an unceremonious end. He had no doubt that the bastards from the banking consortium really had the power to take most of this away from him and render him a figurehead or worse.

Retailing was all he knew from the time he was ten and started working as a stockboy in Warberger's, his father's dry goods store on Buckeye Road in Cleveland. The store was in the heart of a Hungarian neighborhood and the merchandise stocked by Sam Warberger was anything but high fashion. The customers were like family and his father constantly exhorted him to offer them service, quality merchandise, fair prices and credit, if they needed it. His father trusted everyone. But as economic conditions in the neighborhood began to change and Sam was stiffed by a growing number of customers, Barry began to learn it was wiser to trust no one.

He was an only child and Sam and Rebecca Warberger doted over him. Whatever Barry wanted, many of his peers would agree, Barry got. The end result was a selfish, abusive young man who pouted when he didn't get his way.

Barry loved the old store, but as he grew into his teens he knew it was not where his career path was headed.

By the time he went off to college at the University of Pennsylvania the neighborhood was changing and not in a good way. His Dad could hang in there, but not him. Always a brilliant student, he majored in finance, with a minor in computer science, then went to Harvard Graduate School of Business and received his MBA. He was twenty-five years old and ready to make his mark. The first thing he did was change his name from Warberger to Warner.

It was now 1965 and Barry became intrigued by the quick growth of discount mass market retailing and sensed that it presented great future possibilities. With his Penn and Harvard education, he had little trouble landing a spot with Harold's, a twenty-five-store Ohio discount chain headquartered in Columbus. Harold Cohen, founder and president, instantly recognized Barry's abilities and drive. The young man's arrogance reminded Cohen of his own. Within two years, Warner was vice president of operations and ready to strike out on his own.

The two years at Harold's and countless off-work hours scouting other discounters like K-Mart, Zayre's and others had convinced Barry that the key to creating a truly dynamic discount chain was to mate the old concept of department store elegance and service with the fast-paced world of discount merchandising. Shopping in most discount stores, he sensed, was like attending a giant garage sale. His dream discount store would have the pizazz of the cosmetic and perfume department of Bloomingdale's or Saks Fifth Avenue in New York. It would have snob appeal, sell only brand name products and very fashionable apparel. Prices would be competitive, but the accent would be on service.

The name Upscale said it all. He borrowed $50,000 from Sam Warberger and his business plan was compelling enough to convince Euclid National Bank to lend him $250,000. He had no partners.

The first Upscale store opened in 1967 in a strip shopping center in Shaker Heights, about two miles from where the corporate headquarters is now located. Barry personally interviewed every job candidate. He wanted personality, commitment and a genuine desire to please customers. He took teams of interior designers to the finest retail establishments in the country and told them to create a look that was different from anything developed in discount retailing. They did.

While his first store was a smash hit, the start-up was not easy. Many manufacturers were wary of dealing with the brash upstart, especially since they did not know the extent of his pricing policies. Some, including major fragrance, cos-

metic, electronic and watch manufacturers, refused to sell
without assurances he would adhere to their strict pricing
codes. He would not and devised an alternative strategy for
getting the merchandise he wanted on the shelves. Barry
persuaded retailers in other parts of the country to order
excess quantities of the products refused him by the manufacturers and to divert those shipments to him. The other
retailers quickly agreed because Barry paid them a premium
for the "excess" merchandise.

A few minutes after opening the first store, Chip
Holloway, a full-time salesman for a major jeans manufacturer, approached him with the opportunity to purchase gray
market goods designed for sale in Europe at very favorable
prices, including some products that were being denied him
in the United States. Barry jumped at the chance and
Holloway, a short, curly-haired dynamo with boundless
energy, delivered, and the goods started flowing from overseas.

Impressed with Holloway's aggressiveness and ability to
follow through, Warner offered him a full-time job as director of merchandising and sent him first across the country
and then around the world to line up merchandising deals.

It wasn't long before the major vendors, sensing that
Warner would succeed with or without them, acquiesced and
worked out terms to supply Upscale.

The rest was history. Getting money was no problem.
He had five stores in the Cleveland area by the end of the
second year, twenty-five in four years. Developers stood in
line to offer sites and construct buildings. He played one
against the other, deftly extracting the last set of rental con-
cessions from each. No one really enjoyed doing business
with him, but the developers and the suppliers who had once

shunned him sensed that Warner had a winning hand and they wanted to share it.

Chip Holloway and Warner parted company mutually at the end of the third year. The job was too restrictive for a wheeler-dealer like Holloway. Barry said he needed someone with a deeper sense of retail merchandising. For a while, Holloway continued to comb the globe for off-beat merchandise deals that would benefit his friend and other retailers.

Warner took Upscale public in the spring of 1971. The first offering of two million shares at $15 each on the over-the-counter market gave the public a 25 percent piece of the action and made him a millionaire many times over at the age of thirty-one. As the chain expanded at the rate of twenty-five to thirty stores a year and produced a string of record profits at margins unparalleled in discount retailing, the stock split six times.

Barry systematically sold off major segments of his holdings reducing the number of shares he held, but with fanatical Wall Street attention to the stock it kept climbing in value and Warner's net worth soared toward the half-billion-dollar mark, spurring a jet-setting lifestyle that often produced gossip column material.

Life as chief executive officer of a publicly-held company eventually lost its appeal. Divulging financial information to others rode against the grain of his untrusting nature. He grew tired of the endless rounds of meetings with security analysts, of timely reporting and, mostly, of having lost the iron-handed control that came when you owned more than 50 percent of the stock.

By this time Barry owned only about seven percent of Upscale. And fortune smiled again on the brash entrepreneur who always seemed to be in the right place at the right time.

Junk bond mania was suddenly running rampant across the country and the stock market soared on every takeover and buyout rumor. Warner and a group of senior managers decided to jump into the water, too. They cashed in while Upscale was ridden to an all-time high of $65 a share and put very little back into capital required to initiate the LBO.

Warner put up $250 million of the $450 million he received for the remainder of his Upscale stock. Other senior managers and directors chipped in another $20 million. The banks and investment bankers put up a billion and a half in loans and high-risk junk bonds were sold to account for the rest of the $3 billion price tag. One series of bonds for $300 million was the zero coupon variety with a 15 percent interest rate triggered at the end of two years. For the first few months everyone, including the bankers and bondholders, thought it was a marvelous deal. But even more marvelous, Barry was back in control, without having to worry about thousands of individual and institutional investors and accounting to them.

"It's time to go on the air, Mr. Warner."

The squawking sound of his secretary's voice through the intercom shattered Warner's tranquil mood. He rose from the chair and walked slowly to his private bathroom. He was surprised how tired he looked. Where had the years gone? He dampened his face with a rust-colored washcloth, combed his hair and applied some spray from an aerosol can, then straightened his striped tie.

Back at the desk, he slipped on a navy blue blazer with solid gold buttons and walked down the stairs to Upscale's multi-million-dollar TV studio and video production center.

He settled onto a couch next to Mark Spencer, who was scanning notes for the presentation he would make after Warner's customary opening remarks to employees across the country.

"Thirty seconds to air time, Mr. Warner," the director shouted.

"I'm ready."

One of two cameras zoomed to a tight close-up.

Warner's personality changed instantly once he saw the red light illuminated on the camera. Gone was the scowling face that had set the mood for the meeting earlier that morning. He was now Barry Warner, the evangelist, the motivator. While many of his employees despised his often devious and sometimes rough-house management style, they put up with it for one major reason—Upscale paid better and had more substantial benefits than any other company in retailing.

"Good morning my fellow associates," Warner said with a smile. "As you all know, we're facing some tough times these days, and things may actually get worse before they get better. Most of you who have been with me through this wonderful odyssey of more than two decades know that we've had very few setbacks to mar our course. We've done things that no retailing organization has ever accomplished, and you are responsible for these marvelous achievements.

"I just ask that during the coming days you redouble your support and dedication to the principles of Upscale retailing. I firmly believe we will find a solution to the current financial crisis. I just want you to know I'm proud of each and every one of you. We still have the best team in all of retailing, and we'll prove it once again."

As his face faded from the monitor and was replaced by that of Mark Spencer, Warner slipped off the couch and left the studio, wondering if, as the retailing whiz of yesterday, he was really going to be able to pull off one last deal—a deal that would both save the company and keep it in his hands.

Carole Nordstrom flicked off her office TV monitor in the middle of Mark Spencer's opening remarks, which focused on the prohibition of talking with the media. Her first impression of Warner's speech was that it had a hollow ring. Barry's presentation was missing the charismatic fire that usually characterized his Upscale pep talks. Maybe the masses of employees were convinced that Barry could pull success out of his bag of tricks once again, but given her inside knowledge, Carole was beginning to have more doubts than ever before.

As she grabbed her bag and left for lunch, the thought struck her that she might have to start looking around for a bag of tricks of her own.

Chapter Three

A half dozen cars and a large red flatbed tractor-trailer were parked on the edge of Interstate 90 when Patrolman Steve Stafford arrived at the scene of the accident. He looked at his watch and saw that it was exactly noon. Through the windshield of the cruiser he could see a long arcing set of skid marks that ended near the edge of the road. A gaping hole had been torn through a wide strip of guardrail. Broken glass and debris from the vehicle left a track down the grass embankment to a white four-door car that lay upside down in a culvert about 100 feet down from the roadway.

Stafford could hear the sirens of the approaching EMS vehicles. He got out of his cruiser and edged his way down the embankment that led to the culvert.

Thank God there's no fire, he thought as he approached the passenger side of the badly mangled Ford. He guessed it was a 1988 or '89 model. The roof had compressed into the car's chassis. The front wheel on the passenger side tilted limply to the right.

Stafford dropped to his knees, peered inside and saw the crushed remains of a man and woman in the front seat and two children in the back. There wasn't a sound. He didn't expect one. He turned away, suppressing an overwhelming desire to vomit.

Then he got to his feet and walked around to the other side of the car and kneeled again. This time he saw a pair of tiny hands clutching a small doll.

Two members of an EMS crew were running down the embankment toward him. They could see the anguish on his face.

"Bad, huh?" one of them said.

"The worst," Stafford answered. "Looks as if four members of a family were crushed in the car. You're going to need help. I'll get it."

Stafford walked up the embankment and saw traffic creeping past the scene. Twenty or more cars were now parked on the narrow edge of the road, and a crowd was beginning to gather. Sliding into his cruiser, he picked up the microphone and gave dispatch a brief description of the situation. "We'll need some additional help with traffic control," he said. "We're going to be here for a while."

The other EMS crew had arrived and four paramedics wearing pale blue uniforms were working around the car. Stafford knew there was nothing he could do there for the moment. He grabbed a clipboard from the seat and looked up as a muscular man wearing tight-fitting jeans and a navy blue T-shirt approached the car.

"I saw it all happen," the man said.

"Can I have your name, sir?"

"Bryan Burns from Charleston, West Virginia."

"Tell me what happened."

The man formed his eyebrows in an expression of concentrated concern.

"I was rolling down the highway in that rig over there when the white Taurus passed me. It was going pretty fast, maybe seventy, seventy-five. When he got ahead of me, the driver signaled he was cutting back into my lane. All of a sudden the car veered to the right, started skidding, went airborne. It flipped over several times and skidded on its roof into the position where it is now. I can't be sure, but it looked as if there was a young couple in the front seat and two kids in the back. I can't believe anyone survived."

"They didn't."

Stafford asked Burns to remain on the scene and started back down the embankment when an EMS crewman caught up with him.

"We couldn't get a pulse on any of them, patrolman. They're all gone."

Stafford was not surprised.

"Any idea what caused it?"

"A witness said the car simply careened out of control. No other car involved. A bright sunny day, no rain, no snow, a couple of terrifying seconds and a family of four is wiped out. You wonder how the father felt trying to control the car, how scared the kids must have been."

"Yeah," the EMS man agreed.

Stafford went back down to the Taurus, kneeled down behind it and jotted down the number from the Michigan license plate. Somebody would have to notify the family back in Michigan, if there was any left to notify. He hoped it wouldn't be him. Being the bearer of terrible news was the part of his job he hated most.

A fire company from a neighboring town and a large green wrecker bearing the sign "Smith's Service and Towing" had arrived. The time had arrived to begin the grisly task of removing the bodies. Stafford had no stomach for watching the bodies being extricated from the wreckage. "Get pictures from every angle," he instructed a trooper who had just arrived with two Nikon cameras hanging from straps around his neck. Stafford walked back to the cruiser and radioed the license plate information to dispatch. Thanks to computer technology and a nationwide license plate data base, the name of the car's owner would be known in minutes.

It was two-thirty in the afternoon by the time the last of the bodies had been removed from the wreckage. All of the victims were pronounced dead at the scene.

Stafford and five other troopers blocked I-90 while the wrecker backed through the gaping break in the guardrail and down the embankment. A thick cable was attached to the back axle of the Taurus and amid the sounds of whirring winches, the car was dragged out of the culvert. When it was on level ground, a flatbed truck with a crane and winch pulled the car, still upside down, onto the truck and secured it.

Stafford walked to the open window of the truck cab. "Take it to your place," he said to the driver. "Tell Smitty I'll be over early in the morning. We'll go over the car together."

Stafford returned to the cruiser and radioed dispatch that he was on his way back to the post. He was the last to leave the scene. As he pulled out onto the I-90 pavement, the highway patrolman was oblivious to his surroundings. It was impossible for him to get his mind off the two small hands clutching the bloody doll.

Chapter Four

Pedro Cardiz was eating a grilled ham and cheese sandwich at his black oriental desk when Chip Holloway called to say Barry Warner was eager to meet at Commonwealth the next day at two o'clock. Holloway told Cardiz that Warner would be flying into New York on his own jet and would be staying at his Fifth Avenue condo. His own driver could bring him to Commonwealth.

"No, we'll send Ernesto to pick him up at 1:45," he insisted. "What's the address?"

"Nine sixty-five Fifth Avenue."

Cardiz told Holloway that to facilitate the meeting, Commonwealth needed financial and operational information sent directly from Upscale's computer network to Commonwealth's mainframe by the end of the day.

"With Upscale's reputation for data processing and communications, this should not be difficult," he said, then rattled off a laundry list that included a current financial statement, a list of critical payables, and an assessment of short- and long-term cash requirements to meet bank and junk bond commitments and to return store inventory to pre-crisis levels.

"We'd also like a list of your stores and sales levels for each month during the previous fiscal year. So that we can assess the company's merchandising mix, we need a complete list of SKU's handled by the chain."

SKU was an acronym for Stock Keeping Unit, the key inventory measure in retailing. Every single item handled in a store had an SKU. For instance, a navy blue ladies blouse in a size six was an SKU. The same blouse in a size eight was another. A typical Upscale store carried in excess of 100,000 SKU's.

"Holy shit," Holloway barked after hearing the list. "Warner will think you're buying the chain."

"It may come to that," Pedro said. Ever since Holloway's initial call, Commonwealth had assembled a massive database on Upscale, but the information provided by Warner would be used to confirm its own information and determine what level of product penetration Commonwealth could obtain in the retailer's stores.

The Cardiz brothers were tough, talented and a thoroughly ruthless pair submerged in almost total anonymity. Unbeknown to Barry Warner and the rest of corporate America, Ramon and Pedro were among the world's richest and most powerful businessmen.

Ramon, forty-two, and Pedro, forty, were the youngest sons of Raul Cardiz, master of one of Colombia's most powerful drug cartels. Both were born and raised in Cali, but received their higher education in America. Raul Cardiz considered the drug business the same as any other corporate endeavor and wanted the two younger sons to have the best business education possible. Both went to the University of Michigan. Ramon got a law degree at Yale, and Pedro an

MBA in finance from Pennsylvania's Wharton School of Finance. Both decided to stay in the United States.

Raul deliberately kept them out of the mainstream of the drug trafficking business. He felt they could be more valuable finding outlets for the hundreds of millions of dollars being generated annually by the sale of crack and cocaine around the world.

In the beginning, Commonwealth Investment Services was the family conduit for acquiring respectable business enterprises and real estate. Using carefully crafted corporate structures and a web of front organizations, Ramon and Pedro swiftly acquired real estate in New York, Chicago, Los Angeles, Hong Kong, London and Paris.

With their penchant for remaining riveted behind the scene, neither ever attended the closing of one of their real estate deals. As a result, they did a good job of hiding the source of funding.

In the early 1980s, they branched out into manufacturing and quickly acquired a dozen companies in widely diverse fields—including greeting cards, clothing, auto parts, crystal and pottery.

Pedro and Ramon worked well as a team. Ramon, the lawyer, was soft spoken, scholarly and seemed almost gentle. But beneath was a toughness that only occasionally penetrated the surface. On the other hand, Pedro was more vocal and animated, and he possessed a sometimes hot South American temper. His walk was almost like a strut. A few of his close friends called him "The Peacock."

Their management team was small, but talented and loyal. Most were Colombians who wanted to get away from the terror induced by the drug business in their country. All knew where the source money came from for the relatively new venture that would make cutting a deal with Barry Warner and Upscale their biggest coup ever.

The scope of the business empire created by the Cardiz brothers and its capabilities would surprise even the brilliant Barry Warner.

Chapter Five

Carole Nordstrom slammed down the beige receiver in disgust. "I just can't believe this stuff," she said to Missy Schwartz, her staff assistant. "I spend half of my time begging and cajoling suppliers to ship merchandise on credit, when even I don't know whether they'll ever get paid. To be honest with you, I feel a bit like a whore."

She could still hear Billy Ray Sargent's southern drenched words. "Aa'm sorri Carole. But uunless we geht summ fuuunds transfurred, we cain't ship thoose jeans. And that goes for awders in the futah."

Sargent was president of Carolina Textiles of Autryville, North Carolina, which supplied most of Upscale's private label jeans and Levi Dockers look-alikes.

"We give that hillbilly tens of millions of dollars a year in business and he's playing hardball with us," Nordstrom said coolly. "What ever became of loyalty?"

"But you can't really blame him," Missy responded. "Given all the bad press we've had and the fact that we aren't paying our bills on time, if at all, would you sell to us on credit?"

"I guess you're right. I'm just frustrated. This was the tenth call this afternoon, and I don't have any answers. Everyone wants to know when they are going to get paid for their past-due invoices, for the merchandise we want shipped today. What really galls me is that I'm not getting any help from Barry on this. He just says 'Handle it.' "

"I guess we just have to hope Barry pulls this off," Missy sighed. "Not only for our sakes, but for his own. He has a helluva lot more at stake than we do."

Nordstrom leaned back in her hunter green leather chair, tugged at the back of her hair and looked at her watch. It was 4:30. "I'm out of here for today. Maybe tomorrow will be better."

"Let's hope so."

Carole pulled a stack of reports from the large semicircular desk, stuffed them into a brown Gucci attaché case and walked out the door. "If anybody's looking for me, tell them I went home sick, which is really not far from the truth."

The ride to The Village, an expensive condominium development about three miles away, took about seven minutes, one of the reasons she had selected it when moving from Manhattan nearly two years ago.

The security guard saw her white BMW convertible and opened the orange gate. She waved to him, drove another quarter mile past a man-made lake and tennis courts and pulled into the driveway of her two-story townhouse condo.

Nippon and Claiborne, the two Siamese cats named for her favorite designers, were at Nordstrom's feet as she walked in the door and turned off the security system.

"Hi, guys, I'm home for the day."

Nippon rubbed up against her leg and let out a short squeaking sound.

"I'll bet you guys are hungry." They were always hungry, she thought.

She pulled out two small cans of fancy cat food, ripped off the pull-tab lids and dumped the contents into a green plastic bowl. She chopped the food into small hunks with one of the lids, then placed the bowl on the white ceramic tile floor.

"That ought to hold you until breakfast," she said and headed for the bedroom.

The red message light was blinking on the phone answering machine located on a cluttered white night stand next to the bed. The digital display indicated one message. She pushed the "play" button, sat down on the edge of the bed and waited for the tape to rewind and play.

The deep voice was unmistakable. "Hi, Carole. This is Mitch Rudolph in New York. I have some important news for you. Please call me at 1-800-1RETAIL as soon as you get this message—day or night."

Nordstrom looked at her watch. It was a few minutes after five. She dialed the number. Mitch Rudolph answered the private line on the first ring.

"Mitch. It's Carole Nordstrom returning your call."

"I didn't expect to hear from you until later this evening. What are you doing home so early?"

"If you had to talk with angry creditors all day, then try to convince them to ship more merchandise, you'd get home early, too."

"I've been following some of it in the newspapers. Is it that bad?"

"It's the most frustrating situation I've ever had to deal with."

"How's Warner handling it?"

35

"He's running around the country trying to raise money to save the company before next week's meeting with the bankers. He still refuses to budge on the issue of putting more of his own money into Upscale. I don't have to tell you there are a lot of nervous people around Upscale. Say, what was the reason for your call?"

"We need to talk," Mitch said seriously. "And quickly, too. What are you doing for dinner tomorrow night?"

"I'm not planning to be in New York, if that's what you mean. Otherwise, I have no plans."

"No. I'm talking about dinner in Cleveland."

"You're on. But why all the urgency?"

"It's a unique situation and it bears some explanation... but not on the telephone. I'll probably have the client with me, too. You'll understand when we meet. I'll see you in the lobby of the Ritz Carlton at six. Maybe after all these years, we'll finally get something going."

Chapter Six

Bruce Smith was seated be-
hind a huge oak desk sorting through a stack of mail when
State Patrolman Steve Stafford arrived at Smith's Service and
Towing a little past 7:30 in the morning. The size of the office
and the desk befit the figure behind it. Smith was an enormous, barrel-chested man. His vital dimensions were 6'5",
285 pounds.

The contrast between Smith and the ramrod straight
Stafford was drastic.

What a mess, Stafford thought to himself as he quickly
surveyed numerous piles of paperwork strewn across the
desk and the oak credenza behind it.

"You ever clean up this place?" Stafford asked with a
wry smile as he reached to shake Smith's hand.

"Not very often. If I did, guys like you wouldn't have an
opportunity to ask about the mess," Smith answered dryly.
He was the president and sole owner of the company, an
impressive spread located on Route 19, about three and a half
miles north of Waterford and about a dozen miles from the
center of Erie. The 35,000-square-foot L-shaped building

included a wholesale and retail parts operation and eight service bays in the rear. The whole spread occupied five acres.

"Speaking of a mess, you look awfully tired, my friend," Smith said seriously.

"Didn't sleep a minute last night. I just kept thinking about that poor family in the Taurus your guys brought in yesterday afternoon. It was so sudden. No reason for it. Boom. It's over in a few seconds."

"Life sucks."

"Both the father and mother were physicians. Both had finished residencies in Ann Arbor, Michigan, and were on their way to new jobs in New York. They had planned to visit his brother at Cornell University on the way to the Big Apple."

"Quite a waste, I'd say. That ought to bring the lawyers out in full force if there's any liability involved. I just got back in town last night. How did it happen?"

"Coroner says there were no drugs or alcohol involved. It was a beautiful dry day. The doctor just lost control of the car, it did a couple of three-sixties and wound up in a ditch off I-90, just east of Route 19. Four fatalities just like that."

"I haven't had a chance to take a close look at the wreck. It's still on the flatbed in the yard. Let's grab a cup of coffee and take a look."

Few mechanics in western Pennsylvania knew more about cars and trucks than Bruce Smith. Over the years, his expertise had earned him thousands of dollars as an expert witness in liability lawsuits. He worked both sides of the street. Whoever got to him first was the beneficiary of his usual articulate testimony.

Smith and Stafford climbed onto the flatbed parked in the back lot. There was barely enough room for them to navigate around the edge.

"Watch yourself or we'll have another casualty," Smith warned.

"It will be a lot noisier if you fall off this thing," Stafford replied, swiping a look into the blood-caked interior of the car.

"Car ran off the right side of the road on the passenger side, right?" the burly Smith asked as he edged his way around to the left side of the upside down vehicle.

"That's right."

Smith took a cursory look at the suspension and steering mechanism. "This is a no brainer. Look at the tie rod end on the passenger side. It came cleanly out of the socket. How can you steer a car when the rod connecting the front wheel to the steering mechanism is shot?"

"Obviously you can't."

Smith edged in closer and looked at the two pieces, a short arm about eight to nine inches long and the ball that fit into a crimped joint. "This part looks almost new. I'd say it was installed within the last week or so. Look over here. The same mechanism on the driver's side is grimy and warn looking. Probably original equipment."

"If it's new how could it fail?" Stafford wanted to know.

"That's the sixty-four-thousand-dollar question about a part that retails for less than forty bucks. About the only thing that seems possible is that the car ran over a piece of damaged tire on the road and that it got up in there and slammed against the tie rod end, causing the crimp to give way. I've seen that happen on ends that have been in service for thousands of miles. But a new part? Never."

"Maybe it was just a faulty part that failed under stress. Witnesses said the car was traveling sixty-five, seventy miles an hour, maybe more."

"These parts are made to endure, my friend. They just don't fail very often."

"Once in a case like this is quite enough, I'd say."

"Jot this number down on your clipboard," Smith said in a tone that made it sound less like a request than an order. He put the beam from a long black flashlight on the number etched into the longest part of the tie rod end and called out the number. Then he rubbed his hand along the finish of the part. "This just doesn't feel right."

Stafford and Smith jumped down from the flatbed and returned to the office. Smith poured a cup of coffee from a white Braun coffeemaker in a back corner of the room. Stafford declined the offer of another cup.

"Bring that number with you and let's see if we can find who made it. From the numbers and the letters I don't think it's a Ford Motorcraft replacement part," Smith said as he led the patrolman into the busy retail parts section of the Smith operation.

Smith hastily took out a series of book catalogs from major replacement parts suppliers, including TRW, Moog, McQuay-Norris and Strong-Anderson. Each part, he explained to Stafford, had the same letter and numerical designation. Two or three letters at the end of the number indicated the name of the manufacturer.

"Here it is," Smith said with a touch of excitement in his voice. "ES2912SA. That's a Strong-Anderson number. We carry their line, and I'm sure we have that part in stock."

They walked between two long rows of metal shelving stacked about six feet high. Smith stopped about three feet from the end, looked up at the fourth shelf and picked out a green box with yellow lettering.

40

"Here's the critter," he said, taking the part out of the box. "I'm sure you've seen one of these things up close and personal before."

"I know what a tie rod end looks like," the patrolman said with a touch of annoyance in his voice.

Smith led the trooper out into the yard again and back up on the edge of the flatbed. Once again, the two navigated their way around the edge to the passenger side of the Taurus.

"It's subtle," Smith said. "Compare the feel and the texture of the metal on this new one with the piece that came unglued."

Stafford rubbed his hand over the disconnected sections on the stricken car, then did the same with the piece Smith had removed from the box.

"You're right. There is a subtle difference. But couldn't it have come from road wear?"

"You know what I think? This is a very bad copy of a Strong-Anderson tie rod end. I'm sure when we get this to a lab and they analyze the part, they'll confirm my suspicions."

Stafford leaned against the passenger side wheel and was silent for a moment. "If you're saying to me that someone put a phony part in this car and it resulted in a crash that killed four innocent people, this isn't just an auto accident. It's mass murder."

Chapter Seven

Even though Chip Holloway had a way of exaggerating things, Barry Warner figured he had nothing to lose by coming to New York. As his plane approached Teterboro Airport across the Hudson in New Jersey, he just wondered whether the people Holloway was sending him to see really had the wherewithal to help him bail out Upscale. And, if they did, what the ultimate price tag would be.

Warner knew his former merchandising director had long ago graduated from the legitimate world of gray market merchandise to the blatantly illegal business of brokering counterfeit products of all kinds. The new Rolls Royce Corniche he bragged about was testimony to how well he was doing at it.

Holloway was persistent. On several occasions, even when Upscale was doing well, he had casually suggested to the Upscale chairman that Warner could single-handedly improve Upscale's bottom line if he would open his stores to selected products represented by Holloway.

"It's a $200-billion-a-year business worldwide, pal," Holloway had said on one occasion. "You'd be surprised who's buying and selling."

"That gray market stuff was okay when we first started in business," Warner had responded. "We're too big and respectable for any of that kind of stuff now."

When word of Upscale's mounting financial crisis spread beyond the boardroom and made headlines across the country, Holloway was on the phone once again, telling Warner he might have a solution to the problem—if the retailer would free up some valuable shelf space for his client.

"I appreciate the offer, but no thanks," he told Holloway, but filed his private, unlisted phone number in a prominent place in his Rolodex.

As it became obvious to Warner that, aside from selling his real estate holdings at fire sale prices, he could not come close to coming up with what Sculley was demanding, Holloway's suggestion became more appealing. About a week ago, Warner called Holloway in San Francisco and bit the bullet.

Claiming he was just a conduit between retailers and his client, Holloway was vague about the people he represented and the type of deal in which they might be interested. But he assured Warner that his client, a company called Commonwealth Investment Services, had a billion dollars in liquid assets and was interested in talking with him at his convenience.

The long black Commonwealth limousine was in front of Warner's Fifth Avenue condominium at precisely 1:45 P.M Pedro Cardiz was in the back seat, introduced himself and greeted Warner with a hearty handshake.

It took about ten minutes for Ernesto to navigate through the mid-day midtown traffic and arrive at the Commonwealth headquarters. Warner and Pedro talked mostly about the traffic congestion and the convenience of flying in corporate aircraft. Warner told his host about the joys of flying in Upscale's newest jet, the Canadair Challenger, and was surprised to learn that Commonwealth owned two of them.

Warner noticed as they entered the Commonwealth building that the only identification for the entranceway was a small brass plaque on the right side of the gray French door that carried the company name. The security guard tripped the door switch and Pedro motioned Warner to follow him inside.

"Why the super security?" Warner wanted to know when Pedro used the magnetic passkey cards to activate the elevator and gain entrance to the fourth floor suite.

"In our business it is very necessary," Pedro replied.

Pedro ushered him into Ramon's spacious office, where the older brother was seated at a handsome wooden desk positioned in front of the long string of windows. The sun was streaming in.

"Welcome to Commonwealth," Ramon said as he rose from the chair and motioned Pedro and Warner toward a seating area on the other side of the room. There were four wine-colored Italian leather chairs placed around a low antique coffee table. Warner sat down first. Pedro and Ramon flanked him.

"Coffee, tea, a soft drink?" Ramon asked softly.

"No thanks. Not right now."

"Mr. Warner . . . "

"Please call me Barry."

"Barry, we agreed to meet with you here today because my brother, Pedro, and I believe we can have a mutually beneficial relationship with Upscale and you." Ramon's speech was slow and measured. "We know you are a very busy man and under extreme pressure these days. We would not have taken you away from your other duties if we weren't very serious about what we have to propose."

"I appreciate that," Barry said, "but I wouldn't be here in the first place if I wasn't serious about listening to what you have to offer."

"Before we tell you who we are and why we have an interest in Upscale, and why you should have an interest in us, there are a few things I'd like to stress," Ramon said.

"In the event we do not reach some kind of a formal business relationship as a result of this and subsequent meetings, you will forget what you heard and saw here and anywhere else you might go with us."

Warner gave Ramon an affirmative nod.

"As you will learn, we are a very private, but very powerful, organization," Ramon continued. "We deal fairly, we keep our word and we deal on a handshake."

"At some point, if we decided to work together," said Pedro leaning closer to Warner, "it will surely be necessary to involve some other of your people in whatever arrangements are worked out. They will have to be chosen very judiciously."

"I understand," Warner said warily. He had spent enough time with Mafia-controlled clothing manufacturers on Seventh Avenue to know that Ramon was issuing a veiled threat about silence if the talks produced nothing more than conversation. It didn't faze him.

"Secondly," Ramon said, "in the last five days, we have learned an awful lot about Upscale and you personally. How much will probably surprise you. One of the reasons we're so successful is that we carefully screen and investigate the companies and individuals with whom we do business. We don't like surprises."

"Now, we've been doing all the talking. Let's start by your giving us a candid appraisal of the retail environment and Upscale's chances for survival."

Warner was on stage. He stood up, took half a dozen steps toward the middle of the room and faced his hosts. "Well, as you probably are aware, Upscale is not alone in the situation it faces . . . not by a long shot. Much of retailing is in trouble for one reason or another.

"Just look around. B. Altman is history, the Campeau fiasco put Federated and Allied into Chapter 11. Ames grabs Zayre and can't swallow it.

"Majors, like Macy's, are underperforming, and some long-time retailers have just closed their doors. Blooming-dale's is put on the block and nobody is willing to come up with a billion. Companies like ours have taken on enormous debt to finance LBO's. Unfortunately, there's not enough cash flow because of soft sales to pay debt service, keep the stores stocked with merchandise and pay for all the rest, like salaries, advertising, promotions, etc."

"And multi-million-dollar corporate aircraft," Pedro interjected with a smile.

Warner let the remark pass and revved up again. "Frankly, the specialty shops like The Gap and The Limited are doing a much better job of servicing the customer than the traditional department store retailer. The customer is no dummy.

"In our business, discounting, the 'category killer' is killing us. Look around. We sell toys, electronics, books, office supplies and equipment. But today, you have specialists who concentrate on one market segment. They have huge selections and goddamn low prices. They are carving us up aisle by aisle," Warner said, punctuating every point with his hands or fist.

Ramon, fascinated by Warner's presence and blatant arrogance, listened intently. He and Pedro knew a great deal about category killers.

"Our biggest problem was timing. We have been repositioning some of our merchandising, developing more exclusive lines, refurbishing at a record pace, getting rid of marginally profitable stores and reemphasizing service—the key that got us where we're at in the first place. Nobody in the industry does a better job with computers and tracking merchandise.

"We're automated from the warehouse to the selling aisle. We know every day what's sold in every store everywhere. By 6:00 A.M. I can get a total picture of our store operations from the previous day, right down to how much Tampax we sold.

"Timing. The LBO. All that fuckin' interest and a time when business just isn't that good. That's what's hurting us."

Almost in concert the brothers wanted to know what it would take to reverse the tide. Warner returned to his seat and was ready with the answer.

"Two things. Money and time. This whole retailing environment is changing and it's going to take time for the industry to sort it out. The industry is overexpanded. There's a lot of competition, and Wal-Mart is expanding left and right across the country.

"There's no doubt in my mind but that we can make it, but not on the terms demanded by those bankers."

"Money, how much?" Pedro asked, cutting to the heart of the matter.

"Long term... about $300 million. Short term, a holiday on principal and interest payments, a new line of credit and renegotiation of interest rates so we get some breathing room.

"What we have to do immediately is get up to date with our interest payments and get suppliers paid, so that we can get merchandise levels back to normal. When a customer comes into a store and can't find what he or she needs, they go elsewhere. And they may not come back for a long while, if ever."

Ramon left his seat, walked to a rosewood cabinet and popped the tab on a Coke. "Much has been made in the media about your unwillingness to put up additional cash as part of any financial bailout of Upscale," he said. "As I said before, we have learned a great deal about you since Chip Holloway said you might be interested in working with us.

"We know that the reason you have stonewalled has very little to do with principle . . . that even though you have a very substantial net worth, mostly in real estate, you can't convert it into the kind of cash needed now or in the next thirty to sixty days. The term, I believe, is no net-quick assets."

Ramon handed Barry a sheet of paper with a list of Warner's assets and debts.

"You guys are thorough, I'll say that."

"We estimate it would take you a year at a minimum to liquidate the kind of assets that would produce $150 to $300 million in cash, and in this real estate market you'd take a real beating," Pedro said.

"By that time, Upscale might be a footnote on the American retailing scene in a worst case scenario or run by someone else. Most likely you would have lost your multi-million-dollar stake."

"Okay, let's cut out the bullshit. I know you guys do your homework. Let's get down to cases," Warner responded irritably. "Suppose I say yes to buying whatever you are selling. How can you help me raise $250 million between now and next week?"

"I think the best way to start is to take you to our command center, where we direct our worldwide operations," Ramon said. "Come."

The two brothers led Warner out of the office and down the brightly lit corridor to the elevator. Pedro inserted the green magnetic card and pushed "B." In a moment the cab stopped at the basement level of the brownstone.

A security guard with a large shotgun was posted at the entrance to the double doors. There was a buzz and Pedro pulled open the door. Warner found himself facing a giant picture window that separated the room he had just entered from the control room.

On the far wall was a large illuminated map of the world, accentuated by flashing colored lights in various countries. Warner noticed there were great clusters of lights in the Far East and the Pacific Rim, quite a few in South America and Italy and a considerable number in the United States.

On the right side of the illuminated map was what appeared to be a changeable directory, the kind frequently found in airport terminals. On the floor of the center, dozens of men and women were hunched over computer terminals with blue screens.

"I don't know what I'm looking at, but it's pretty impressive," Warner said.

"What you are looking at here is the command center for the world's largest product counterfeiting operation. That's what Commonwealth is all about," Ramon said. "The red lights on the board indicate the plants we own. The green are subcontractors who produce for us. Orange represents videotape duplication centers, and purple locations are where we do audiocassette duplication. Yellow represents printing plants where packaging is duplicated.

"The people at the computer screens are tracking the counterfeit cargo as it is heading from the manufacturing facilities to our various distribution centers, which are represented by the blue bulbs."

"Amazing."

"That's why I said at the outset of our discussions that if nothing materializes from our conversations, you have never been here. We and this place do not exist."

Ramon and Pedro took Warner to the floor of the control center. "Any idea how big the counterfeit business is?" Pedro asked.

"Holloway said something one day about $200 billion a year worldwide."

"That's a fair number, probably a little low. The fact is nobody really knows for sure. We probably have the best handle on it."

"Last year, we moved $20 billion worth of merchandise worldwide, nine of it in the United States alone. Estimates of counterfeit sales in America alone range from $80 to $100 billion annually; 5 to 8 percent of all the products sold in the world are counterfeit."

"I really had no idea it was this big," Warner said with astonishment. "Who's selling this shit? I mean how do you get it to market?"

"You'd be surprised," Ramon answered with a smile. "Show me a retail operation of any magnitude and I'll show you counterfeit products on the shelves. You may well have some in your stores. Obviously, most of the retailers are oblivious to what is counterfeit and what is not.

"On the other hand, we have a lot of customers who buy counterfeit products from us on an ongoing basis and enjoy the extra profit margins they produce," Ramon continued.

"Take a look at the map and I'll give you an overview of the world of counterfeiting," Pedro said. Warner thought he sounded like a tour guide at Disneyland. "Obviously, a large part of our manufacturing comes from the Far East and the Pacific Rim.

"Electronic parts, apparel, luxury goods, auto parts, sporting goods, consumer electronics, athletic goods, pharmaceuticals and other products come from this area," he said, making a sweeping motion in front of the electronic map with his arm, in an arc that included Japan, Taiwan, the Philippines, Indonesia, Hong Kong, Singapore, Malaysia and Thailand. "Brazil is our biggest source for sporting goods. Mexico produces apparel and sporting goods. Italy is big in apparel, leather goods and consumer electronics. There are few countries out there that don't have some counterfeiting operations.

"We do a lot of it right here in the United States," Pedro continued, pointing to the forty-eight states on the big map. My guess is that $10 to $15 billion of the coun--terfeit products sold in this country are produced right here."

The tour finished, Ramon suggested they move on. On the fourth floor, they turned left out of the elevator instead of right toward his office. About halfway down the hall, they stopped in front of a pair of paneled doors. Pedro inserted a red magnetic card into the slot and opened the right door to the Commonwealth conference room.

From about the four-foot level, the room was surrounded by row after row of polished oak shelving against a background of cream-colored grass cloth. Warner had been in hundreds of sample rooms, but he had never seen anything like this.

He quickly sensed that what lined the shelves was the largest collection of counterfeit products, or knocks, the world had ever seen. Warner walked around the room picking up item after item. Eveready batteries. TDK audiotapes. Nike and Reebok athletic shoes. Ford Motorcraft, GM and AC-Delco auto parts. Dial Soap. Johnson's Baby Shampoo. Brand name cosmetics, sportswear, sporting goods. Stacks of prerecorded audiotapes. Nintendo games. Dozens of first-run movie titles on videocassettes. He guessed there were more than 1,000 items on the shelves. As far as he could tell, the packaging looked like the real thing.

Pedro and Ramon sat silently as Warner explored the shelves. Finally, the retailer looked at his watch. It was 4:00 P.M. His mouth felt dry.

"I'll take that soft drink now, if you don't mind," he said.

"I think we're all ready for a break," Ramon said as he picked up the phone and instructed his secretary to bring in an assortment of soft drinks.

Pedro got up, walked to a far corner of the conference room and returned to his seat with two large plastic bags. One had the highly recognizable Upscale logo emblazoned diagonally across the center. The other was a plain poly bag.

"This morning we sent one of our people out to Stamford to visit one of your stores and do some shopping, and this is what he brought back," Pedro said as he dumped the contents of the Upscale bag on the table. He brushed those items to one side of the table. Products from the other bag slid onto another segment of the table.

"Compare these." Pedro's words sounded almost like a command. "As far as we know all of the products picked up at your store are legitimate. The remainder on this table are not."

Warner silently sifted through the products, making a careful comparison of each. With the naked eye he couldn't tell the difference.

"Very impressive."

"We thought you'd be impressed," Ramon interjected. "Barry, we are not only counterfeiters but—and you may chuckle at this—we run a quality operation. By that I mean we try in every conceivable way to emulate the real thing. Sometimes, of course, it is impossible. We always come close."

"We are constantly checking the product quality and the packaging. We're selfish. If it looks real and feels real, there's a lot less chance of our getting a consumer recognizing it's a counterfeit and our getting caught.

"We're simply in the business of manufacturing and distributing products, only we're very quiet about how we do it. We just let someone else pay for the product development, package design, marketing and advertising," Ramon continued.

"Look," Pedro said. "There are some people out there in this business—just as there are in any business—that give the industry a bad name. They counterfeit birth control pills and other pharmaceuticals, military helicopter parts, faulty auto parts and counterfeit toys that do not meet minimum safety standards. A lot of children have been hurt. Counterfeit aviation parts are so authentic no one knows it until there's an accident, like the one that recently killed a TV traffic reporter and her pilot.

"Obviously, we're operating outside the law, but it behooves us to avoid anything that calls attention to ourselves and the people who sell the products we produce."

Warner slowly took a sip from his Diet Coke. Somehow, he knew he was in the right place.

Chapter Eight

Carole Nordstrom was in a state of mental limbo and had been ever since returning Mitch Rudolph's call the previous evening. What Mitch had in mind must be unusual or the man considered to be the top retail executive recruiter wouldn't take the time to fly to Cleveland just to introduce her to a potential employer.

The question kept regurgitating in her mind. Why was Mitch being so unusually secretive. It wasn't his way.

The dull buzz of the intercom broke her train of thought, and she hastily picked up the receiver.

"It's Harry Carlson of Turning Point," Missy Schwartz announced. "Says he needs more information before they can ship the current order."

Nordstrom knew what that meant. Carlson wanted to know when Turning Point could expect payment for $2 million worth of junior sportswear.

"Tell him I'm in a meeting and will get back to him later. In fact, I don't want to take any more calls this morning."

It was more than eight hours until her meeting with Mitch, and she had to do something to kill the time.

Nordstrom picked up the latest computer printout on out-of-stock merchandise. It was nearly a half-inch thick.

"Incredible," she said out loud. "Incredible."

She remembered that when she arrived at Upscale fifteen months ago it was unusual for the report to contain any more than three or four pages. The company had the most sophisticated reorder system in retailing and plenty of cash in those days. Items were rarely out of stock and if so, just for a few days. Now the report was nearly fifty pages—a sign of Upscale's deepening financial plight. Out of stock meant lost sales and unhappy customers.

With exceptional looks, brains, a commonsense approach to management and a genuine concern for people, Carole Nordstrom had been a winner as long as she could remember. Now, as she studied the report, she was frightened that her career reputation would get mired in the growing mess at Upscale.

She was high school homecoming queen and valedictorian of her class in a small town near Milwaukee. She was school president and voted most likely to succeed by her classmates.

Like Barry Warner, Carole Nordstrom grew up in a retailing family. Her father, Henry, had operated a small department store that featured women's apparel. As a teenager, Carole spent much of her free time working for him in virtually every capacity in the store. She had an affinity for the business, and by the time she was a senior in high school, she was entrusted with buying several important lines. Then Carlson's, a big discount chain out of Oklahoma, parked a 100,000-square-foot store on the outskirts of town and essentially dried up business in the downtown area, as the giant retailer had done everywhere it went.

Carole watched as her father struggled to keep the family business going. He tried everything. New lines, promotional events, longer hours, stressing personal service. Carole even offered to drop out of high school and to cash in her college endowment fund to help Henry Nordstrom remain in business. He would not hear of it.

The saddest day of her young life came one evening at dinner when Henry Nordstrom announced to his family that he was closing the store and would take a job as a traveling salesman for a women's apparel maker.

Fortunately, Henry Nordstrom had prepared well for his daughter's education. With a splendid academic record and sufficient funds, Carole had her choice of virtually any campus in America. She chose Miami University in Oxford, Ohio, a sleepy rural town in the foothills of southern Ohio, because it had a strong retailing program. Originally, she majored in retailing with a minor in fashion merchandising, but by the time she was a senior, Carole decided she might want to combine a career in retailing with fashion design.

After graduation from Miami, Carole spent a year at the Fashion Institute of Technology in New York City, where she studied fashion design and illustration, apparel arts and textiles.

She nearly broke Henry Nordstrom's heart when she told him, in the summer of 1975, that she would not be returning to Milwaukee, where she had three job offers. She decided instead to relocate to Boston as a management trainee with Julie Marshall, a fast-growing 200-store chain specializing in trendy and expensive clothing for women.

Carole spent six years at Julie Marshall. There was no fashion design, but she got a real education in retailing and fashion merchandising. Julie Marshall Cohen, founder and president of the chain, picked her out of a class of fifteen trainees as a shining star of the future.

Within a year, Carole was Cohen's administrative assistant. Julie promoted her to eastern regional vice president at the end of the third year, with an annual salary of $75,000, and two years later moved her into the executive suite as one of three executive vice presidents. At the age of twenty-eight, she was earning well in excess of $100,000 a year and being groomed to succeed the founder.

On a warm summer day in July, 1979, Julie called Carole into her office and told her the awful news. She had been diagnosed with pancreatic cancer and had only months to live. Carole was devastated. Julie had treated her like a daughter, and she wondered how the chain could survive without its founder.

When word leaked out into the retail community about Julie's terminal illness, the headhunters began swooping around the executive suite like vultures. One of them was Mitch Rudolph, whose firm, Mitch Rudolph and Associates in New York City, had handled middle-level recruiting assignments for the chain.

Carole had spoken to him on the phone a number of times, but they had never met.

During a conversation related to recruiting a division manager, Rudolph suggested it might be appropriate for the two to meet the next time Carole was in New York. Nothing special, he said.

A month later, Carole visited Rudolph in his fortieth floor office in the General Motors Building at 58th St. and Fifth Avenue. Rudolph knew a great deal about her ability, but until he saw her walk through the door he had no idea how beautiful she was.

They sat facing each other at a round glass coffee table. Mitch—tall, handsome and muscular with sandy gray bangs across his forehead—was coatless. Even sitting in the chair he was an imposing figure. Mitch was immediately impressed with her soft, genteel manner and wondered how she would survive in the cutthroat business of high-powered retailing.

Mitch and Carole talked for almost an hour about her career at Julie Marshall's, how much she liked Boston, how much she enjoyed her work, how her life had changed since she began dating a young Harvard professor. She was amazed at how easy Mitch Rudolph was to talk with. They continued their conversation over cocktails at the Palm Court in The Plaza.

"Have you thought about what life might be like at Julie Marshall once the old gal is gone?" Rudolph asked after the waitress had brought each a vodka martini on the rocks and a plateful of finger sandwiches.

"Not really. Right now, I have an enormous amount of responsibility. With Julie just available for limited consultation, I'm almost totally responsible for day-to-day store operations. I don't have much time to think about the future.

"I'm just dedicated to making life as simple as possible for Julie during whatever time she has left. We're all like family."

"I can understand that," Mitch said. "I've known Julie since she began expanding. We've placed a number of people with her and with few exceptions they've felt just the way you do. But I also know that Julie's two sons have no interest in the business. The minute she's gone, they'll peddle the chain to the highest bidder. You'll quickly find out that there are few Julie Marshall Cohen's in the real world of retailing.

Personally, you might want to lay the groundwork now for life after Julie Marshall."

He explained his operation and asked permission to discreetly consider her for a number of upper level management positions being handled by his firm.

"I'm not going anywhere right now," she said in an uncharacteristically sharp tone. "Frankly, I'm a little offended by the whole tone of this conversation. Julie is still very much alive. Let's drop it."

Mitch Rudolph was right. Two months after Julie Marshall Cohen died, her two lawyer sons announced a deal to sell the chain to The Allen Pearlman Group of Texas for $110 million.

On the day she was to meet Allen Pearlman to discuss her future with the chain, she received word that Professor Alan Harvey, the man she had been dating for almost a year, had been killed in a commuter plane crash in South Carolina. In her grief, she decided it was time to leave Boston for good.

She gave the new owners four weeks notice, gave up her apartment, sent the furniture into storage and returned to her parents' home in Milwaukee to ponder life without Julie and Alan. Mitch Rudolph's pursuit was almost relentless, and it became annoying to the point she refused to talk with him about the future of her career and possible job opportunities.

Carole found the time spent with her parents, Henry and Penny Nordstrom, very comforting. Henry Nordstrom, doing quite well in his role as a midwest sales representative for a hot line of sportswear, offered to underwrite a new retail store for her in the Milwaukee area. While the thought of owning her own business was tempting, Carole knew it would be too restricting.

Then the call came from Merrilee Gardner, a former executive at Julie Marshall's, inviting Carole to an interview at Bloomingdale's in New York. Four weeks later she was ensconced in an office on 59th Street as a vice president in store operations.

One of the first people she called when she got to the Big Apple was Mitch Rudolph . . . to apologize for being so elusive while she was in Milwaukee.

While there was never anything romantic about their relationship, Carole and Mitch became good friends. They dined together occasionally and often took in the Knicks and the Rangers.

After she settled in at Bloomies, Rudolph peppered her with potential job opportunities, but she never even consented to an interview. While she didn't necessarily see it as an end-all position, she was happy at Bloomingdale's. By the end of the fifth year she was a senior vice president, considered one of the bright young stars in retailing and earned in excess of $350,000 a year.

Two years later Barry Warner unexpectedly entered her life. She had just completed a speech at a National Retail Federation seminar at the New York Hilton when Warner, who was in the audience, cornered her and, to Carole's amazement, virtually offered her a job on the spot.

Carole said she was flattered, but preferred to remain in the East.

Warner pursued her relentlessly. After several telephone conversations in which she continually professed her happiness at Bloomies, Warner finally convinced her at least to visit Upscale, assuring her she had nothing to lose.

Carole went to Cleveland on one of Upscale's corporate jets and spent three days being wooed by Warner.

Barry told her about the recently completed LBO and said he was looking for someone who could eventually be groomed as chief executive officer. He talked about introducing an entirely new line of Upscale signature clothes. She could even help design them and supervise manufacturing operations in the Far East. Then he dangled a $250,000 signing bonus, a $750,000 annual salary and $1,000,000 in stock options in front of her. She agreed to come to Cleveland.

Despite his reputation as a blatant womanizer, Barry was on good behavior during the courtship. But once she was on board, he kept fabricating reasons for their being together. Carole was wary and kept her distance. Warner was unusually patient. Finally, over cocktails in the small bar at Giovanni's one evening during which he quickly consumed four vodka martinis, Barry made his move. He told Carole what a great future she had at Upscale, put his arm around her, pulled her close and began massaging her thigh with his other hand in the vicinity of her crotch.

The normally reserved Nordstrom yanked his hand from her lap and nearly went ballistic. "Fuck-off. No more passes, ever," she said sternly putting her nose right into his face. "If you do, I'll plant my knee right in your groin and you'll never forget it."

"I promise," Barry stuttered.

Barry did not take rejection lightly. It was the only promise he kept.

Chapter Nine

Pedro Cardiz took an urgent phone call in his office, and when he returned Barry got a little more insight into the counterfeit business.

"Customs grabbed a container of computer boards with pirated operating system chips already in place. Probably worth about $500,000," he told Ramon, who shrugged it off as the price of doing business.

"Happen often?" Warner wanted to know.

"Let's put it this way," Ramon answered. "The odds against that happening are a helluva lot better for us than the odds you play on the black jack and craps tables in Las Vegas." Warner's gambling habits were legendary. He had been known to drop a quarter of a million on a very cold night at Caesar's.

"The chances of U.S. Customs doing a 100 percent inspection on a container or airport shipment are less than one in a hundred, and we like those odds," Pedro said. "With some three hundred ports in the United States, plus a large number of gateway airports and the expansive borders with Canada and Mexico, enforcement and detection are virtually impossible. I'll give you an example, the Port of Los Angeles handles more than 1.5 million incoming containers a year. That's like finding a needle in a haystack."

Pedro explained that powerful computer networks had simplified the paperwork process in international shipping to the United States. "Certain information, such as specific country of origin or first time importer, might trigger a 100 percent inspection. Some shipments and containers are just selected at random, but the key is still the customs inspector.

"On any given day, an inspector might look at hundreds of shipment files. A lot of it's hunch and experience. Sometimes failure to sign a piece of paper, whether deliberate or not, will trigger an inspection. You just don't know.

"The customs inspectors are human just like everyone else. They have good days and bad days. Guy has a fight with his wife or girlfriend and doesn't get laid. His mind might be a million miles away on the day he reviews paperwork covering a counterfeit shipment. On another day, he might spot something suspicious and pull the container for 100 percent inspection.

"In the course of a year," Ramon interjected, "we might lose $20 to $30 million in cargo to customs inspectors. We don't like to lose any, but considering the volume we do, we can live with it . . . and more if we have to . . . just as long as they can't trace it to us."

Warner's microscopic attention span was legendary, but he was fascinated with the conversation and wanted to learn more, especially how Pedro and Ramon got into the business. He got his chance when Pedro talked about the Custom Service's preoccupation with snooping out illegal drugs and the fact that every container from his native Colombia was searched.

"From Colombia?" Warner asked inquisitively. "Why aren't you into drugs instead of counterfeiting?"

"Our family still is," Ramon answered, then explained that Commonwealth was originally organized to funnel laundered drug revenues into more legitimate enterprises. "Pedro and I have never actually been involved in the distribution end of the business."

"We still act as a conduit for some of the drug money," Pedro explained. "A great deal of that money, more than a billion to be exact, was used initially to fund Commonwealth. Now we're pretty much self-supporting. Once in a while we have to call on some of our brothers in the drug trade when there's some unpleasant enforcement to be handled."

Pedro told Warner that the intensifying war on drugs was one of the stimuli for the counterfeiting operation. With the U.S. government marshalling its forces against drug cartels, there was somewhat of a vacuum when it came to searching for regular imported merchandise.

It had been Ramon's idea in the first place, he said, to bring some order out of the chaos in the international counterfeiting arena. With a global network of its own plants and reliable subcontractors, the venture could control product quality and broaden the avenues of distribution from the street corners of Hong Kong, New York and other major cities to the shopping malls of America.

"We presented the idea to my father, and he gave it his blessing," Pedro said. "It took us about four years to build the network you saw on the wall in the basement. We're really starting to roll.

"The real skill in this business is to create enough confusion in the paperwork so that it is virtually impossible to determine where the product originates and who the real intended customer is. That's what a lot of those people operating computers are doing. It's the highest form of organized confusion."

"Let me give you an example of what Pedro is talking about," Ramon said. "Investigators from a Paris detective agency were stymied for three years as they trudged through nine countries trying to break one of our units specializing in perfume.

"That's because the product was produced in Israel, the bottles came from Italy and Spain, and the packaging was done in Mexico and England. Of course, the money came from us, but it was channeled through banks in the Bahamas and Switzerland. When they finally put it all together, it caused some inconvenience, but we regrouped and were back in the counterfeit fragrance business in a big way. The important thing is that they never were able to connect anything to Commonwealth."

Barry looked at his Rolex. It was nearly five o'clock and they had been at it for nearly three hours. He thought it was time to get down to the bottom line.

"No question about it. You guys have an impressive operation, but how do we put all this together in a package that will get me the money I need?"

Chapter Ten

It was just before six o'clock when Carole turned the white BMW convertible onto West Third Street and pulled in front of the Ritz Carlton. A doorman in a black tuxedo greeted her and presented a ticket for valet parking.

Two more doormen in the same garb held open the double doors to the ground floor foyer and told her the lobby was on the sixth floor.

Carole turned right out of the elevator on six, walked across the marble floor and immediately spotted Mitch sitting at a round glass-topped table for four just inside the bar area. He was nursing a Cutty Sark on the rocks. He stood up, put his arm around her and kissed her lightly on the cheek.

Nordstrom was wearing a red raw silk dress, fashionably cut three inches above the knees. A custom-made geometric-shaped pin was snapped on the lapel.

"You look stunning. I love that outfit."

"Thank you. You don't look so bad yourself. I can't remember the last time we got together.

"Too long. About six months."

Carole sat next to Mitch in a low-backed chair covered in a light-blue-and-beige-striped pattern. A harpist was playing "Sunrise, Sunset," from *Fiddler on the Roof.* Early evening sunlight was splashing into the room through sheer drapes covering four large windows.

Nordstrom ordered a Smirnoff on the rocks with a twist, Mitch a second Cutty.

"Listen, there are a couple of guys joining us for dinner at seven. I've reserved a private dining room so we don't have an audience for our little get-together."

"Why all the secrecy, Mitch? You've never been that way before."

"Frankly, I've never quite been in a situation like this before."

"Tell me about it," Carole said leaning forward on her elbows.

"On Monday morning, I receive a call from a guy who says he's executive vice president of Union First Bank in Cleveland, asking if he can stop by at two to discuss a recruiting assignment. I'm not doing anything at two, so I tell him to come right ahead.

"When Peter Cosgrove gets there the first thing I ask him is how he got my name. He says they checked around and found out that I have a great reputation in retail recruiting. They want to work exclusively with our firm and they want to move fast. He swears me to secrecy and we get down to the nitty gritty.

"He says the bank is looking for a top-flight retailing executive to become CEO of a large chain, if the bank has to pull the plug on current management for failure to pay back some healthy loans.

" 'That chain wouldn't be Upscale, would it?' I ask. He confirms that it is, but says the whole operation is on the

Q.T. I said it may be, but there are plenty of rumors flying that Barry Warner was on his way out, if he doesn't come up shooting with some big bread."

Mitch paused to take a sip of Cutty.

"Go on."

" 'You may be in luck,' I said. 'And you may not have to look very far. There's a young lady at Upscale who's very qualified to step right into Warner's shoes.' "

"That's unbelievable," Nordstrom said shaking her head in amazement.

"You can say that again. Anyway, I told him about your background and gave him a copy of the latest resumé we had on file. I told him you wouldn't come cheap. He said money was no object. Two hours later, he calls and asks me to set up an appointment to meet you in Cleveland. Given my past history as a headhunter with you, I thought it best to say as little as possible until I was here."

Carole thought for a long moment. "I don't know, Mitch. It's Union First Bank that's trying to scuttle Upscale. I still work for the company. Don't they call consorting with the enemy treason?"

"Oh, come on, Carole, unless I miss my guess Barry's a dead player. He doesn't have a real friend in the world, certainly no one willing to come up with the kind of bread needed to make this thing fly. This could be an incredible opportunity for you."

"But, it also could earn me the reputation as a traitor in the industry. Look, Barry is paying me $750,000 a year to help keep Upscale a viable entity. There are a lot of people depending upon me to help keep this thing alive and Barry at the helm."

"You didn't listen to me eight years ago when we had a discussion about your future after Julie Marshall Cohen was gone. What do I have to say now to get you to keep an open mind about this? Barry doesn't give a shit about you, or anyone else for that matter. You and I know that the major reason he hired you in the first place was that he wanted to get into your pants. When that didn't happen, he turned against you. As for the people who are depending upon you . . . they'd probably have a better chance with you at the helm."

"I know, but there's such a thing as loyalty."

"Loyalty to whom? The only things Barry Warner are loyal to are his wallet and his dick. I've handled more than a dozen former Upscale executives who displayed the utmost loyalty to that prick, only to be unceremoniously discarded when they outlived their usefulness or wouldn't go to bed with him. Why do you think we've never worked for him?"

"I've never asked myself why."

"Look, you have nothing to lose," Mitch said, sensing that Carole was wavering. "We'll have a nice dinner and see what they have to say. Who knows? I may be wrong. Barry may pull the rabbit out of the hat and there'll be no opportunity at all."

After almost an hour they moved to a small private dining room just off the main lobby. Dan Sculley, chairman and CEO of the bank, and Pete Cosgrove, generally regarded as No. 2 in the hierarchy, were already seated, sipping on Tanqueray martinis.

After the introductions, Nordstrom took a seat between Sculley and Cosgrove and directly facing Mitch. They ordered another round of drinks and when the waitress left, Mitch got up and closed the door.

"I think we all agree that this is a highly unusual situation," Mitch said. "Given the circumstances, Ms. Nordstrom has expressed serious reservations about even being here. I have assured her that all this will be treated in a highly confidential manner."

"There are only four people in the world who know about this meeting, and they are all in this room," Sculley said in a resonant voice. You can be sure that if anything leaks out it won't be from us. Frankly, this whole situation is touch and go right now. The last thing we need is Barry Warner claiming that we're tampering with one of his top executives. Does that reassure you, Miss Nordstrom? It is Miss Nordstrom, isn't it."

"Very much so, Carole responded with a smile, but inwardly curious about the tone of Sculley's question. Almost as a reflex, she glanced at his hands. There was no wedding band. She was surprised that it pleased her.

Tall and well-built, Sculley was an imposing figure, with sharp facial features, a ruddy complexion and a shock of wavy brown hair that looked almost windblown. Dressed in a tan, lightweight double-breasted Hugo Boss suit, Carole thought he looked more like an advertising agency executive than captain of a major bank.

"I assume, Miss Nordstrom, that you are well aware of Union First Bank's role in financing the LBO of Upscale."

"Very much so. Barry Warner talks about it all the time."

"I assume you also know that Barry Warner and I don't exactly share a mutual admiration society. In fact, I'm the first to admit I just plain don't like the guy. It's as simple as that. I also don't think Upscale is going anywhere with him running the show. Frankly, I'm taking that position and so are the major bondholders."

"That means," Cosgrove interjected, "if Barry Warner doesn't come up with enough money to satisfy our demands, there are not too many pleasant options for him. He can go Chapter 11 and lose control to the courts; or he can deal with us to protect his investment. Our terms for putting in more money and restructuring the debt are plain and simple."

"Goodbye Barry," Mitch said impulsively.

"Precisely," said Cosgrove, the prototype of an accountant with a rapidly receding hairline and black wire-rim glasses that hung midway down his nose.

"That means we must have someone in place to take charge immediately," said Sculley, who was having a hard time keeping his eyes off her.

"And what happens if Barry Warner surprises you and comes up with enough money to get you off his back?" Nordstrom asked.

"Good question," Sculley said with a smile. "Frankly, we think it is highly unlikely. First of all, we know it would take months for Barry to get liquid enough to put more of his money in Upscale. Secondly, given the condition of many of the country's banks and their reluctance to commit to anything but a sure thing, finding an alternate source of funding would be very difficult. I assure you, even with new management and an infusion of cash, no one would call Upscale's future a sure thing."

"But what if he does," she persisted.

"Well, then all bets are off for now. He still calls the shots," Sculley replied in a tone that indicated he didn't believe it would happen.

"Let's look at the menu and order," Mitch interrupted.

When the waitress appeared a few minutes later, Carole and Mitch ordered sautéed chicken breast with grain mustard and tarragon sauce. The bankers selected New York strip steaks with bordelaise sauce.

"For starters, bring us an assortment of blue points, shrimp and smoked Scottish salmon, and another round of drinks," Mitch said. He could afford to go first class on this one. A placement fee for the chief executive officer of a company like Upscale would bring a six-figure commission.

They talked through dinner. Sculley said he was impressed with Nordstrom's background, but wanted to know why she had soured on Warner.

Carole thought for a moment. She knew how she felt about Warner, but didn't know how far to go.

"Look," she finally answered. "I still work for Barry and feel a little uncomfortable about this entire situation. I may still wind up as his executive vice president."

"Let's just consider this a conversation among friends," Sculley reassured here.

Carole folded her arms in front of her and, ignoring Mitch and Cosgrove, looked squarely into Sculley's deep brown eyes. "The guy doesn't tell the truth. He made all kinds of promises, but aside from paying me $750,000 a year, he's failed to deliver. He just won't give up control. He has to be in on virtually every merchandising decision. The business is passing him by and he doesn't know it.

"In spite of severe difficulties resulting from our poor cash position and suppliers demanding cash up front, I'm trying my darnedest. I've invested too much in my career and I don't want to be remembered as one who went to the bottom on the Good Ship Upscale without a helluva fight."

"Two questions," Sculley said, silently admiring her beauty and spunk. "First, can a new management team turn Upscale around? Second, would you consider heading up that management team, if the job were offered to you?"

Carole sat motionless for what seemed like an eternity, framing the answers in her mind. More than anything, she knew she wanted the challenge of running Upscale. That prospect had brought her to Upscale in the first place. But the circumstances were different now. She wondered how she would be perceived in the industry if she helped push Barry off the ship.

"Yes to the first question," she finally answered. "Providing there is enough funding to do the job and a free hand to replace some of Barry's hand-picked associates in management. Some are just as out of touch as he is.

"To the second question, the answer is I just don't know. Don't get me wrong. I'm flattered that you're even talking to me. I'm not playing games here. There's an issue of ethics and loyalty and I'm wrestling with them. This has come up so suddenly."

"We certainly can understand that," Cosgrove said. "Frankly, we've just begun our search. You're the first person we've talked to. Obviously, there will be others."

"Hopefully, we'll talk again sometime next week . . . after we've had a chance to get Barry to the conference table," Sculley said.

It was after ten when Sculley and Cosgrove got up to leave. Carole shook hands with the executive vice president first, then Sculley. The warmth of the handshake and the touch of his hand excited her and she wanted to preserve the moment.

Mitch and Carole lingered in the dining room after the bankers departed, sipping Grand Marnier. Mitch told her how well he thought the evening had progressed, what an opportunity it might be for Carole.

"You just want that big commission," she joked.

"You might be interested to know young lady, that I get paid a very handsome fee whether or not they hire you or anyone else."

"Then I don't have to feel guilty if I turn them down."

"Be serious Carole. If you're offered the job I think you'll take it. For more than one reason."

Finally, Mitch accompanied her to the front door of the Ritz Carlton and waited until her car arrived. She kissed him lightly on the cheek and thanked him for thinking about her . . . and the lovely dinner.

On the way home to Beachwood, Carole thought it was amazing how easily Mitch had read her and what she was thinking about the opportunities the evening presented.

Chapter Eleven

"The first stop is Norfolk," Ramon shouted to Barry over the sounds of the screeching jet engines as the Boeing 737 lifted from the New York La Guardia runway. "We want to give you a first-hand look at why detection is so difficult."

Little more than an hour later they were taxiing toward a private hangar at Norfolk International Airport. A driver in a nondescript gray Ford Taurus picked them up as they alighted from the plane. The brothers climbed into the back seat. Warner sat next to the driver.

Before leaving Ramon and Pedro the previous afternoon, Barry had agreed to a one-day tour of Commonwealth facilities, which the brothers felt was critical before getting to the deal. They wanted Warner to appreciate the magnitude of what they were about to propose and assimilate how he would incorporate what they had in mind into Upscale's business.

They came out of the airport grounds, turned into Interstate 64, then swung onto I-564, past the giant U.S. naval base that dominated Norfolk's economy. They finally exited onto Terminal Boulevard, which they followed right onto the docks at Virginia International Terminals.

They passed the Container Control Center, made a series of turns between rows of colored containers and ultimately wound up on the dock. Warner and the brothers stepped out onto the dock, where three ships were simultaneously being unloaded by giant twin cranes. As each container was being lowered toward a resting place on a chassis pulled by a tractor, four stevedores wearing hard hats scrambled around the truck and chassis to provide guidance for the crane operator, looking down through the Plexiglas floor of his cab, perhaps 100 feet in the air.

"If one of those containers lets go, there won't be much to pick up," Warner observed.

"It happens once in a while, and that's why these guys are pretty well paid," Pedro said.

"We run our own trucking company, which not only serves our business interests but generates substantial legitimate revenues for our firm. There's one of our tractors, the one with the green and yellow trim," Ramon said pointing to the rig just below the crane.

Back in the car, the driver made several quick turns and pulled in front of a long, one-story tan building. They left the car again. It was hot and humid and Warner impulsively removed his glen plaid suit jacket and flung it into the back seat of the Taurus.

Inside the building a dozen workmen driving forklift trucks unloaded wooden crates from the containers and shifted them to other trucks on the opposite side of the terminal. Pedro walked over to a stack of crates, examined the numbers on top and told Warner they contained leather goods from Italy.

"Some of the merchandise is legitimate. We often mix legitimate and counterfeit merchandise in the same containers to make the bogus products more difficult to detect."

Pedro said the arriving cargo would be trucked to Commonwealth's processing and packaging centers throughout the Southeast, the nearest of which was in Charlotte where the group was headed next.

"One of the keys," Ramon said, joining them after a chat with a supervisor, "is not to do too much in any one facility. In the event an employee starts putting two and two together we have ways of dealing with them. It only happens rarely."

On the ground in Charlotte, shortly after one, there was a slight delay while they waited for ground transportation. The embarrassed driver said he was held up by summer highway construction.

There was no name on the nondescript brick building in an industrial park on the north side of the city, only the street number on the glass door. Ramon pushed the buzzer.

A heavy-set man in gray trousers and a navy blue polo shirt came to the door. Warner noticed that he, too, was obviously of Colombian heritage. Pedro introduced him as Guillermo, the facility manager.

Guillermo led them to a large video editing suite with no windows, where a technician in shirtsleeves was sitting in front of a big color monitor. As scenes flashed across the screen, his fingers worked tiny levers on a control panel the size of a secretarial desk. Warner recognized Robert Redford on the monitor and inquired what the technician was doing.

"This is a DeVinci color correction system," Guillermo explained matter-of-factly. "On the other side of that glass wall you'll find 35mm motion picture footage being fed into the system. It happens to be a pirated copy of a new movie that will be released in video stores within the next few weeks.

"The technician here is color correcting the film as it is being electronically put on videotape. With this system, we're able to assure that the dubs will be about as perfect as they are when they come directly from the producer."

Warner wanted to know how Commonwealth got a copy of the film.

"There are many ways," Pedro answered. "Sometimes, we are forced to steal them from local theater film distribution depots, or intercept couriers who deliver them. We also have sources within the movie industry who feed us copies used for screening and marketing. In a number of markets, we operate legitimate movie theaters. We only need the release print for the time it takes to process the film-to-video transfer, about the actual length of the movie."

"Mind-boggling," Warner said, throwing his arms into the air. "The movie production company spends millions to produce the film, spends millions more marketing and promoting it, and finally gets it out onto the marketplace on VHS; in one fell swoop, you guys steal the print and make copies. The only investment you guys have is the cost of this equipment and the dubbing machines."

"Precisely," Pedro said as Guillermo led them into a clean room where technicians in white lab coats were mass producing dubs of movies on high-speed dubbing equipment. "But we're not only in this business. Our take from the thousands of video stores who deal in pirated tapes is about $500 million, about a third of the total business."

"I suppose you already know that we do a sizeable video rental and sales volume in our stores," Warner volunteered. "We do it for two reasons. First, of course, is the profit motive. Secondly, it's a traffic builder.

"The customer comes in to rent the tape, then is back a second time for return. We get two shots at the customer to purchase something."

Guillermo explained that after duplication the tapes were shipped to another location for boxing, labeling and shipping.

"Again," Pedro said, "it's part of our divide-and-conquer theory. Don't let anyone see too much."

In his office, Guillermo produced a couple of boxes of *E.T.* and asked Warner to select the one containing the pirated tape. Warner looked closely and finally admitted he didn't have a clue.

"With sophisticated camera work, retouching and high quality printing, we are able to make a near perfect duplication," Ramon said. "Once we get our hands on the box and labeling, we can have our product in video stores within forty-eight hours. It's driving the movie industry nuts. They're trying everything to thwart us, but we're always a step ahead of them."

Finally, Guillermo took them to an area where bogus audiocassettes were being duplicated. It was an impressive operation. Printers turned out labels and applied them to tape shells. Other machines loaded tape into the shells. Banks of duplicating machines recorded the tapes, which were then automatically shrink-wrapped.

"These machines record blanks from the master at sixty-four times the regular playback speed," Guillermo explained. "This is much simpler than the movie business. We simply purchase high quality compact discs at the music store down the street and produce a master."

The last stop on the trip was a large warehouse building on the other side of Charlotte, which Ramon said housed Commonwealth's packaging facility.

"We handle packaging for regular legitimate customers and our own counterfeit packaging. Because we have so many different customers, no one here suspects that it all isn't legit. Besides, most of the people employed here are mentally handicapped. They are taught to perform one or two simple functions and that's it. We don't ask them to think and they don't ask any questions."

Barry and the Cardiz brothers finally talked turkey on the way back to New York.

"The deal is simply this," Ramon said, pouring a vodka on the rocks for Warner. "You agree to stock our merchandise in your stores, assuming that you can get them on the shelves without any problem. In return, we'll advance you the money you need.

"As far as the financial deal is concerned, it's going to be with you personally. We'll advance you the money to put on the table as the carrot that will pull the banks into the deal. Whatever you need—$250 . . . $300 million. Just to make it legitimate, we'll ask you to put up an equivalent amount of Upscale stock as collateral. We also have to establish an interest rate, say 8 percent. It's mostly for show, but we'll expect quarterly payments of half the amount due.

"Now, for every dollar of counterfeit merchandise that passes through your stores, we'll credit your account with 20 percent. We ship $100 million worth of goods, the balance drops by $20 million.

"For instance," Pedro said, "we've analyzed your auto service and parts departments. The best we can figure is that the average store moves $400,000 worth of parts a year. Six hundred fifty times $400,000 equals $260 million. Since auto parts represents one of our strong suits, we think we can funnel $30 to $50 million in volume through these units."

Ramon told Warner that Commonwealth would make an analysis of every department in which it has products to sell. "We'll start in auto and work our way slowly through other appropriate store departments. Of course, you can veto any product category. We think it will take no more than three years for you to earn back the $300 million."

"How long do you hold my stock hostage?"

"We'll release it in $100 million increments," Ramon answered.

"And if I want to bail out before the end of three years?"

"You can pay down your obligation at any time," Pedro answered with a smile.

"What happens at the end of the deal?"

"We take a walk and you resume purchasing everything from legitimate sources. Or, we renegotiate a new deal in which, you, Barry, share in the profits."

Ramon and Pedro waited for Barry to respond. He took his time, not wanting to appear too eager.

"Without giving the terms a lot of study, the numbers appear to be workable, but do you think we can pull this off without going to jail?"

"A legitimate question," Pedro answered. "We don't want it to happen any more than you do. We take extraordinary security precautions. We're careful who we deal with, careful who we share information with. You have to adopt the same precautions."

"First," Ramon said slowly, "we move very slowly and test your systems. We have the resources. We have the time. This is not a one-shot deal. We're not going to take unnecessary risks.

"All of the merchandise will be ordered and shipped through legitimate distributors and manufacturers that are actually fronts for our operations. In many cases, the counterfeit goods will be mixed with legitimate merchandise."

"That's our end," Pedro interrupted. "What about yours?"

"I've given it some cursory thought," Barry answered. "Our barcoded order entry and automated warehousing system is tailor-made for this operation. Products move in and out of our warehouses and to the stores without anyone usually knowing what's in the cartons.

"The timing is beautiful. Because so many of our traditional sources are drying up the supply, we can legitimately buy from your front guys and return very slowly to some of our regular suppliers. That way we leave no traces when it's over.

"Aside from a handful of executives whose departments are affected, we should be able to limit exposure to the scheme," Warner explained.

"Do we have a deal?" Ramon asked.

Barry thought he knew the answer, but wanted to leave the door open to change the terms. "I'll get back to you in a few days—after I've had a chance to sleep on it and consult with some of my key associates."

Chapter Twelve

The two FBI agents pulled up to the front of Smith's Service and Towing in a nondescript, light blue late-model Chevy Caprice, looking like a couple of businessmen making a sales call. Eric Albert, the resident agent in Erie, led the way through a doorway on the left side of the building, which opened into a small suite of offices housing Bruce Smith and his buying and accounting staffs. He had been there before. Virtually every law enforcement officer in Erie County knew Bruce Smith.

Steve Stafford was already in the office, dressed in a pair of light blue Levi Dockers and a navy blue cotton crew neck shirt. It was his day off, and he had just driven the few miles from his home in Waterford.

"Hal's had some experience in what we're going to be talking about today," Albert said as he introduced Special Agent Hal Spear of the Detroit FBI. "Besides, since the victims are from Michigan and the accident occurred here, it's pretty certain that most of the investigation will be centered in the Detroit area."

Smith bolted out of his chair before the visitors could be seated. "I don't know about you guys, but my stomach says it's time for lunch."

"I'm sorry we're late, but Hal's commuter plane was delayed by storms in Cleveland," Albert said.

"Come on with me," Smith said. "I'll take you for a ride in the best American-made car in my memory."

Outside, they got into a shiny black Cadillac Seville STS. The two agents sat in the back.

"Business must be pretty good to afford this," Albert said.

"It's leased. Payments are only $625 a month. Uncle Sam pays for a good part of it . . . Sorry guys," he said, remembering the identity of his passengers.

The four entered the Main Street Cafe, a small but homey little restaurant with eight or ten tables and a counter in the rear. The wood-paneled walls were painted blue and plastered with signs advertising various specials.

Smith suggested cheeseburgers and French fries. "The fries are the best I've ever had, made from potatoes grown in the neighborhood." All took his advice.

"I've briefed Hal on the accident and your conclusion that a phony tie rod end may have caused it," Albert said, getting to the subject of the meeting.

"We're very interested because this ties in with an investigation we've been conducting out of our office for almost three years," said Spear, who identified himself as an assistant agent-in-charge of the field office.

"I know there are phony parts out there," Smith said. "Every once in a while someone shows up at our place and offers us a deal. Sometimes they'll call them overruns. Other times they might say they bought out the stock of a failing parts retailer and are liquidating the stock. I tell them to pound salt."

"It's a lot bigger than a bunch of carpetbaggers selling parts at the back door of places like yours," Spear said, announcing that he was going to give the trio a brief education about the counterfeit auto parts business.

"It's big, so big that it costs the Big Three automakers more than three billion a year. When you add the bogus parts for the foreign producers, that figure could swell to five or six billion.

"Counterfeit parts show up literally everywhere ... parts retailers, major auto service centers and service depots for big fleet operators like auto rental firms, which must order parts on short notice and shop for the best price on a day-to-day basis.

"We all know that one of the most blatant markets is the body shop. The auto insurance industry regularly turns its cheek on the widely used custom of substituting phony parts for the real thing."

"The only thing that matters to those guys is to get the job done at the cheapest price," Stafford interjected.

Picking up again, Spear said, "Auto parts counterfeiting is a global business. In fact, the people at General Motors tell us that 40 percent of all GM replacement parts sold in the Middle East and almost half in the Far East are counterfeit. Half of all counterfeit auto products sold overseas are manufactured in the United States. The economic impact is staggering, with some experts estimating that the manufacture and sale of bogus parts costs us 240,000 jobs in this country."

"I had no idea it was that big a deal," Smith said with astonishment. Sensing there was more to come he hollered to the waitress to put on another hamburger.

Spear started again. "Despite our efforts and those of U.S. Customs, I'm afraid to say it's not getting any smaller."

Besides the United States, he told the group, producing countries include Spain, Italy, India, Korea, Japan, Taiwan, Mexico, Canada, Great Britain and more. Components, he continued, include ignition parts, small engine parts, wheel covers, grilles, fan belts, filters, bearings, brake shoes and parts, rubber products, spark plugs, crank shafts, shock absorbers, steering assembly parts, etc.

"We've seen some bogus brake and transmission fluid that's so powerful it actually eats through aluminum," Spear explained. "There are also counterfeit engines on the market. They're bought at junkyards, cleaned, rebuilt, spray painted, relabeled, crated and sold for a fraction of the prices automakers charge for new replacement engines."

Spear went on to explain that many of the counterfeit products manufactured off-shore and shipped into the United States are generic. Once in the hands of distributors, they are put into U.S.-made cartons that are exact duplicates of those used by legitimate manufacturers.

Raids against manufacturers in the United States and abroad have done little to stem the tide, he said. "It's like putting a finger in the dike and trying to prevent a flood."

Albert's beeper went off and he excused himself to make a phone call. He returned in a minute to say that he had to respond to a bank robbery in Erie. Smith said he would take Spear back to his place and, if necessary, to the airport.

The agent from Detroit picked up where he left off, focusing now on General Motors and its two brands of replacement parts—AC-Delco and Mr. Goodwrench.

"Goodwrench parts are sold only by authorized GM dealers, the AC-Delco brand in a wide variety of outlets that range from neighborhood service operations like Smith's to K-Mart and other mass market discounters.

He pointed out that GM has explicitly warned dealers that those caught selling counterfeit Goodwrench parts risk losing their franchises.

"They are also spending millions on advertising campaigns that urge consumers to 'Look for Genuine GM Parts.' Unfortunately, dealers and consumers can't tell the difference by just looking at the boxes. The bogus packaging is just like the real thing."

"Well the problem here is not only a matter of dollars and cents," Stafford interrupted in frustration. "Four innocent people are dead. Fuck the money. It's a matter of life and death."

"You're absolutely right," Spear answered patiently. "The sad thing is no one knows how many deaths have been caused, though there are reports that at least two fatalities resulted from bogus brake shoes made of sawdust."

Spear quickly turned back to the money issue, pointing out that the losses were not only the result of lost sales.

"I don't get it," Smith said.

"Automobile manufacturers annually pay millions for product liability claims, resulting from accidents, some of them fatal. In many cases, the failures result from counterfeit components, which the complainants charge were the genuine article. Years after the accident, it's hard for the manufacturer to prove otherwise."

"This may sound a bit naive, but why can't we do a better job of tracking down these counterfeiters?" Smith asked.

"There's no simple answer," Spear replied, "but a major factor is priority. Various law enforcement agencies just have very little time to be proactive in dealing with the multibillion-dollar counterfeit industry.

"In fact, most attempts at breaking up domestic and foreign counterfeit rings have been undertaken by the automobile manufacturers and legitimate parts makers. Customs and the FBI usually respond if they show us the way."

Spear explained that in 1987, the Detroit FBI office, spurred by the U.S. Attorney for Michigan, decided to take the initiative, largely because the counterfeit auto parts business was having a tremendous impact on the Michigan economy.

"With the help of General Motors, one of our agents was put into business as an AC-Delco distributor. In a sting operation called 'Partsman,' our agent made contact with dozens and dozens of persons who sold counterfeit parts at the wholesale level. Many of the deals consummated with these people were captured on videotape," Spear said.

Spear told the others that the sting operation continued for three years. It culminated when dozens of agents, assisted by experts from GM and other automakers, raided forty plants in fifteen states. In all, government agents carted off sixty trailerloads of parts worth more than $30 million.

"The perpetrators ranged from hard-core criminals to sophisticated businessmen who were considered the 'pillars' of their communities," Spear said. "Some of the stuff was very good. In fact, one of the reasons experts from the automakers went along on the busts was to verify the parts were bogus."

The group left the table and returned to the service center, where the owner led Stafford and Spear out into the yard. The wreckage of the Taurus was still upside down, but covered by a royal blue tarp. Smith pulled back the plastic cover.

"It's no wonder there were no survivors," Spear said in shock as he walked around the compressed vehicle.

Smith motioned the FBI agent to the front wheel on the passenger side of the car and pointed to the broken tie rod end.

"This was the culprit," he said. "Almost brand new. When it came apart, the doctor lost control at high speed and that was all she wrote."

"Bruce said the tie rod end installed on the car carried the serial number of the Strong-Anderson brand," Stafford volunteered. "He stocks the real thing and compared the two for me. There was just something about the feel and look of the part that wasn't right."

"I assume you have close-up photographs," Spear wanted to know.

"We have it documented from every angle. I have a set for you in Bruce's office."

"Good. I'd like to take the broken tie rod end with me for lab analysis in Washington. If Bruce can spare a genuine Strong-Anderson part with the same part number that would help, too."

"No problem," Smith said with a wry smile. "I'll just deduct the $17.81 it cost me from next year's income tax. There's no charge for the labor. It'll take a couple of minutes for one of my mechanics to take it out of the car here. I don't do tie rod ends anymore.

"By the way," Smith said. I had two visitors looking at the car yesterday. One was an insurance adjustor for Premier Casualty. The other guy was a personal injury lawyer representing the family in Michigan. He was making noise about a product liability suit. I told him he was wasting his time."

Fifteen minutes later, one of Smith's mechanics came into the office with the severed tie rod end wrapped in plastic bubble pack and a box containing a new part for the Taurus. Smith handed them to Spear. "Here are the photos and copies of our reports on the accident," Stafford said. "Phone number for the doctor's father is also in there, in case you want to contact him."

"It's going to take us some time to unravel all of this," Spear said. "We first have to determine where the part came from and who installed it. Hopefully, that will lead us to bigger fish."

Chapter Thirteen

Carole Nordstrom had slept fitfully, her mind a kaleidoscope of flashing images relating to Barry Warner, Dan Sculley and the potential of becoming president of Upscale, a job that had more or less been promised by Warner when he hired her. When she finally dozed off into a deep sleep, the alarm sounded. She hit the snooze button several times, then finally disengaged it. She fell back to sleep and awoke about nine.

"I overslept," she said drowsily on the phone to her assistant. "Be there in an hour or so."

"I wouldn't hurry. Nobody of any importance seems to be here," the assistant said. "Jeff Weinstein's secretary says they're all at a meeting at Barry's house."

Nordstrom's first thought was one of paranoia; she had been excluded from whatever was happening because Warner had learned about her clandestine meeting with Cosgrove and Sculley. She quickly dismissed that thought. She sensed that Warner was up to something he didn't want her to know about. Why else would the No. 3 executive in the company, at least on the organizational chart, be excluded?

As distant as they had become, exclusion was not something that had happened in the past.

Carole decided that confronting Barry over the issue would display a measure of insecurity, give him the opportunity to be abusive. In the tight little, gossipy world of Upscale's top management, she would ultimately find out what it was all about.

Showered and dressed, Carole was filling the water bowl for Nippon and Claiborne when the phone rang. It was Mitch Rudolph. He expressed surprise that she answered the phone.

"Was expecting to get your answering machine."

"You almost did. I'm just getting ready to leave for the office. Overslept a tad."

"Probably needed the extra sleep."

"The only thing I missed this morning was the opportunity to talk with more unhappy vendors. Anyway, the pleasure of this conversation?"

"I have some good news for you . . . I hope," Mitch said enthusiastically. "Dan Sculley called just a few minutes ago and told me to call off the rest of the search. You really wowed them. The job's yours, if you want it. And providing, of course, that self-proclaimed Mr. Wonderful doesn't come up with a miracle, which Sculley assured me is quite unlikely.

"Sculley says they'll work out the details later, but it will be a much better deal than you have right now. He told me to emphasize that he keeps his promises. By the way, I probably shouldn't be telling you this but Sculley wanted to know whether there was anyone special in your life."

Carole took a deep breath. Getting snubbed by Barry made the decision a lot easier. "Tell Mr. Sculley I accept, but I won't order business cards just yet."

Barry Warner and his tennis-playing buddy, Tony Hartley, were just finishing a second set of tennis when the others began to arrive.

"There's orange juice, bagels and coffee at the gazebo," Warner shouted across the court to Mark Spencer and Jeremy Todd. "I should be finished in a couple of minutes."

Todd, Spencer and other Upscale executives knew the gazebo well. It was an open-air, octagon-shaped wooden structure tucked away in a wooden area of Warner's Hunting Valley estate. Warner used it during summer months for small executive conferences or for general entertaining. He thought its isolated location made it a perfect place for the hastily called Thursday morning meeting.

By the time Warner arrived, still in his white Fila tennis outfit, the others were assembled around a large white table with a glass top and wicker legs and trim. In addition to Spencer and Todd, senior vice president for merchandising, the group included Jeff Weinstein, senior vice president and chief financial officer, and Walter Hood, senior vice president for store operations. Hartley, Warner's confidant, took a seat off to the side.

Warner poured a tall glass of orange juice from a crystal pitcher and took a seat in a white wicker chair at the head of the table.

"I asked you to come here today on rather short notice because, aside from me, you have the greatest stake in the future of Upscale," he started, his tone dead serious. "You are the key players who mortgaged yourself to the hilt to participate in the LBO. I think you deserve to know where we're at now, our chances for survival and how we can assure it.

"Frankly, the picture does not look very bright for a conventional solution to our financial dilemma. The banks are playing hardball. Dan Sculley of Union First Bank has a big hard-on for me and he makes no bones about it. He's made it clear the pricetag for a Union First bailout is another major investment by me or my head on a silver platter.

"As you know, I've stonewalled on the issue of putting more money into Upscale. I've already invested $250 million. The fact of the matter is that even though I have a substantial net worth beyond that investment, most of it is in real estate. Given the state of the real estate market today, it would take months, maybe even a year, to raise the kind of cash Sculley is talking about. I'd take a substantial beating. Be that as it may, I'm not in the least bit inclined to put up one more dollar. Period.

"As for delivering my head on a silver platter, I'm not much for committing suicide. That means I'm going to fight like hell to stay alive, to save my investment and yours," he said emphatically, pounding his fist on the glass tabletop. "None of the alternatives are very pleasant."

"I don't think what you've said is a surprise to any of us," interrupted Jeremy Todd, youngest of the assembled executives. "I sense we're in the final seconds of the game and we need a 'Hail Mary' play to win it. You must have some suggestion or you wouldn't have asked us to come here this morning."

Todd's voice carried a touch of irritation, largely because of a lecture he had received from his wife no more than an hour earlier. She had exhorted him to challenge Warner to put up more of his wealth to protect Todd and all the others who had scraped up millions for their share of the LBO.

With most of their assets tied up in untradable Upscale stock, the Todds were having trouble existing on Jeremy's $350,000 annual salary. His wife said she expected other executives were having troubles, too, because of the high interest rates on notes signed to raise LBO capital.

"Look, Jeremy," Warner said coolly, "I know that you and the rest of the gang here are uptight, but what you have collectively invested in this company is a mere pimple compared with what I have at stake.

"Now, there's an option, but it involves some risk, which, personally, I'm willing to take. I believe it's the only viable solution left. If we don't take advantage of it, my guess is that we'll all lose our jobs and what we've invested in the company."

"Let's hear it," Mark Spencer said.

Warner looked around the table. There was the customary scowl on his face. Warner knew each of the participants well. They represented only a fraction of the management team that had put up a share of the buyout dollars. He had carefully selected them for inclusion in the meeting because their departments would be critical to implementing any deal with Commonwealth.

As arrogant as he was, Warner knew it would be impossible to engineer the deal by himself.

He pledged each attendee to secrecy, with a veiled threat that any breach of the meeting's content might be hazardous to their health. Then, without naming names and being vague about the details, Warner told them about the potential deal—counterfeit merchandise for cash.

"Unbelievable," gasped Mark Spencer, the graybeard of the Upscale organization. "I'm not sure I want to be part of this, Barry."

"I'll second that," Jeff Weinstein said strongly.

One by one, Barry went around the table, reminding each of the executives about his particular investment—the personal debt each had incurred. He stressed how Upscale's computer network, its automated ordering system and state-of-the-art warehouses made detection almost impossible.

"Anyone know what the penalties are for trading in counterfeit goods?" Mark Spencer asked snidely.

"Plenty," Walter Hood answered quickly.

Warner had heard enough. "Fuck you all," he shouted. "My balls are in a vise and so are yours. If I go down, you all go down with me. I don't need your permission to make this deal. I control the company. But your cooperation will make it a lot easier.

"Anyone who feels strongly about not participating can submit their resignation right now."

The silence was deafening. Warner looked around the table, waiting for the first defection. There was none.

"Okay," Barry said, his voice more conciliatory, "from this moment on we can limit our little secret to those assembled at this table. The more people who know about it, the more chance for a leak. We don't want that. Any further conversation with me regarding operational matters will be on a one-on-one and need-to-know basis."

"What did I miss at Barry's house this morning?" Carole asked Jeremy Todd over lunch at Charlie's Crab, a fashionable fish house around the corner from Upscale.

"How did you know about the meeting?" Todd blurted, then was immediately sorry he had responded that way to the question.

"You know as well as I do the walls around Upscale have ears. I didn't know it was such a secret."

"It was really nothing. Barry wanted to bring a select group of LBO investors up to date on his attempt to arrange financing. Since you are not in that group, I assume he saw no reason to invite you."

"Shareholder or not, I am still executive vice president of this company and I should know what's going on," she said with frustration. "Do you want to share that information with me?"

Realizing that he was in a tight situation because he reported directly to Nordstrom, Todd decided to extricate himself in a hurry.

"Afraid not, Carole. You'll have to get that from Barry Warner."

Back at Upscale in the afternoon, Warner knew he needed to buy time to pull everything together; there was no way he would be ready for Sculley and the other bankers on Monday afternoon.

He telephoned his lawyer, Seth Garfinkel, and in typical Barry style ordered him to postpone the meeting until at least the following Friday. When Garfinkel protested that Dan Sculley wouldn't like it, Warner raised his voice and said very succinctly, "Just do it," then hung up abruptly.

The next call was to Pedro Cardiz. "I'm ready to make a deal," Warner said eagerly, "but there are a couple of points I'd like to go over with Ramon and you, including the scope of our merchandising categories. We're very low in a number of categories, and this is a perfect time to fill in with products from your distribution. Can you make a meeting in Columbus, Ohio, on Saturday? Besides, there's something I want to show you."

Chapter Fourteen

Dr. Gerald Freeman was bitter and FBI Agent Hal Spear sensed it. He couldn't blame him.

"Look," the noted internist said after his secretary had put through Spear's call, "I've turned the entire matter over to my attorneys and they've already engaged the best personal injury law firm in the state. We are going to sue the shit out of whomever was responsible for killing my son and his family. Those two young doctors had so much promise. And the beautiful children . . . ," he choked.

"I can understand how you feel," Spear said sympathetically. "We're just trying to find out who was responsible for this horrible tragedy. We suspect a counterfeit part may have failed, causing your son to lose control of the car. We've sent the part to our lab in Washington for analysis."

The physician, in his office in Birmingham, Michigan, a trendy suburb of Detroit, told Spear he did not know where his son had the car serviced, but that he was always meticulous about keeping his car in good repair.

Spear told him he needed information on where the son banked and the account numbers, the latest statements and credit card numbers and statements.

"Unless he paid cash for service on the car," Spear said, "one or the other should tell us who repaired the steering system."

Dr. Freeman apologized for being abrupt, gave the agent the name of his attorneys and said he would call immediately and instruct them to provide any information he requested.

Sitting jacketless with the sleeves of his blue oxford cloth shirt rolled up to mid-arm, Spear spent the next two hours in his small office poring over logs and inventory records of the parts seized by fellow agents in the 'Partsman' sting operation. Every conceivable part found on an automobile or truck was seized in the raid on forty-five plants, but there was not one mention of tie rod ends. That meant the sting net had missed some of its targets, or counterfeit tie rod ends came from off-shore.

He called U.S. Customs headquarters in Washington, D.C., but had no better luck getting information on bogus tie rod ends being shipped into the United States.

Weary from studying the log sheets and records, Spear was about to leave the bureau when a one-page fax transmission arrived from Worthington & Worthington, the Freeman law firm.

It listed the names and numbers of young Dr. Freeman's bank and credit card accounts and noted that since it had been little more than a week since the fatal accident, all of the victim's checks had not yet been returned from the bank. Ditto for credit card statements. Checks and statements for the previous two months would be messengered to the FBI office as soon as they were collected.

Spear called the security department at Motor City Bank and arranged to review the victim's accounts the next morning.

"This won't take long," Spear told the leggy assistant vice president who ushered him into a small, sterile-looking conference room on the seventh floor of the Motor City Bank building. Inside the room she handed him a bulging manila envelope containing Dr. Robert Freeman's checks and bank statements for the past month and VISA and MasterCard statements for the past two months. She noted that it was near the cut-off date, and the cancelled checks for the month had not been mailed.

Spear took off his navy blue suit jacket, hung it meticulously on another chair and thumbed carefully through dozens of light blue checks, which covered everything from a deposit on a new apartment to clothing purchased at Brooks Brothers.

There was nothing remotely connected with any automobile service. The agent asked if he could look at checks for the past three months and was told it would take two or three days at a minimum to pull microfilm copies.

Next he studied the VISA statement, which contained a potpourri of charges, but nothing for an auto repair. He picked up the MasterCard statement and scanned the long list of charges.

"Bingo," he half-shouted. "June thirteenth. A charge for $235.75 to Rollins Brothers Auto Service in Ann Arbor."

Ramon, Pedro and a third man walked out of the executive aircraft terminal at Port Columbus Airport just as

Barry was pulling up in a rented powder blue Cadillac Sedan DeVille. As the trio entered the car, Ramon introduced the stranger as Mark Garrettson, director of midwest operations for Commonwealth.

Barry spent most of the twenty-five-minute drive telling his guests the significance of their trip to the Upscale Columbus Distribution Center.

"It's the most automated distribution center in all of retailing," Warner said. "That's what makes this deal so intriguing."

He explained that Upscale was the first major mass marketer to insist that every vendor put a barcode on every item or tag. No barcode, no business with Upscale. It was that simple, vendors were told.

Warner told how he had spent millions to equip each store with point-of-sale, or POS, cash registers to develop inventory management systems that are the most accurate in the industry. Instead of ringing up each item, the sales associate scans a barcode on the product or tag. When scanned, he said, the tag produces a veritable fountain of information on each SKU, including product category, style, size, color, price, promotional considerations, etc. When the sale is recorded, the item is immediately withdrawn from the company's massive inventory records. Each night after midnight, information on every store is processed in the mainframe in Beachwood. By 6:00 A.M., every executive has a total chain sales picture, as well as information on groups of stores and individual units.

"Our tight inventory control procedures dictate that virtually every item sold in any of the company's stores pass through one of the two identical warehouses. The other is just outside Kansas City," Barry explained. "In many cases merchandise moves from trucks on the incoming side of the dock to the trucks on the outgoing side without ever physically coming into the warehouses. It's called cross-docking and it's very efficient."

The assistant distribution center manager, a heavy-set dark-haired man in his mid-fifties, was stunned when he saw Warner walk through the door with the three guests, but it was typical Barry. In less trying financial times he was constantly on the road visiting stores and other facilities and never gave advance notice. Not knowing when or where he would materialize kept associates on their toes constantly.

The three men with him, Barry told the assistant manager, were principals of a South American firm with plans to build a similar automated warehouse. Barry excused the executive and said he would personally conduct the tour.

"One thing you'll notice here is that we have very few employees," Warner explained, walking briskly. "That's because every pallet or large carton that enters the center carries a barcode, which identifies the contents.

"Once a pallet or case of product is placed on one of these automated conveyors, infrared scanners read the barcode and automatically dispatch it to its proper picking location in our thirteen-story storage tower. Conversely, when orders are picked, computers direct our automated pickers to the proper location and the process is reversed, right down to putting it on the correct truck. There is almost no human intervention."

"Brilliant," Ramon said enthusiastically.

"Very impressive," Pedro shouted over the noise of the conveyors.

"Is this place always this busy on a Saturday?" Mark Garrettson wanted to know.

"This place goes twenty-four hours a day, seven days a week, 365 days a year. We never close," Warner responded.

Forty minutes later the four were aboard Commonwealth's parked Boeing 737 at Port Columbus Airport eating lunch and putting the final touches on the deal.

The call on Saturday afternoon came as a complete, but very pleasant surprise. It was from Dan Sculley.

"I'm having some of our senior bank officers and their wives for a cookout this evening," he said. "Even though it's a little late notice, it would be great if you could drop over. The dress is very casual."

"I'm very flattered," Carole said, pulling herself up on a patio chaise lounge. "But how did you get my unlisted number?"

"I put in an emergency call to Mitch Rudolph. Is there a problem?"

"No problem at all. I'd love to join you. Can I bring anything?"

"Just yourself."

Carole was delighted to know that Sculley's home was in The Woods, about two minutes from her condominium, and pretty sure about one thing—Sculley wasn't married.

All of the other guests were there when Carole arrived at eight, wearing a pair of skin-tight designer jeans and a red and black plaid blouse tucked in at the waist. A white alpaca sweater was slung over her shoulders. All heads turned when Sculley led her onto the beautifully landscaped terrace and started introducing her to his associates and their wives.

The only other person she knew was Peter Cosgrove, who was there with his wife, Lisa, a chunky woman with long black hair. Carole thought she didn't look as if she belonged to a man who was just a heartbeat away from heading a huge financial institution.

Sculley poured Carole an Absolut on the rocks and took her on a tour of the grounds, including the large oval swimming pool surrounded by a black ornamental wrought iron fence. The lot wasn't huge, but the landscaping was magnificent. They sat on a white wooden bench just outside the pool gate.

"You have a lovely place here," Carole said softly, resisting an urge to take the banker's hand.

"I built the place about three years ago . . . after the divorce. My wife got the mansion on Shaker Boulevard. The three kids live with her."

"How long were you married?"

"Just short of twenty years."

Carole volunteered that she had never been married.

"I'm sure you've had many opportunities."

"Only one that really mattered. But he was killed in a commuter plane crash. That was a long time ago. Since then, I've really been wrapped up in my work."

Carole couldn't remember how long they had been talking when Sculley suggested they rejoin the others on the terrace. A young waitress in a white blouse and black skirt was serving hors d'oeuvres. Carole ate a water chestnut wrapped in bacon, then tiny pieces of marinated chicken and pineapple that had been charbroiled on a skewer. Sculley handed her a fresh drink and excused himself to supervise the grilling of the steaks.

Peter Cosgrove cornered her. "I assume you've heard that the showdown meeting with Barry has been postponed until next Friday, at his request."

"Frankly, I hadn't heard. I haven't seen much of Barry the last week or so. Besides, I haven't really been on the financial side of the loop. I guess he feels that since I wasn't part of the LBO group, I don't need to know," she said, remembering the Thursday luncheon conversation.

"We're still confident that one way or another we'll get control and extremely pleased that you've agreed to work with us when we do."

"It certainly will be a challenge . . . if it happens."

"We have pretty close ties with the banking and investment capital world. We haven't heard an inkling about the possibility that Barry can raise the kind of money that will keep him in the picture."

"I know he'll take it hard if he loses control."

"Maybe we'll teach him some humility."

"If you want my opinion, Barry will never be humble . . . no matter what happens."

The other guests departed just before midnight. Sculley asked Carole to stay for a nightcap, which they sipped in the banker's magnificent mahogany-paneled study. At two, Sculley walked her out to the oval driveway and opened the door to the BMW convertible.

"I'd like to see more of you, if that's okay," Sculley said.

"I'd like that too, but I think we'll have to do it in private until this thing with Upscale is decided one way or another."

Chapter Fifteen

Barry Warner was euphoric about the deal, but the weekend numbers didn't do much to cheer him at six-thirty on Monday morning. He searched through the regional results with an on-line terminal in his home office and didn't find a single section of the country in which Upscale wasn't hurting badly. The phone rang just as he turned off the computer.

"Who the fuck is calling so early?" he said out loud to no one.

"Barry, it's Mark. Sorry to call you so early, but I wanted to catch you before you went out to the tennis court." Mark Spencer's voice sounded tired. "I've got something I'd like to talk over with you, and it's probably best done outside the office."

"If it's about the numbers, I've already seen them."

"I've been through them myself. Pretty awful."

"Look, Tony and I will be finished about eight-thirty. Give me a few minutes to shower, and I'll meet you in the gazebo at nine."

When Barry arrived at the gazebo, Spencer was seated in a large wicker chair, sipping coffee from a gold mug emblazoned with a distinctive looking black logo. He was wearing a pair of navy slacks and a white cotton crew neck sweater.

There were dark fleshy circles under his blood-shot eyes.

"You look terrible, Spencer," Warner said.

"I feel worse than terrible."

Warner poured coffee from a brown ceramic pot into an Upscale mug and sat down across from the No. 2 man at Upscale.

"I can't go along with it, Barry."

"Go along with what?" Warner responded tartly.

"The plan you outlined at the meeting the other morning. I know we're in desperate condition, but breaking the law to solve the problem will just create far more problems in the long run. I respect you and appreciate what you've done for me, but I've invested too many years in this industry building a reputation and I'm not about to throw it all away."

"You know, Mark, if this thing goes down the drain you're going to be a multi-million-dollar loser. I don't think you can afford that."

"I've factored all of that into my decision. I'm sixty years old, I don't need the stress."

His face flushed, Barry took a deep breath and stood up. "How can you, of all people, do this to me after what I've done for you? You were nothing but a drunk. But I gave you a chance when no one else would touch you with a ten-foot pole. This is the thanks I get. You really have gall."

"Integrity is a better word, Barry," Spencer bristled, refusing to be intimidated by Warner's bluster.

"Call it whatever you want, but I want you to know I think you're an ungrateful prick."

"I'm sorry you feel that way."

"Did you say anything to Irma?" Warner asked, returning to his seat.

"No, I just told her that this entire financial situation and the way we are performing has me depressed. She said maybe it was time to take a walk."

"The timing is really fuckin' great," Warner responded with hostility.

"I've given this a lot of thought and believe the best course for all concerned would be to announce that I'm taking early retirement because of health reasons."

"Okay, Okay. I don't have any problem with that, but for the time being I want you to get lost. Take Irma to my place in Palm Beach for the next week. Tell flight operations you want to leave this afternoon. I'll tell the staff you're stressed out over the entire situation and need some time away. At this point everyone will understand.

"When you return I'll get Human Resources working on fulfilling your retirement package."

"I'm sorry about this, Barry," Spencer said offering his hand.

Warner turned abruptly and walked out of the gazebo.

The impact of Mark Spencer's decision began to settle in as Warner drove his two-seater Mercedes convertible to Upscale. Warner admitted to himself that it was a major blow to his plan to resuscitate the company. He had counted on Mark to make the counterfeit deal work; now he had to formulate an alternative plan and do it quickly. You don't replace a seasoned executive like Mark Spencer overnight.

He thought about the possibilities. Jeff Weinstein was a brilliant financial strategist, but had very little practical retail experience. Walter Hood, head of store operations, was a pusher and very adept at squeezing the last ounce of performance out of every store manager, but he was generally regarded as a prick who would sell his own mother if it meant adding $9.95 to a store's register tally.

And then there was Carole Nordstrom, probably the most qualified of all. However, the fact that she was not part of the LBO posed a problem, and Barry knew he could never confide in her about the counterfeiting scheme. Still, without telling her all of the details, she had to be part of the scheme to get new merchandise into the stores.

"This entire situation has gotten to Mark Spencer," Barry said to his secretary, Sadie Young. "He's depressed, shell-shocked, beaten. I told him to take a few days off with his wife and stay at my place in Palm Beach. Call the housekeeper and tell them the Spencers will be there late today and to take good care of them.

"Check with Fern about Mark's schedule for the week. Get me a breakdown of what he has on tap. I know he was scheduled to go to Jacksonville tomorrow for the opening of our new prototype store. I wasn't planning to attend, but under the circumstances maybe I should be there. Tell flight operations I'll leave at ten tomorrow morning. By the way, if anybody asks about Mark, let's just say he's under the weather."

Barry then tore a page from a yellow legal pad that contained the names of the executives who had been at the gazebo meeting on Thursday. Pedro Cardiz wanted information on them for future reference.

He handed the list to Sadie. "Have personnel get me updated resumés on these people and throw in Carole Nordstrom's, too. You know enough about all of them. Add any personal information you can think of, such as home addresses, names of wives and children, hobbies, etc. And tell Jeremy Todd I'd like to see him as soon as possible."

Jeremy Todd was just ending the weekly marketing department executive staff meeting when he was summoned to the chairman's office. Jacketless, he grabbed a white legal pad from his desk and headed down the corridor and up a flight of stairs to Warner's huge penthouse office suite, the only one on the fourth floor of the building. Todd always had a white legal pad with him. He was continually taking notes and always writing follow-up memos to meetings and conversations. One Todd memo, carefully directed, could trigger an avalanche of paperwork.

Warner had chided him on the note-taking and memo-writing on more than one occasion, finally telling him that if he stopped using so much paper he could single-handedly save the environment.

"Let's sit over here," Barry said, motioning his chief marketing executive to an area composed of four cream-colored Italian leather chairs and a square teak coffee table.

"You won't need that this morning," said Warner pointing to the legal pad. "The less we put in writing about this matter, the better off we'll be. That means no memos. Period.

"Now, we're ready to proceed with the matter we discussed at the gazebo last Thursday," Warner said quietly. "It's going to be tricky because we have to involve Carole . . . without her knowing what's going on. Working with Carole, but keeping her essentially in the dark, you are going to be the point man for this operation. The job essentially involves coordination with our new suppliers."

"How do we get started?" Todd asked eagerly.

"Very slowly. It's going to take a few days to iron out the details and begin implementing the program, but within a week or two we should have some merchandise flowing into the pipeline. We must phase it in in such a way that we don't alert our major manufacturing suppliers that something not kosher is taking place.

"As far as Carole is concerned, I'll touch briefly on my plan to involve more distributors in our merchandise mix when we get together later."

Warner was exceptionally cordial when Nordstrom entered his office. He even apologized for the stress she was undergoing and suggested that things would soon be getting better. Barry's upbeat mood didn't surprise her. She had seen enough of his Dr. Jekyl and Mr. Hyde personality in the past.

Jeremy arrived five minutes late for the meeting, equipped as always with his legal pad. This time Barry put no prohibition on his using it.

"I wanted to get together with you to discuss a couple of matters," Warner said at the outset of the meeting. "First, Mark Spencer is a little under the weather, and I've instructed him to take some time off. The pressure of the entire situation has taken its toll on him, as it has on all of us."

"Any idea how long he'll be out?" Carole asked with concern.

"I don't know how long he'll be out of action—and between us, there's a chance he won't return to his role as president. Right now, it's a day-to-day thing. He's pretty emotionally beat up. That means we'll all be under the added burden of picking up some of Mark's pieces. I'm going to Jacksonville to take his place at the grand opening."

"You know we'll do anything we can," Jeremy said.

"Getting the shelves stocked again is my major concern," Warner said. "Once customers get in the habit of shopping somewhere else, you may never get them back. While we have a short-term problem right now, we must plan for the long term. I'm planning to be around for a while yet.

"As a stop-gap measure—and this is very confidential—I've made arrangements with independent distributors who stock a number of the lines in which we are currently lacking, most notably fragrances, auto parts and athletic shoes. I'm trying to work out arrangements in other categories as well.

"Within the next forty-eight hours, I'll need an updated report on major out-of-stocks in those areas I mentioned, so that we can get the merchandise flowing into our stores as quickly as possible. I'll be arranging a meeting with a representative of the distributors within the next few days, and we'll discuss procedures at that time."

On the way back to her office with Todd, Carole expressed shock at the news that Upscale would be buying regular merchandise from distributors to fill its out-of-stocks.

"If we can't pay our regular vendors, how are we ever going to pay these new suppliers?" she asked.

Todd just shook his head as if he didn't know.

Chapter Sixteen

The agents did not call for an appointment, but by the time they arrived at Rollins Brothers the next afternoon they had assembled a short background on the firm and its operator, Bud Rollins.

Rollins Brothers was founded in 1935 by Cyrus Rollins and had been in the family ever since. Ownership passed from the founder's son, Cryus, Jr., and then to his son, Bud, who bought out his father in 1987. Dun and Bradstreet reported the firm paid its bills on time, and the IRS said it earned more than $125,000 the previous year.

As they drove to Ann Arbor from downtown Detroit, Hal Spear and John Crenshaw, a young agent assigned to work with him, agreed that it was highly unlikely that Bud Rollins would knowingly jeopardize a more than fifty-year reputation in the business by dealing in bogus parts.

"But you never know," said the blond-haired, blue-eyed Crenshaw, just two years out of law school.

"You're absolutely right," Spear agreed. "Sometimes those who appear to be the most honest turn out to be the biggest crooks. Look at some of the people we picked up in the 'Partsman' sting. On the surface they were real solid citizens."

"There's nothing like the lure of the easy buck," Crenshaw said. Rollins Brothers was located on Stadium Street, not far from the University of Michigan campus. The exterior of the one-story brick building and the landscaping were immaculate. They pulled the beige Chevy Caprice into the driveway on the right side of the building and parked the government-issue car in a small area reserved for customer parking.

It was a hot summer day and a large overhead door leading to the garage area was open. They walked in. The inside was spotless, with five service bays on each side and a wash rack at the far end of the building.

A young man in a starched gray work shirt with a "Rollins Service" patch over the pocket greeted them at a free-standing service desk located near the front of the building.

"I'll tell Bud you're here," the young man said nervously when both produced their FBI credentials.

A few minutes later, Rollins came out to greet the agents and motioned for them to follow him into the office, a modest-sized space about fourteen-feet square. A large gray metal desk was on the far wall. A black leather chair and gray credenza were behind, and two metal chairs with leather seats were in front. An IBM computer with a monochrome screen was on the credenza. The agents took the two seats.

"We're sorry to bother you during the heart of your business day, but the matter we have to discuss is very important," Spear said solemnly. He removed a copy of Dr. Robert Freeman's MasterCard statement from inside his brown suit coat pocket and kept it folded.

"Ten days ago, a couple from Ann Arbor and their two children were killed in a traffic accident in Pennsylvania and . . . "

"Dr. Bob Freeman . . . a terrible tragedy," Rollins said, interrupting Spear in mid-sentence. "He was a good customer. As a matter of fact, he was in here not too long before the crash. The daily paper said he lost control of the car and went off the road. The guy was a workaholic. Maybe he fell asleep at the wheel."

"That's what we want to talk with you about," Spear said. "This credit card statement we obtained from his bank shows that Dr. Freeman charged $235.75 worth of service here on his MasterCard on June 16, 1992. Can you tell us what you did to his car?"

"Sure, just a minute," Rollins said confidently. He turned toward the credenza and began typing on the computer keyboard. The search took just seconds.

"Here it is, Dr. Freeman's complete service file on the 1988 Ford Taurus."

Rollins tapped on the page-down key until he reached the final file entry on Freeman's record. "That's right, it was June sixteenth. He complained the car was not handling well, and we replaced the right side front tie rod end. Charged him $35 for the part and $49 for the labor. I personally test drove the car, as I do on most of our repaired vehicles, and we corrected the problem. We also tuned the car and replaced the oil. The total amount was what you said . . . $235.75."

Crenshaw noted the information on three-by-five file cards, the standard FBI issue.

"The tie rod end . . . where did you get it?" Crenshaw wanted to know.

"We don't stock many parts here. Just costs too much to carry all that inventory. We buy from a couple of sources, but mainly from Partsmania over on Washtenaw Avenue. They're part of a big chain and generally give us the best prices." Rollins turned and looked back at the screen.

"Our records show it was a Strong-Anderson part, and it did come from Partsmania. We keep very accurate records here because we try to ascertain the profitability of every job, no matter how small. You want to know what I paid for the part?"

"That won't be necessary."

"What does this have to do with me anyway?" Rollins asked, getting right to the point.

"First of all," Spear answered sharply, "the outer tie rod end you installed failed at high speed and that caused Dr. Freeman to lose control of the car and crash."

"That's bullshit. Strong-Anderson is a quality manufacturer of automobile replacement parts. A new tie rod end simply doesn't fail after a few hundred miles."

"We have no doubt about the quality of *real* Strong-Anderson parts," Crenshaw assured him. "But we have a strong suspicion that the part your company installed on Dr. Freeman's car may have been counterfeit."

Rollins's mouth dropped open. "That's un*fucking*-believable," he said, visibly shaken.

"Don't get me wrong. We're not intimating right now that you or someone in your organization knew it. We're just stating what we suspect about the part. We've sent the part that failed along with a legitimate Strong-Anderson part to Washington for analysis and should have a report very quickly."

Spear took a stack of pictures from his attaché case and thumbed through them for Rollins. He stopped at a close-up

117

of the broken outer tie rod end. "See right here, the ball joint came out of the socket."

Spear asked the owner if he could be sure that it was a Strong-Anderson part that was installed on the doctor's car.

"We service fifteen to thirty cars a day here, and they all usually require some parts, which we get from Partsmania and other suppliers. I have eleven mechanics. I don't do any of the work myself anymore. To be honest with you, I don't remember whether I saw the box and the part that went into the car. We have an on-line terminal connected electronically to the Ann Arbor Partsmania store. We just tap in what we want and within an hour they deliver it to us. They have great customer service."

Spear wanted to know who ordered the part. Rollins said it was either himself or his nephew, Rodney, the young man who had greeted the agent at the desk. Rollins said the part was installed by one of his best mechanics, a young man named Jim Davis, working in Bay 7.

"We'd like to talk with him later," Spear said.

"No problem."

"Have you ever had any problems with the parts ordered from Partsmania?"

"Nothing of any consequence. No supplier is perfect. Once in a while we get a lemon part and Partsmania—and all of our suppliers, for that matter—replace it immediately. We guarantee our work."

"The guarantee didn't do Dr. Freeman and his family much good," Crenshaw interjected snidely.

"Is there any way one of your mechanics could substitute a counterfeit part for the real thing?" Spear wanted to know.

"Why? For what reason? These guys are well paid. Most have been with this company for ten, fifteen, twenty years. Ernie in Bay 10 is starting his twenty-fifth. We've been in business for a long time and we hope to be here a lot longer.

"Believe me when I tell you we've had the opportunity to purchase counterfeit parts. Every three or four weeks we're offered some deal on parts at prices that are unbelievable. At those prices the parts are either stolen or counterfeit. I don't have anything to do with them."

Spear finally asked Rollins to bring in Jim Davis, the mechanic, and asked the owner to leave the room. The interview with the blond-haired mechanic didn't produce much more than the conversation with Rollins.

"We deal with a lot of parts every day," he said softly. "You take the old parts off, put the new ones on. I assume what Bud or Rodney orders and the parts store sends over is the right part. There's nothing special about a Strong-Anderson or other brand of tie rod end, if it's the right part for the right car. I just put the right part on the right car."

By the time Bud Rollins returned to his office, the two agents were ready to leave.

"If there's anything else I can do to help, please let me know," Rollins said, as he walked the two out into the sunlight.

"We may be calling on you again," Spear said, squinting. "In the meantime, we'd appreciate it if you keep our visit confidential. We've asked the same of Jim Davis. At this point, we don't want to awaken any sleeping dogs."

Chapter Seventeen

"Thought with the meeting coming up on Friday we'd better get our ducks in a row," Barry Warner said to lawyer Seth Garfinkel and Gary Cardwell, an investment banker from New York, over lunch at the Cleveland Racquet Club.

"You've been very elusive the last four or five days," the thin, wiry Garfinkel replied between gulps of chicken noodle soup. "Where do you stand on the financing?"

Warner knew he had to be elusive because he was not prepared to bring his two friends and advisors into the inner workings of the deal.

"I've had some discussions with an outfit in New York about getting some financial help. We are close to a deal. It involves my putting up a sizeable amount of Upscale stock as collateral, in return for $250 to $300 million, which I will then lend to Upscale. Right now, I don't want to go into a lot of details, but the deal feels comfortable."

"Who are these guys, anyway?" Garfinkel asked in surprise.

"A couple of South Americans who have a lot of excess cash."

"The company's name is Commonwealth Investment Services. They have over a billion dollars in liquid assets."

"What's in it for them?" Garfinkel probed.

"They get interest on their money and a first option to buy the company from me."

"Sounds clean enough," Cardwell offered.

"I don't know," Garfinkel said quizzically. "I'd like to know more about it . . . see something in writing."

"In due time, Seth. Let's drop it."

Garfinkel knew enough to abandon the line of questioning. Barry always told you only what Barry wanted you to know.

"I want to keep Dan Sculley guessing as long as possible," Warner told the duo. "That means no tips, no leaks. I want to play out the string with him. Get him to make a speech at the meeting. Get him to make a commitment on the record as to what the bank will do if I put up my own money. Get him to say what will happen if I don't."

"Word on the street right now is that he's telling people there's no way you'll come up with the funds necessary to keep control of the company. If I know Sculley, he's tapping every banking source around the world to find out what you're up to," Cardwell said.

"I don't think it's any secret that he has been actively seeking candidates for your job," Garfinkel interrupted. "There's even a rumor that his lieutenants have been talking to people inside the company about life when you're history."

"That's a crock of shit. I have a pretty loyal management group. Even though some of them are pretty ambitious, I know I'd get the word."

"It should all be academic come Friday," Cardwell said.

"Seth, I want you to take the lead in organizing the meeting," Warner ordered. "Put together an agenda. We'll need a report on current sales trends and prospects for the short-term future, an update on our cash position, and a report on the current state of our inventory. Carole Nordstrom can help you with that. Let's make it as bleak as we can. I want to get as much as I can out of those bastards."

"I don't think you have to exaggerate," Garfinkel replied soberly. "It's pretty bad as it stands now."

Cardwell was instructed to prepare a five-minute summary of the LBO, of which he was the architect. It was to include how much had been paid back, how much was still owed and what Upscale needed in terms of relief.

"I can do it off the top of my head," he responded.

"Then we'll turn the floor over to Mr. Sculley and let him make an ass out of himself," Warner said gleefully. "We'll let him think he's on the brink of victory. Then I'll land a $300 million punch on the prick's nose."

Garfinkel raised the question about dealing with the media, which he said would be out in force for the meeting.

"Fuck the media. We are a privately held company and have no financial reporting responsibility to anyone, except the banks, bondholders, shareholders and the IRS. For now, the only comment we're going to have is no comment. I don't want anyone to be optimistic in any way; I just want to take Sculley by surprise. We'll work out some kind of statement after the meeting, when we know the exact terms."

Cardwell stopped at the men's room on the way out of the club, and Garfinkel cornered his client. "Barry, I'd still like more details about the deal. We've been friends and business associates for too long for me to let you go off half-cocked just for the sake of protecting your ego."

122

"Get off it, Seth. I'm a big boy. When I need your advice I'll ask for it . . . and pay for it."

A long rectangular box was in front of the door when Carole Nordstrom arrived home from work. She walked in, turned off the security system and pushed Nippon and Claiborne away from the door, fearing that the two declawed felines would escape into the cruel outdoors. She carefully reached outside and pulled in the white box.

At the kitchen table she slid the card from under the red ribbon and opened it. The note was from Sculley.

> *Enjoyed being with you on Saturday night. Hope we can do it again soon. If you want to call me at the bank, my private number is 621-3397. Unlisted number at home is 831-7791. Dan.*

She opened the box and was touched by the sight of a dozen long-stemmed red roses. She couldn't remember the last time anyone had sent flowers. Carole put the flowers in a clear crystal vase, set it on the kitchen table, poured a full glass of Night Harvest wine and sat on the hunter green living room couch.

She was thrilled by Sculley's interest. It was mutual. The few hours she had spent alone with him were the most tranquil she could remember in years. She found him attractive physically, but there was much more to it than that. There was a gentleness, a depth of kindness, a keen intellect and inquisitiveness. He was the antithesis of any man of power she had ever met.

But as Carole sat there sipping the wine, she was perplexed by the conflict between what had the potential for a budding relationship with Sculley and her duties at Upscale.

The conversation with Barry and the revelation that he was going to buy from new distributors continued to bother her, especially how he planned to pay for the merchandise.

There must be more to it, she thought. It must be part of a greater plan to save the company. But, what was the plan and why wasn't she a part of it? She suspected Jeremy Todd knew a lot more than he was saying. She was determined to find out what was going on, even if it eventually cost her the current position at Upscale.

Carole told herself to move slowly, then picked up the white princess phone and dialed Sculley's private office number at the bank. He answered on the second ring.

"Hi, it's Carole Nordstrom," she said nervously. "Thank you for the lovely flowers."

"What a pleasant surprise. Where are you?"

"I got home a little early."

"I'm just finishing up a meeting, It'll be about five more minutes. Give me your number and I'll call you right back."

Carole poured herself another glass of wine and waited for Sculley's call. It took about ten minutes.

"I thought if you're not doing anything special for dinner tonight, I might reciprocate for the cookout Saturday night," she said cheerfully. "Besides, I need to practice my culinary skills. They're getting rusty."

"I have a meeting that will last until about seven. How about half past eight?"

"Fine, the guard at the gate will direct you to my place. Tell him your name is Van Dorn. We can't be too cautious these days."

"I like your way of thinking."

"While you're on your way here, you might consider the possibility that Barry Warner may have more lives than a cat."

* * *

Carole was in the driveway of the condo when Sculley arrived in a red Porsche Carrera. She motioned him to pull in behind her BMW convertible.

"Thought a stuffy banker like you would be driving something a little more conservative than that," she chided as he got out of the car.

"I left my conservative wheels at home. This is my summer fun car. I stopped home for a few minutes to check the mail and change clothes. Didn't want to look too stuffy in my dull banking attire.

He was wearing a pair of khaki pants and a kelly green Jack Nicklaus shirt with a golden bear emblem on the lapel.

"This is strictly casual," Nordstrom said. She took his hand and led him through the garage and into the condo. Nippon and Claiborne were at the door.

"I'm not sure I'd call what you have on casual," he said. She was wearing sand-washed silk pants and a tunic with a gold contour belt adorned with a cheetah buckle. Sculley thought she looked stunning.

"It's just a little something I picked up in New York the last time I was there. Nippon and Claiborne say 'hello' to Mr. Sculley."

"Dan, if you don't mind."

She put ice, vodka and lemon peels into two short glasses and placed them on a tray along with a basket of assorted crackers and small bowls of chicken, egg and tuna salad and led Sculley out onto the patio.

They settled into a pair of high-backed white metal chairs with matching cushions made from material that looked as if it were copied from an abstract painting.

"So you think Barry may have nine lives," he said.

"Well his demeanor was a little mellow this morning. That's not typical Barry. He's usually arrogant, confident and smug. Today he acted as if he didn't have a care in the world. He told us he had lined up some alternate sources of merchandise and that should help our out-of-stock position."

"That's interesting. Did he tell you how he was going to pay for it?"

"Not really," she said. "He told us we'd be getting more details in a few days."

"Maybe he's just raising a smoke screen."

"A smoke screen for what?"

"I'm just speculating, But I know we've touched base with virtually every banking source in the world with resources to help bail him out and not one of them has reported being approached recently by anyone representing Barry. That's strange."

"I guess all of the suspense will be over on Friday."

"Let's hope so."

"You've seen my resumé, but I've never had a look at yours," she said smiling, deciding to change the conversation. "Give me the short version."

He told her about growing up as one of six children in a small Oklahoma town, where his father owned the local bank. He was the oldest and the only boy, and he relished the big brother relationship with his younger sisters, who were there to cheer him on when he starred on the high school's football, basketball and track teams.

"We weren't rich by any stretch of the imagination," he told her, "and it sure helped when I won a football scholarship to Oklahoma State. Remember, my father still had five girls to put through college."

He said he had no interest in pursuing a career in banking. Instead, he received a degree in business administration with a major in marketing and took a job as a trainee with J. Walter Thompson Advertising Agency in Chicago. A month after he was promoted to junior account executive, he received a panic call from his oldest sister telling him that his father had died of a heart attack on the golf course. After the funeral, his mother asked him to return home to run the bank. Having enjoyed the good life in Chicago, he had one goal when he returned: to sell it for the best price and get out of Oklahoma.

A funny thing happened, though, he told Carole. He liked banking. With the marketing skills he learned at Oklahoma State and three years at J. Walter, he began innovating and promoting. The bank began growing.

"Within five years, Community Federal had grown from its main office and a tiny branch to the fastest growing institution in the state, with ten offices and assets of $200 million. All across the country, banks were merging in droves. Sculley said he had two choices: to be an acquirer or be acquired. The family voted to sell out. Sculley took his two million, put it in tax free municipals and became executive vice president of Midwest National Bank in Chicago, the bank holding company that had purchased the family bank.

"I think I've exceeded the short version," he said smiling, "but to make a long story short, we merged and merged and acquired and acquired. One day I wound up in Cleveland as chairman and chief executive officer of the whole thing."

"I'm curious about one thing," said Carole, who was totally captivated by Sculley's story. "Why all of the distaste for Barry Warner?"

"It goes back to the days in Oklahoma and a shifty little guy named Harry Gilbert. who owned the local department store called Gilbert's. On Saturdays, the rural folks were lined up into the street trying to get into the store.

"One day Harry Gilbert came into my dad's bank with a proposal to expand his inventory. Said he needed a short-term loan of a million dollars. Trusting soul that my old man was, he approved the loan. After all, everyone in town knew that Harry Gilbert was doing a land-office business.

"Harry took the million dollars and disappeared. A month later, creditors from around the country descended on our little town and forced the store into bankruptcy. They settled for five cents on the dollar. The biggest loser was the bank. I think the stress from that deal finally took its toll on my father.

"In a strange way, Barry Warner reminds me of Harry Gilbert."

Chapter Eighteen

The call from the FBI lab in Washington came in just as Hal Spear and John Crenshaw were getting ready to leave the crowded white-collar-crime-squad bullpen for Findlay, Ohio. Spear took the call in his small office. The conversation between the agent and the senior metallurgical technician was brief. Spear nodded his head a few times, thanked the caller and hung up. Then he returned to the bullpen, initialed the Bud Rollins interview notes and handed them and a stack of three-by-five interview cards to a clerk for filing.

"That was a call from Washington," he told Crenshaw as they walked out the door. "The technician said we had a case; the part from the car was a fake. They ran scanning microscope tests on the samples of both the broken part and the new one I picked up in Erie. He said the real Strong-Anderson part was made of high quality cold-rolled carbon steel. In his own words, the knock-off was made of 'shit.' He said the gauge of the metal crimping the ball was thicker on the real part. A detailed fax is on the way. You have to admire Bruce Smith. He took one look at the part and said it was a phony."

Morning rush-hour traffic was just winding down when they pulled out of the downtown Detroit area on their way to the headquarters of Strong-Anderson in Findlay, a small city of forty thousand located in the northwest quadrant of Ohio, about a hundred miles south of Detroit. Crenshaw was behind the wheel, and the usual summer construction projects on I-75 slowed them down.

Spear was slumped in the corner trying to nap, to recoup an hour or so of the sleep lost during the night because of the inevitable argument with his wife, Helen, about his continuing a career with the bureau.

Being an FBI agent was all Hal Spear ever wanted. When he graduated from Duke University Law School, all of the other hotshot graduates headed for the big law firms and large starting salaries. Spear opted for the bureau.

During his first assignment in Boston, he met and married Helen, whose father was managing partner in one of the city's premier law firms. At first, she was enamored of the fact that her husband was an FBI agent, but as her two brothers graduated from law school and entered the high-paying world of corporate law, she began carping at Spear to accept her father's offer to join the firm. She never got anywhere.

When their two children were old enough to start school, she wanted them in private institutions, which Spear could not afford as a young agent. She got her way about private school only after her father offered to pay the tuition. Year after year the bickering got worse. It never even lessened when Spear received a choice promotion as assistant agent in charge in Detroit, heading the white collar crime unit.

Now, it was unbearable. He finally told her last night that he had no intention of leaving the bureau now . . . or in the near future; he liked the challenges the job presented, and he was damned good at it. With all of the crooks in the world, someone had to be the good guy. If she didn't like it, he would cooperate in giving her a divorce.

Spear awakened drowsily from a forty-five-minute nap just as they were passing a sign that said Findlay was thirty miles away. "This should be an interesting session this morning," he said to Crenshaw. "Their head of security is a former FBI agent who left the bureau in 1986. He said we wouldn't believe the struggle they've had with this counterfeit stuff. He told me this was the first time they've heard of a fatality resulting from a knock-off of one of their parts, though he couldn't swear it had never happened before."

"My guess is that it happens more often than they think, or even would admit," Crenshaw said, taking a drag of a Marlboro.

"With forty to forty-five thousand traffic fatalities a year in this country, I'm sure you're right," Spear said. "One thing you can be sure of, the auto companies and parts manufacturers aren't going out of their way to publicize the dangers."

Spear was surprised at the large turnout in the Strong-Anderson conference room. The woman at the head of the table, a striking redhead in a beige Evan Picone suit, was Maude Strong, the president and daughter of the company's founder, who was now chairman of the board. Others she introduced were three attorneys from the company's law firm in Chicago, two principals from a private investigating firm out of Indianapolis and the company's senior vice presidents for sales, marketing, engineering and public relations.

"Your report about the unfortunate accident in Pennsylvania brought home our worst fears that this continuing plague of counterfeiting would finally take a toll in human lives," Maude Strong said in a strong, husky voice. We stand ready to help you in any way possible to bring the people responsible for this to justice."

Spear brought the group up to date on what he knew about the accident and the subsequent investigation, including the morning call from Washington verifying that the tie rod end was a fake.

"It's funny you should mention Partsmania, which happens to be a fairly large customer of ours," Maude Strong said. "About six months ago one of our sales managers noticed that sales volume with Partsmania had slowly eroded to the point that it had dropped about 20 percent over the previous three months.

"We called in the salesman and he couldn't explain it. Business at Partsmania was strong and all of our other major parts retailers were increasing volume with us rather than decreasing it. It just didn't make sense.

"Then over a period of two months, Strong-Anderson received dozens of letters from repair shops and consumers complaining about poor quality," Maude Strong said.

"As you can imagine, we take customer complaints very seriously. We followed up each of the letters, and there was one common denominator—all the parts in question were purchased from Partsmania. That's when we turned the matter over to the law firm that has represented us in other counterfeit matters."

"I'm sure you know the counterfeit parts business is enormous," one of the lawyers piped in.

"We know," said Spear. "We're from Detroit."

"The counterfeiters are very clever," the lawyer continued. "They'll never just load up a store with counterfeit parts. They'll find a way to subtly integrate them into a supply of regular parts. You go into a store one, two, three, four times and you get a genuine Strong-Anderson part. The fifth time the box contains a counterfeit. Or, maybe you never get a phony."

The lawyer reached down to the floor next to his chair and pulled up two sets of boxes. One set included boxes labeled as Mr. Goodwrench parts, marketed through GM's dealer network. The other set contained two green and yellow Strong-Anderson boxes. He shoved them across the table to the agents and asked them to identify the real boxes. Neither could tell the difference.

Spear wanted to know what the company had done about Partsmania and was told that Strong-Anderson's PI firm had purchased dozens of parts at every one of Partsmania's stores and found many counterfeit parts of surprisingly good quality.

One of the principals from the PI firm told the agents about an undercover operation now under way at the Partsmania warehouse near Detroit, but said no move has been made yet because they've been unable to pin down the source of the counterfeits.

"We want to blow the whole thing out of the water at one time," the investigator said. "It's necessary to nail the suppliers of the parts as well as the retailer. Otherwise the counterfeits will just show up elsewhere."

Spear turned the questioning to the origin of the counterfeit parts. The PI said he thought most were coming from the Pacific Rim, though it was possible that counterfeiters in the United States and other parts of the world were involved.

"The counterfeiters know all the tricks," said the other PI principal, who identified himself as a former U.S. Customs supervisor. "The bogus parts or goods are shipped into the United States in bulk, with no identification number, no packaging. They may be listed simply as auto steering parts. That way, there's no trademark infringement.

"Once the stuff gets off the dock, it's shipped to a facility where serial numbers are stamped onto the parts, and they are packaged in incredibly good replicas of the original packaging."

A pretty, dark-haired receptionist brought in a tray of deli sandwiches, and the meeting continued without a break until about two o'clock, by which time Spear had heard enough and decided to get back on the road.

All agreed that, for the present, super secrecy was the prudent approach.

"No need to alarm the general public at this time," the preppy-looking Strong-Anderson public relations executive said. "Of course, we're a publicly held company and have the shareholders to worry about, too. Word of this kind could cause a panic."

Maude Strong had an uncomfortable look on her face, wishing that her PR advisor had never made that statement in public.

Spear and Crenshaw spent another half hour with the lawyers and private investigators to review their files, then headed for Detroit, convinced that the next step was a visit to Partsmania.

Chapter Nineteen

It was a typical grand opening party with plenty of hoopla and, as Barry Warner suggested, a minimum of speeches.

"Let the store and the merchandise speak for itself," Barry had said on more than one occasion.

And that's what he essentially told the guests at Upscale's new Jacksonville prototype store in a brief welcome that lasted about a minute.

As Barry had expected, the media were out in force, but not necessarily to look at the new fixtures. He had taken a calculated risk when he allowed public relations to announce that he would personally appear at the grand opening, rather than Mark Spencer, who was reported ill.

"I'll be a target, but will take my chances one on one," he said in vetoing a press conference.

The first reporter to corner him was a reporter for the Associated Press, which had a request from the *Plain Dealer* in Cleveland for coverage of the event and comments from Warner on Friday's impending showdown meeting with the banks. He was quickly joined by a stringer from the *New York*

Times and a writer from the *Wall Street Journal* who had flown in from Atlanta.

"Have you been able to line up financing to keep Upscale out of bankruptcy?" the AP reporter asked.

Warner always marveled at the stupidity of some reporters and their inane questions. Why, he thought, would I ever answer that question even if I had the answer.

He decided to be patient and charitable and to throw a curve ball at Sculley and the other bankers.

"I think there's very little likelihood of your finding Upscale in bankruptcy," Warner answered. "As you can see from our new concept store here in Jacksonville, we are definitely thinking in future terms. We plan to be around here and elsewhere across the country—with the same ownership and management.

"As for financing, we are presently in negotiations with two large West Coast financial institutions and one foreign investor. We are confident something positive will happen by our Friday meeting."

"Can you give us a hint on any names?" the *Times* stringer inquired.

"I don't think that would be appropriate."

"What about the rumors that the bankers have already started recruiting your successor in anticipation you will fail to line up financing?" the *Wall Street Journal* reporter wanted to know.

The questions kept coming from the group assembled around him, and Barry kept volleying with non-answers. Finally, a local TV reporter interrupted and asked if he could talk about the new store concept, to back up some of the footage his crew had shot.

"Sorry guys," he said turning to the print media, "have to tend to business. This guy wants to talk about some matters that will get customers into my store."

He motioned to the TV reporter and crew to follow him and walked out of the tent erected in the parking lot and into the store, knowing full well that the business about the west coast banks and foreign investor would send Dan Sculley on a wild goose chase to verify the information.

Dan Sculley's early-morning call awakened Carole from a sound sleep.

"What time is it?" she moaned.

"Five after six. Look, I'm sorry to call so early, but I just saw the *Plain Dealer* and have an important question. Barry told reporters at your store opening in Jacksonville last night that he has two West Coast banks and a foreign investor interested in providing financial assistance to Upscale. Just wanted to know if you heard any scuttlebutt along those lines."

"I'd probably be the last to hear about it. All I know is what I told you Monday night. Barry appeared to be confident things would work out."

"It's too early in the morning to check out west coast sources. If American banks are involved, I'm sure we'd have gotten wind of it. The foreign side is a little tougher."

"I guess you won't have to wait too long until you find out."

"I don't like surprises," Sculley said. "Do me a favor. If you hear anything around Upscale today, please get in touch. Otherwise, I'll call you at home this evening. Sorry for the early wake-up call. Bye."

Carole shut off the snooze alarm, which had been set for seven, and decided to sleep in, then resume the session with Jeremy Todd, which had ended at 2:00 A.M. Both had left Upscale exhausted after identifying hundreds of items that could be purchased from the new distributors.

But she could not fall back to sleep. There was something about the new arrangement that bothered Carole, especially Jeremy Todd's enthusiasm for replacing long-time vendors with strangers, known only to Barry Warner. She sensed that Todd knew a lot more about the arrangement than she did, but was stymied in finding an approach that would get him to open up.

Chapter Twenty

Jim Davis, the Rollins Brothers' mechanic, had agonized for two days and two nights about whether to share his secret with Mike Garber, his future brother-in-law and manager of the Partsmania store in Ann Arbor.

Davis didn't want to get into any trouble with the FBI for spilling the beans about the visit two days earlier, but reasoned he didn't owe anything to the feds. He decided to tell Garber. How far he wanted to take it was his business.

He called work, left a message he would be a little late and then waited until eight o'clock for the Partsmania store to open. At Davis's suggestion, Garber took the call in his office.

"Remember the story in the *Ann Arbor News* several days ago . . . about the family of four killed in a traffic accident in Pennsylvania? It was all over page one. The parents were both doctors at the University of Michigan Hospital."

"You had to be blind to miss it. Why?"

"I repaired their car just before they left for the East. It was an '88 Ford Taurus. Replaced an outer tie rod end. Two FBI agents came to visit us the other day. They talked to Bud and me. Said the tie rod end failed, causing the driver to lose control.

"Our records show it was a Strong-Anderson part and we got it from your store."

"It's too bad about the crash, but isn't that Strong-Anderson's problem?" Garber asked.

"It would be, except the FBI thinks the part was counterfeit."

"There must be some mistake. I've been with Partsmania for six years. We sell only branded parts. That's part of our appeal. I just can't believe it."

"Hey, I'm not taking sides here. I'm just reporting what I know. And, by the way, you didn't get this information from me. Understand?"

Joe Longo listened intently as Mike Garber relayed the conversation between Jim Davis and himself.

"Any other information?" Longo wanted to know.

"No, just what I told you. Except that Jim Davis—he's my future brother-in-law—said the agents asked him to keep their visit quiet."

"Let's keep it that way for now internally. In the meantime, I'll get in touch with Strong-Anderson and see what they have to say."

When Joe Longo hung up, he didn't call Strong-Anderson. He dialed directly to the posh Hassler Hotel in Rome and asked the operator to connect him with Sonny Longo, his father, the owner-president of Partsmania, who was vacationing in his native Italy.

Sonny Longo, a black-haired, tall, muscular man in his early sixties, was just getting serviced by a high-class Italian hooker when the phone rang. His first inclination was to let it ring. But, on the fourth ring, he reached over and picked up the phone.

"Dad, it's me, Joe. I need to talk to you." The connection wasn't the greatest.

"I'll call you back in an hour," Sonny said and hung up the phone.

Sonny Longo handed the bimbo three hundred American dollars, showed her to the door and said he'd see her tomorrow at the same time. When she was gone he remembered he forgot to ask her name. He took two small bottles of Finlandia vodka from the mini-bar, put three ice cubes in a glass and emptied the two vodkas. The first sip burned all the way down.

Sonny dialed Partsmania via AT&T USA Direct, told the American operator his credit card number and waited for an answer. He thought AT&T USA Direct was the greatest advance in travel convenience since the airplane. You no longer had to deal with foreign hotel operators and get screwed by the second on toll charges.

"We have a major problem, Dad," Joe Longo said breathlessly as soon as they were connected. "I have Billy and Danny here in the office, but don't want to put on the speakerphone because someone might overhear the conversation." Billy and Danny were Sonny's youngest boys.

"So what's the problem?" Sonny asked, the vodka already making him mellow.

Joe outlined the scenario, and Sonny didn't like it one bit. "Good thing I'm not around to take the heat," he said firmly. "I'm sure you'll be hearing from the feds very soon. Just how and when is the question."

"We have a half million in Strong-Anderson stuff in the warehouse right now," Joe said. "About a fifth of it from our friends in Korea. Right now, it's all integrated with the legit merchandise."

"Any way to sort it out quickly?"

"Take a week."

"That's no good. What about the stores?"

"About the same amount."

"My gut reaction is we clean out the Strong-Anderson warehouse stock tonight, but only the product categories in which we go both ways. Leave the 100 percent legit categories alone. Probably fill two semis. I take it most of the stuff is on pallets."

"Correct."

"With forklifts it should take a couple of guys three or four hours tonight, after the warehouse is closed. As a matter of fact, Billy and Danny both can drive forklifts. Let's use them. Call Tony Riggio at Allied Trucking and tell him you want to store the semis at his place for a couple of weeks. Make sure the rigs are locked."

"That will leave us with only two semis to handle our regular store restocking programs."

"Call Penske Leasing and rent a couple of trucks for a month."

"What do you suggest we do with the stores?"

"We can't worry about 125 stores right now. We'd get too many of our own people suspicious."

Then Sonny gave his oldest son instructions on how to deal with the FBI, if agents showed up.

"You gotta be very careful about what you say. Be polite. Don't piss those guys off. Help them out, but don't tell them anything except that we've had a lot of complaints about Strong-Anderson parts and we're phasing them out as a supplier. That's why the inventory is so low. That'll confuse them."

"Great thinking, Dad."

"They'll certainly want to talk with me. Tell them I'm on an extended overseas vacation and not expected back for a month. That'll buy us some time. Tell them you're my son, but you just do what you're told. After you've handled the warehouse tonight, tell Billy and Danny to get lost for a few days."

"What about the rest of the stuff in the warehouse?" Joe asked.

"My guess is that the FBI will limit themselves to Strong-Anderson. By the way, call Lee Ling and tell him to hold any further shipments until we notify him. And tell him in no uncertain terms we don't ever want to see another tie rod end from him."

Chapter Twenty-one

The silver and white Lear Jet touched down at County Airport right on schedule. Barry Warner was in the executive jet reception area to greet Mark Garrettson, whom he had met over the weekend with Pedro and Ramon.

"He looks just like a cop," Barry said to himself as he saw Garrettson stoop through the door of the Lear and slowly walk down the steep retractable stairway, a gray glen plaid suit jacket slung over his shoulder. He was tightly built, about six-foot, 185 pounds, Barry thought.

Warner led the director of midwestern operations for Commonwealth to his two-seater Mercedes convertible, told him to buckle up and gunned the car out of the parking lot, leaving Garrettson's hair in wind-blown disarray.

"Ever been to the Cleveland area before?" Warner asked.

"Never had the pleasure."

"Unfortunately we won't have enough time to show you the sights this trip. Maybe the next time you're here. Do you play tennis?"

"Played a little when I was a kid, but not in a lot of years. Took a slug in my right shoulder during a shoot-out with a pair of bank robbers when I was with NYPD.

"It's restricted my mobility."

"How many years were you on the force?"

"A dozen . . . long enough to make lieutenant and earn a law degree on the side."

"How did you land at Commonwealth?"

"I'd had enough of police work. New York is a jungle, as I'm sure you know. After the shooting incident, I put a high priority on living to a ripe old age. Even though I had a law degree, I didn't want to practice law or work as a prosecuting attorney, though I had opportunities to do both. I decided to give corporate security a shot. Commonwealth was looking for a security director and hired me. The starting salary was twice what I was making on the force."

"And now, if you don't mind my saying it, you're on the other side," Barry remarked, smiling wryly.

"I guess you might say that," Garrettson answered coldly, "but I gave up on idealism a long time ago. I just look at this as a business opportunity. And, as you will come to find out, the people I work for are a helluva lot more moral than some of the so-called giants of business and industry, including some of the sleaze on Wall Street and in the savings and loan industry. They do business on a handshake and they keep their word."

Carole Nordstrom and Jeremy Todd were already at the gazebo, sipping coffee and eating the bagels and cream cheese that had been put out by Warner's full-time cook.

The large white wicker table was filled with the order documents they had created during the past forty-eight hours. It was decided that the initial orders would be presented to Upscale's new supplier manually, so they could discuss any discrepancies or problems with Garrettson. Once the format for ordering was established, most of it would be done electronically from Upscale's mainframe network directly to Commonwealth's data processing center near Chicago.

Garrettson had received a briefing on the two principal Upscale players during the ride to his home. He knew Todd was aware of the counterfeiting plan; Nordstrom was not. The ex-cop gave each a smile and a warm handshake and said he hoped this was the start of a long and mutually rewarding relationship. He handed each an expensive-looking business card that proclaimed him as president of Retail Distribution Services, Inc.

On cue from Barry, Garrettson explained that his company represented a number of distribution centers that supplied a wide variety of general merchandise to retailers ranging from single mom-and-pop operations to some of the largest retailers in the country. By having a central ordering location, which redirected the orders to the appropriate warehouse, he explained, there was a tremendous savings in paperwork, which reduced the costs for all concerned. No company was more efficient in supplying the needs of retailers, he bragged.

Garrettson was smooth, and Warner was sure he would make a good impression on the savvy Nordstrom, who sat there silently, listening to Garrettson's spiel. Warner sensed that Nordstrom was buying the package when she told Garrettson that Upscale desperately needed all the help it could get in filling its shelves.

Still, Nordstrom wondered silently why Warner had opted for this route and what kind of financial deal Barry had cut with Garrettson and the people he represented. The subject of terms never came up in the discussions.

The meeting lasted for three hours. Nordstrom and Todd took turns covering the categories Garrettson's group would supply. The match between what Commonwealth's could initially supply and Upscale needed wasn't perfect, but Nordstrom estimated the hard-strapped chain would get 90 percent of what it needed.

Garrettson said the process of supplying Upscale would be very easy because everything would be delivered directly to Upscale's two distribution centers and then funneled out to the stores in the retailer's trucks.

Merchandise would be on the road to Columbus and Kansas City within three days, which meant it could be in the stores the following week.

Finally, Garrettson stuffed a three-inch-thick packet of orders into his black attaché case and said that for an initial period all inquiries should be directed to him personally. His director of management information would be getting in touch with Nordstrom in the next few days to make arrangements for handling future orders by Electronic Data Interchange, he explained. Carole told Garrettson she didn't understand much about computers; Jeremy would be the contact for implementation.

Barry thought the meeting went well and said so to Garrettson on the way back to the airport. The ex-cop was not so sure.

"There's something about your Ms. Nordstrom that bothers me," he said. "I'm not one hundred percent certain she buys what we're trying to do."

Chapter Twenty-two

The twelve-car caravan followed by a white moving van pulled up in front of the gray two-story Partsmania office building and distribution center at 8:00 A.M., just before starting time. The complex was located in Metro Industrial Park, a few miles from the runways of Detroit Metropolitan Wayne County Airport. Spear heard the roar of the jet engines as he got out of the FBI-issue car and motioned for the others to follow.

There were about forty people in all, including twenty agents, Strong-Anderson engineers, the two PI firm principals and an attorney from the auto parts manufacturer's law firm. Spear was dressed in a gray pinstriped business suit. The rest of the agents wore blue jeans or other casual pants and dark blue "raid" jackets with the letters FBI emblazoned on the back. The others were also in casual clothes.

A moving van, also lined up by agents working for Spear, was in the convoy, ready to haul the parts and records seized during the raid. Spear sent the moving company equipment people and three hired forklift operators around to the loading dock on the side of the building.

The raiders followed Spear through a single glass door into a small reception area. A middle-aged woman, obviously shocked by the entourage that had engulfed the room, slid open the glass window and in a piercing tone demanded to know what was going on.

"FBI," Spear shouted, flashing his badge. "We have a search warrant, and we're executing it."

The raiders barged past her through a set of double doors and down a long corridor. In the process, they almost trampled Joe Longo, who stepped out of his office to check on the commotion.

"What's going on here?" he shouted.

The FBI jackets gave him the first clue. "Who's in charge here?"

Spear identified himself.

"I'm Joe Longo," he announced. "What's this all about?"

He was dressed in a pair of tight-fitting black pants, a white shirt with subtle gray and maroon pinstripes and a garish-looking flowered tie. He had an arrogant look on his angular face.

Disliking him immediately, Spear stepped directly in front of the black-haired Longo until they were nose to nose.

"We have a warrant to search your facilities and we're going to do it."

"On what grounds?"

"Trafficking in counterfeit auto parts."

"That's ridiculous."

Spear shoved the warrant into Longo's hand. It had been approved the previous afternoon by the U.S. Attorney's Office and signed by a federal magistrate.

"You can read it all right here," Spear said.

Longo looked over the document. The contents did not surprise him.

Fanning out into the warehouse, the agents ordered all of the employees out into the parking lot on the side of the building. One agent logged all of the names and job descriptions. Another photographed all of the doors and obtained general shots of the interior, documentation to be used later if anyone claimed the agents damaged the facility.

The crispness of the place impressed Spear. The walls were light blue and framed aisles of navy blue racks that reached to the ceiling. Until they were ordered to stop, yellow forklift trucks darted in and out of the aisles. The place was brightly lit with overhead fluorescent fixtures. A long conveyor belt ran down the center aisle.

The lay-out looked very much like that on the diagram provided by the PI firm.

After the initial encounter with Spear, Joe Longo heeded his father's advice and tried to be helpful.

"Believe me, we have nothing to hide," he said to Spear. "I think you'll find what you're looking for down that aisle. We try to organize our inventory alphabetically. Makes it easier when we put the stuff away and pick it for our own stores and wholesale customers."

Longo offered forklift drivers to aid in the search, but Spear declined, saying he brought his own.

Armed with razor knives, the squadron of agents descended on the Strong-Anderson boxes. They were closely followed by engineers from Strong-Anderson, there to separate the real parts from suspected counterfeits.

"Get anything that looks suspicious and bring it out here," Spear barked. "We'll set up a command post at the end of this aisle and photograph anything that doesn't look right, then load it into the truck."

Moving swiftly into the bookkeeping and data processing departments, Spear and five agents ordered all personnel to leave the building and photographed everything.

The agents systematically examined the files, searching for any records that dealt with the purchase and sale of automobile steering components and other parts manufacturers.

The contents of entire drawers, which contained regular and cellular phone records and check stubs, were hastily shoved into corrugated boxes, which were tagged and photographed. The agents also seized dozens of back-up computer tapes and volumes of printouts.

A massive pile of cartons was assembled in the middle of the bookkeeping department. Two agents created a long line and summoned the movers to load the cartons into the van.

The remainder of the agents questioned office and warehouse people about vendors and procedures. Spear walked into Joe Longo's large office and found him behind a huge cherry desk, talking on the telephone.

"Be with you in a minute," he said, putting his hand over the phone.

Spear took a stack of three-by-five note cards out of his coat pocket and waited for the owner's son to hang up. He looked around the office. The trappings, including expensive grass cloth and tasteful paintings, were handsome.

"You have a key for your father's office?"

"Sure."

"I'd like to have it."

"No problem. You won't finding anything of interest in there."

Longo opened the center drawer of his desk, pulled out a gold key ring with a single key dangling from it and handed it to the agent.

151

Spear's interview with Longo was brief. Vehemently denying that the company dealt in counterfeit parts, Longo blamed the Pennsylvania accident on shoddy merchandise produced by Strong-Anderson and strongly suggested the agent raid the manufacturer if they wanted to get to the bottom of the case. In fact, Joe Longo told Spear Partsmania was so unhappy with Strong-Anderson, it was phasing out the company as a supplier.

The agent dutifully noted Longo's comments on his cards. In the end, he got about what he expected. When Spear asked Longo where his father was staying in Italy, the son declined to answer.

The interview completed, Spear and another agent moved to Sonny Longo's office. More opulent than his son's, the senior Longo's office featured French provincial furniture more suited for a living room than a place of business. An enormous desk, barren except for a large Rolodex, dominated the room. Spear took the Rolodex and, finding no other files of any kind, left.

In the warehouse, dozens of green and yellow Strong-Anderson boxes were strewn everywhere. Agents systematically ripped off the shrink-wrapping on pallets, cut open taped cartons, slipped out randomly selected boxes, then took out the contents for inspection by Strong-Anderson engineers.

By noon, the raiders had searched through more than fifty lines of parts, but the experts from the auto parts manufacturer couldn't pinpoint one part that was an obvious counterfeit, nor could they find a single steering component part for any car in the center.

An angry Spear called an end to the search, but ordered agents to take one of each component for further analysis by the scientific center in Washington. Three agents boxed and inventoried the items while another photographed the premises a second time to document the place when they were finished.

"Find anything interesting?" Longo asked the departing Spear.

"I'm sure you knew we wouldn't," the agent responded icily.

"We just run an honest business here."

"Yeah," Spear said. "Tell that to the family of the four killed in the Pennsylvania traffic accident. You haven't seen the last of us."

Chapter Twenty-three

Samantha Henderson, the busty black business reporter for Channel 3, shoved a microphone into Barry Warner's face as he stepped out of the topless Mercedes in front of the Upscale headquarters. A cameraman a few steps behind focused on his face. "We have a report that says you're going to step down today and give up control of Upscale," Henderson said.

Having tangled verbally with her in the past, Warner's first inclination was to shove the microphone aside. He took another tact. "Read my lips," he said loudly, so that another group of reporters could hear. "You're full of shit," he mouthed silently.

"Hope you can use that on the noon news," Warner yelled as he entered the double glass doors.

He imagined that Dan Sculley had endured the same gauntlet when he arrived for the meeting, but couldn't imagine him giving the media such a creative retort.

Warner felt great. He had reversed his usual morning polarity. This time it was an aggressive roll with his live-in, Jennifer, and then two solid sets of singles with Tony Hartley. He was ready for Dan Sculley and anyone else who turned up for the financial showdown.

He stopped at his office to check phone messages and found a dozen from the media, which surprised him. He thought the entire Cleveland-area media corps was assembled in his parking lot.

Laura Green, the chunky, red-haired vice president for public relations and advertising, ducked into his office. She had a pretty face but Warner thought she was built like an orange traffic-control barrel and had said it to her once, reducing the PR executive to tears.

"Thought we'd better touch base before the meeting started," she said in a husky voice. "I assume that we will continue our 'no comment' policy until we have something on which to comment."

"We'll issue some kind of a statement when the meeting is over. All I can say is stand by and we'll take things as they come. I already made things tougher for you on the way in here by telling Samantha Henderson she was full of shit."

"She can get pretty aggressive."

"Before you do anything else this morning, alert the video department that I will probably address the troops in the field when the meeting is over. Hopefully, I'll have some news that will be a quick morale booster."

"Does that mean I'll have a job tomorrow?"

"You'll have a job tomorrow," Warner said smiling.

Barry looked at his watch. It was a minute to ten, time to make his entrance into the Upscale executive conference room. Instead of walking through his office door, he decided to take the long way around and enter from the other side.

"Gentlemen," he said cheerfully to the dozen people congregated around an ornamental coffee cart containing fancy pastries and silver pots of regular and decaf coffee.

Barry made the rounds, shaking hands with everyone in the room. He didn't waste any words on Sculley or Cosgrove, both of whom were dressed in identical dark blue double-breasted suits.

"I wonder if those two assholes from the bank had the same mother," Barry whispered to his attorney, Seth Garfinkel, who had just motioned for everyone to be seated.

The conference room was a showplace, framed with impeccably matched cherry wood, which matched the large rectangular conference table. Four long skylights in the ceiling flooded the room with sunshine. Works by Picasso, Miro and Chagall lined the walls. At one end of the room, double cherry doors were opened, revealing a large projection screen.

Barry took a seat at the head of the table and was flanked by members of his executive and legal teams. Sadie Young, his secretary, was at his right elbow, ready to take notes. Dan Sculley and his entourage were at the opposite end of the table. The air was tingling with tension.

"In the interest of moving things along in an expeditious manner, we've prepared the agenda that has been placed at your seats," said Barry, opening the meeting. "If there are no objections we'll proceed on that basis. Now, let's get comfortable," said Barry, standing and removing his tan lightweight suit jacket. The others joined him.

"I assume we're here for the same reason," he continued, "and that is to resolve this financial crisis and allow Upscale to regain its place as one of America's most successful retailers. I would hope we could conduct business here today without any of the rancor that has characterized some of the press accounts of our problems." He stared directly at Dan Sculley.

"I am sure you are all well aware of our financial difficulties and what they are doing to our ability to conduct business on a normal basis. Many sources of supply have dried up, unless we pay in advance. Our cash reserves are being depleted at the rate of three million a day. At that rate we'll be out of money in a month."

Warner turned over the meeting to Jeff Weinstein, the young fleshy-faced chief financial officer, whose sagging suit trousers reflected the success he was having on a diet. Weinstein's ten-minute slide presentation on Upscale's financial position made it painfully clear that the one-time star of retailing was in serious trouble.

"In my judgment, we need a new line of credit of about $350 million, a moratorium on loan repayment, a reduced interest schedule for eventually repaying the loans and some relief in paying the money due on the zero coupon bonds," Weinstein concluded.

"Is that all?" Sculley asked, scowling.

"I guess so," Weinstein answered meekly and returned to his seat.

Sculley bounced to his feet and started pacing. The room was silent for more than a minute while he framed his thoughts.

"And if we give you all of the things you are asking for, what will management of Upscale do to assure us that this isn't just another ploy to pour more money into a sinking ship?"

"I'll answer that question for Mr. Sculley," said Warner, on his feet too. "The retail climate appears to be improving. With a chance to restock our stores, rebuild confidence with our suppliers and get a little breathing room in loan payments, which are choking us, we can turn this around very quickly."

"I think we've heard that song before," Sculley said with a wave of disgust. "Let's cut out the bullshit and get down to facts. Personally, I think that when you put together the LBO, you overstated the potential for cash flow and the ability to repay the notes and bonds.

"Secondly, we're not terribly happy with the management of a company in which we have a lot of money at stake. I'm sure that comes as no surprise to Mr. Warner. Frankly, I'm not one to throw good money after bad. I can only foresee two scenarios in which we would alter terms of the original loans and bonds and set up a new line of credit as large as you're asking."

"And what might those scenarios be, Mr. Sculley?" Warner responded smugly, knowing full well what was coming next.

"Nothing has changed. We have made it quite clear that our terms for renegotiating the original loans and providing a significant line of credit are contingent upon Mr. Warner showing good faith in his company by matching our own commitment with a significant one of his own."

Warner paused, picked up a glass of water from the table and sipped slowly.

"If he doesn't and Upscale has no other source for the money it needs, I'm afraid we'll have to take drastic measures," continued Sculley.

"That includes Mr. Warner giving up day-to-day control and being replaced by a new CEO of our choosing. Mr. Warner doesn't lose anything but operating control, *and* his handsome salary. He still maintains his majority interest in the company."

"That's a pretty steep price to pay," said Seth Garfinkel, who was sweating profusely because he knew that if Barry went, so would his law firm, which billed Upscale in excess of $2 million a year.

"Putting $350 million more on the limb is also a pretty steep price to pay," Sculley said sarcastically.

"And what happens if I refuse your generous offer?" asked Barry, amused by the scratching between Garfinkel and Sculley.

"Your company is in default," said Sculley, pointing directly at Warner. "You're probably looking at bankruptcy, either Chapter 7 or 11. Either way, you'll probably lose most of your original investment."

"That doesn't give us much maneuvering room," Warner responded with a cold stare at Sculley.

"If you don't mind my saying it, you've done all of the maneuvering you're going to do at our expense," exploded William McBride, the rotund, silver-haired bond representative seated next to Pete Cosgrove. "We're going to get this one way or another and do it quickly. We're one hundred percent behind Mr. Sculley and the banks."

Ready for the kill, Barry left his seat again and moved quickly toward a white chalkboard. He picked up a red marking pencil and put two headings on the board. On one side he penciled "Warner" and on the other "lenders," then drew a line down the middle. On the Warner side he put a dollar symbol but no amount.

"I agree, Mr. Sculley, it is time to cut the bullshit. Let's deal in specifics."

Sculley looked uncomfortable in the wake of Warner's aggressive posture.

"Suppose I change my mind and decide to put up the money you request, give me the specifics of your deal," Warner insisted.

Sculley reached down into his attaché case, pulled out a manila folder and extracted a white sheet of paper, which he never expected to use.

"First of all, the new line of credit will be for 150 percent of what Mr. Warner chooses to invest in Upscale at this time. The repayment terms will be prime, plus two."

Barry penciled in $300 million-plus LOC—for line of credit.

"Second, we will take one third of the outstanding balance of the original $1.5 billion in bank loans and convert them to a stock position in Upscale. Our investment will be about $500 million. That will substantially reduce the loan. Interest on the remaining balance will drop from a flat 11 percent to prime, plus two. There will be a six-month moratorium on the payment of interest and principal."

Barry scribbled notes on the "lender" side of the board to reflect Sculley's comments.

"As for the bonds, Mr. McBride says a majority of the bondholders have agreed to reduce the 15 percent zero coupon bonds to 11 percent and give Upscale a six-month reprieve on repayment.

"And, since our bank and the other lenders our bank represents would now hold a substantial position in Upscale, we propose to expand the board from nine to thirteen members. The additional members will be appointed by us. And finally, we would want much closer reporting from management to the board."

"Is there anything else?" asked Warner, making the final notations on the board.

"That pretty well covers it."

Excusing himself, Warner motioned his secretary to come with him. Outside the conference room, he told her to type the notes in the same format he had outlined the material on the board.

Barry walked back into the room about ten minutes later and handed copies of the typed notes to Sculley and Cosgrove. Sadie Young passed them to others in the room.

"Do these notes accurately reflect your proposal?" Warner asked Sculley and Cosgrove.

"Exactly," Sculley said pushing the paper aside.

"You've got a deal. I'm in for $250 million."

Seeing that Sculley was stunned, Warner smugly called a brief recess so that each side could huddle concerning drafting of an announcement to the media.

Chapter Twenty-four

Sculley spent the entire time conversing with Cosgrove and McBride. The obviously disappointed banker admitted he had misjudged Warner; he was not mentally prepared for the turnabout that had just taken place.

"Where is he getting the money?" Cosgrove wondered.

"I don't care if it's the last thing I do on earth, I'm going to find out how Warner came up with it," Sculley said angrily. "I guarantee you it's not coming from a bank, or we'd have known it."

"Maybe he has some rich friends," Cosgrove murmured.

"How many people are running around with a spare $250 million to lend a friend whose company is going down the drain?"

"Let's face it, Dan," said Cosgrove, putting a hand on Sculley's shoulder. "You threw down the gauntlet and Barry picked it up and ran with it. You've known all along that he's a big-time gambler. He apparently picked up the dice and rolled them."

"Well, he's not seen the last of us. With our four seats on the board he'll squirm and justify every decision. Being a lender is one thing. Being a part owner is another."

Sculley turned to a yellow legal pad and started doodling. He was angry at himself for not anticipating something like this. He was concerned about Carole Nordstrom and her reaction, but more important how the entire situation would affect their budding relationship. He could not see sneaking around town whenever he wanted to see her.

Warner restarted the meeting with an announcement that the first $125 million installment would be in the bank on Monday; the second, three weeks from that day. Sculley said once the first installment was in hand, the bank would immediately activate the new line of credit.

"There's only one other matter we need to address," Warner said. "Wording of the press release . . . and how to handle the horde of media that are presumably here to see me carried out like a gored matador. A lot of them will be disappointed."

"I've penciled something I think will work for all of us," Seth Garfinkel said, interrupting his largest client. "This is about as simple as it gets. I'll read it.

"Upscale Corporation and its lenders and bondholders agreed today to terms that will relieve financial pressures on the 650-store discount department store chain and allow it to resume normal relations with vendors and other creditors.

"Under terms of the agreement, Barry Warner, founder, chairman and chief executive officer, has agreed to purchase an undisclosed amount of stock from the company treasury. The proceeds will help Upscale meet its current and future financial needs.

"In response, the lenders, led by Union First Bank, will initiate a new $375 million line of credit and take other steps to reduce debt and interest payments resulting from the leveraged buy-out of the company. A portion of the $1.5 billion in outstanding loans will be converted into ownership in the chain.

"Bondholders have also agreed to a moratorium on interest payments and a reduction in the interest rate earned on the bonds."

Noting there wasn't a single objection to the wording, Warner made a suggestion: "Unless someone has the insatiable desire to stand up before the media today, I suggest that we have this statement typed, duplicated and distributed. I, for one, have no desire to amplify what Seth has so ably articulated.

"No one will get any additional details from the people at Upscale. I would hope Mr. Sculley and his associates feel the same way."

The word flashed through Upscale's headquarters—Barry had backed down, put up the money and retained control of the company. There was a collective sigh of relief in all but one office. Carole heard the word from Jeremy Todd, who had talked with Jeff Weinstein, the only senior manager at the meeting besides, of course, Barry. Todd said Barry would be addressing corporate staff in the amphitheater at 1:00 P.M., the rest of Upscale's employees via satellite an hour later. While she had never underestimated Barry's resourcefulness and grit, the news was certainly not the best she had ever received. Carole always knew that Dan Sculley's offer was contingent on Barry coming up with the shorts. His attitude the past few days had given her the uneasy feeling that he would somehow pull off retaining control. It was a feeling she had expressed to Dan Sculley during a late night phone call hours before the meeting. During the conversation, Sculley had been almost too sure that Barry would be a footnote in Upscale's history by lunchtime. She tried to caution him not to underestimate a man who had created a retail dynamo and was fighting to save it.

In the final analysis, she thought, it wasn't the end of the world. She still had a job that paid her three quarters of a million dollars a year, and she still had Mitch Rudolph on the prowl looking for a new job, if she decided to move on. At least she wouldn't have to deal with creditors any longer.

The only unknown in the equation was the future of the relationship with Sculley. It was obvious they liked each other, but, as they discussed options after midnight, neither relished the thought of clandestine dinners or restricting their seeing each other to their respective homes. No relationship could flourish under those constraints and, more than anything else, she wanted it to flourish.

Carole knew he would be disappointed with the morning's outcome, and she desperately wanted to comfort him. But she knew he wouldn't risk calling her at the office, and it would be early evening before they spoke.

The amphitheater at Upscale headquarters was spectacular. Illuminated by a giant curved skylight, it sloped upward in a semicircle with thirty rows of forty theater-style seats. It was used mainly for large staff meetings and for national conferences, where managers were brought to Beachwood for seminars on merchandising and motivation. With nearly two thousand hotel rooms within a half-mile, there was usually no need to hold most national meetings anywhere but corporate headquarters.

Two Betacam video cameras were set up in front of the podium, a last-minute decision allowing Barry to address the entire chain live. By a few minutes before noon, more than two hundred corporate staff people were crowded into the front rows. A rousing, standing ovation occurred when Barry entered the room and continued unabated for five minutes. The news traveled fast.

"Thank you for the vote of confidence," Barry said, motioning the crowd to be seated. He was all charm, his voice clear, sharp and confident.

"I wish all of you across the Upscale family could be here in Beachwood today to share this special moment, but addressing you in the field via our video network is the next best thing.

"This morning we reached agreement with our lenders to provide the funding that will keep Upscale on the path to future success and retain the present management to lead the way."

The audience was on its feet again, showering Barry with a thunderous round of applause.

"Throughout this ordeal, I have consistently said I would not . . . would not . . . invest any more of my own funds in an attempt to shore up this company. It was my feeling that the financial institutions with whom we have been dealing have far greater resources. They have profited significantly from our success in the past, and I felt they should bear the entire risk at this time.

"They did not agree with me. But the more I thought about it, the more I became convinced that I could not walk away from the people who have meant so much to me and have contributed so much to the success of our company. This morning, I agreed to purchase an additional $250 million in Upscale stock, triggering a new $375 million line of credit," Barry said, triggering another standing ovation.

"The media will probably say that Barry Warner caved in to the banks," he continued after finally calming down the troops. "I don't look at it that way at all. I look at it as repayment time—repayment for all of the tireless efforts all of you have put forth in the past to make this one of the crown jewels in retailing. I could not just walk away and leave you with an uncertain future.

"There's no question that our image has been slightly tarnished by the events of the past several weeks, but with your help that will change quickly. Our stores will soon be stocked with the right merchandise in the right quantity for our customers.

"Thank you for your continued dedication and support. I honestly believe we have an extremely bright future together."

The audience exploded into another standing ovation that lasted a full five minutes. Then, one by one, the corporate staffers shoved their way to the podium to shake Barry Warner's hand.

Moving slowly through the crowd to the podium, Carole mentally gave Warner grudging respect for his ability to manipulate the rank and file in his organization. But she didn't buy his story one bit. She was convinced that he was motivated by only two things—money and ego.

One of the last to reach the podium, Carole shook Warner's hand firmly. "I told someone the other day that you can't count out Barry Warner," she said. "You're like a cat with nine lives. I guess you proved that once again today. Nice going."

* * *

It was just after seven when Dan Sculley called Carole's condominium. "We tried," he said softly. "I'm sorry it didn't work out the way we planned it. No one was more surprised than me."

"I told you not to underestimate the guy. He's arrogant and ruthless, but he's smooth, and he usually gets what he wants. He had the employees eating out of his hands this afternoon."

"How do you feel about it personally?"

"When you don't have something, you don't have it," she said philosophically. "I always thought your proposition was sort of a long-shot deal anyway. I still have a good job and am sure I can find a better one in the future, if I desire. In the meantime, let's forget about Barry Warner for the time being. I'm cooking up some dinner and you're the guest of honor."

Sculley arrived at eight, bearing a brown kraft bag containing bottles of red and white wine. The enthusiasm of Carole's impulsive embrace when he entered the door almost sent the bag crashing to the floor.

"I'm so glad you're here," Carole whispered, while shooing Nippon and Claiborne from Sculley's legs.

"Frankly, there's no place I'd rather be."

"Then, let's make a deal."

"Anything you say."

"Let's spend an evening without talking about Upscale, Barry or banking."

"Sounds wonderful."

They drank chilled Absolut vodka and dined on veal cordon bleu and wild rice, washed down with a velvety smooth Côte de Rhone. Then they settled tentatively on the living room couch to sip a 1969 port and listen to a retrospective of Tony Bennett classics.

Uncharacteristically, Carole decided to make the most of the moment.

"Be back in a few minutes. I have another good idea," she said. Before Sculley could respond, she disappeared quickly through a door off the living room.

A few minutes later Sculley looked up and saw Carole standing in the doorway, wearing only a sheer knee-length nightgown, and with a wry smile sheepishly wiggling a finger for him to follow.

"Don't be bashful," she said coyly as he shyly answered the summons and followed her into the bedroom. "I've never been this forward in my life, but figured one of us had to take charge of the moment."

"I just didn't want to come on too strong," Sculley said apologetically.

Regardless of who initiated it, they were soon lost in a tender wave of passion that both knew would change their lives forever.

Chapter Twenty-five

Sonny Longo was still struggling to get back to sleep two hours after his son Joe had called to report on the FBI raid at Partsmania. The kid finally got something right, he thought to himself when Joe gave him the news that not a single counterfeit Strong-Anderson part was discovered among the remaining stock. Longo loved his kids but knew that somewhere along the line they had failed to develop his zeal for details. He was a devout believer in the adage that you never assumed anything. If you gave someone an assignment, you kept checking and checking to make sure it was done . . . and done right.

No one questioned his motives. What most employees, including his sons, detested was the heavy-handed, insulting way he did it. But that was his style. He was a large bully who could be outrageous one moment and then docile as a lamb the next. Those around him never knew what the mood of the moment was going to be. All in all, he was not a very likeable person.

Longo tossed and turned in the comfortable king-sized bed in the $700-a-night room. Sonny had plenty on his mind, and the FBI raid was not the largest problem by any means. He figured the worst thing the feds could do was fine him and put him behind bars. But he knew the latter was a remote possibility because very few people went to jail for trading in counterfeit merchandise. In fact, Sonny remembered reading just a few weeks ago about eighteen people nabbed in a counterfeit athletic shoe ring out west, doing $50 to $100 million a year in volume. Not one of the eighteen went to jail.

His greatest fear at that moment centered around Ramon and Pedro Cardiz . . . polished and smooth, but the most ruthless pair he had ever encountered. Cross Ramon and Pedro and get caught and the chances were very good you wind up on a slab in the morgue, or maybe just disappear forever.

Commonwealth Investment Services came to the rescue four years earlier when Longo's Partsmania chain was in deep financial trouble. Longo, who had gambled away a small fortune in the casinos of Atlantic City and Freeport, was on the brink of going Chapter 7, personally and corporately, when Ramon and Pedro interceded in one of their first bail-out deals.

The brothers advanced Longo $25 million, enough to get Sonny even with his creditors and establish a cushion to meet current expenses. The interest rate was 12 percent, very fair by the prevailing bank standards at the time.

In return, Longo agreed that Partsmania would purchase a minimum of $1.5 million a month in bogus auto parts. A major provision of the deal concerned exclusivity. Longo was forbidden to purchase counterfeit parts from any other supplier at any price.

The Cardiz brothers never feared competition as such. What frightened them was the possibility that other counterfeit suppliers, whose quality standards were not as high as theirs, would get a foothold in Partsmania. That could create a scenario in which inferior counterfeit products might come to the attention of law enforcement officers and the spillover could impact Commonwealth. Nobody would benefit.

The brothers also put a lid on Sonny's prodigious gambling activities.

Once the financial deal was made, Ramon and Pedro literally vanished from the scene. They turned over day-to-day contact to Mark Garrettson. As long as Sonny met his purchase commitments there was no need for either brother to get involved in the details. Neither had spoken to him in more than a year.

In fact, the last conversation came on the day Longo repaid the final installment on the $25 million note, which gave him the option of ending his association with Commonwealth. However, in return for a continuation of the exclusivity arrangement, Ramon agreed to drop the price of parts purchased by 20 percent. It was a good deal for both sides, especially for Longo, who sold most of the counterfeit parts at near his regular markups. Another 20 percent was another 20 percent.

The initial deal with Longo had been singularly important for the fledgling Commonwealth counterfeiting operation. The auto parts business was one of the most lucrative in all of retailing, and there were many other players to share the booty. Landing Partsmania, one of the fastest growing regional chains, was a coup for the brothers.

In the darkness of the hotel room, Longo wondered why he had not let well enough alone and stuck with Commonwealth as a sole source. In four years, Partsmania had received its usual share of customer product quality complaints, but not one customer had raised the issue about bogus parts and products.

Commonwealth's product line was broad, but dealt mainly with mass market–type items, like brake shoes and rotors, ignition parts, wheels, motor oil, antifreeze, air and oil filters, shock absorbers, resistors, transmission and brake fluid, etc.

The initial appeal of dealing with importer Lee Ling was that the manufacturers he represented in Korea produced specialty parts, like steering components. They were not highly advertised items, and Sonny could make a longer dollar on these parts than he could ever dream of turning on normal Strong-Anderson parts. He had learned something from the Cardiz brothers: sprinkle the counterfeits with regular merchandise. .

The deal took shape when Sonny received a call from Ling in Korea, asking whether he was interested in selling some products under the Partsmania private label. Ling had said he could provide the parts at considerably less cost than Longo was paying domestic suppliers and would even pay to design and print the Partsmania boxes.

Sonny and Joe flew to Seoul, met with Ling and his manufacturers and came away with two deals: one to produce private label products and the other to supply the counterfeit Strong-Anderson parts. Partsmania's legitimate products would be packaged and shipped from Seoul. The bogus items would be sent to the United States in bulk to avoid trademark infringement and then packaged in Los Angeles and shipped to the Partsmania warehouse.

It was Joe who finally convinced Sonny that no harm could come from making the deal. "How the hell will Commonwealth ever find out," he had said at the time.

"None of the parts we'll be buying from Korea compete with the stuff they are supplying us."

Sonny's principal concern was that publicity on the FBI raid might reach Ramon and Pedro, in which case he could be in deep shit. Sonny was not anxious to return to Detroit.

"Kill the motherfucker."

Pedro Cardiz was pacing his office and shouting at the speakerphone about five feet away. The sleeves on his blue oxford cloth shirt were rolled up to mid-arm and his shirt collar was opened. A blue and red paisley tie dangled loosely from his neck.

Mark Garrettson had just read him the contents of a small four-paragraph article that appeared in the *Chicago Tribune*, containing sketchy details about the raid at Partsmania and its link to the traffic deaths in Pennsylvania. The story said agents were looking for bogus steering components. The article noted that Partsmania had twenty-five stores in Illinois, ten in the greater Chicago area.

"Kill the motherfucker," Pedro shouted again, his face reddening in anger. "If you don't get it handled, I'll take care of it myself."

"Let's get some more facts before we act hastily," Garrettson cautioned.

"That greedy bastard Longo. He can't get enough. We don't supply him with steering components. That means he deliberately broke the agreement, which forbids him from dealing with other manufacturers. I won't stand for it."

"I understand the way you feel, Pedro, and I'm not saying I don't feel the same way. Give me twenty-four hours to check it out and I'll get back to you with a plan."

"Look," Pedro said in a much calmer voice, "we've nailed down the Upscale deal and a big part of it hinges on our ability to place millions of dollars worth of auto parts into their 650 stores. I'm not going to let Sonny Longo create any heat for us.

"He was a big deal when we started four years ago. Now his $18 million in volume wouldn't make a pimple on his fat ass."

"You're right, Pedro. You're right. The FBI may not have found anything this trip, but chances are they'll be back and nail his ass before long. We don't want to be a part of it."

"You have the twenty-four hours you requested. By then I want a plan."

Garrettson hung up the phone and reread the article. He knew exactly where to start.

Chapter Twenty-six

The disappointment of coming up empty at Partsmania and another midnight harangue with his wife put Hal Spear in a foul mood when he walked into his boss' office to review the Partsmania case.

Art Dixon, the gray-haired special agent in charge of the Detroit FBI office, sensed Spear's mood and decided to get right to the heart of it.

"Your wife on your ass again about getting out of the bureau?" the older man asked.

"How'd you guess?"

"Looks like it's getting to be an every night occasion."

Good friends since they both arrived in Detroit three years earlier, Spear and Dixon, fifteen years his senior, had frequently talked about their personal lives. Dixon knew all about Spear's marriage problems and tried to intercede with his wife, only to be rejected out-of-hand by the younger agent's spouse.

"It's coming to a head pretty soon," said Spear, as he poured a cup of black coffee from Dixon's silver thermos.

"I'll try to talk with her again if you think it will do any good," Dixon said.

"The only thing that will satisfy her is my agreeing to leave the bureau and joining her family's fucking law firm. I'm not about to do that. Period."

Wanting to get the discussion about his married life behind him, Spear quickly changed the subject to the raid. They briefly discussed the possibility of selectively raiding Partsmania stores, but Dixon quickly dismissed the idea. If they cleaned out the warehouse, he reasoned, they probably picked the stores clean of Strong-Anderson counterfeits, too.

"What's your alternative?" Dixon wanted to know.

"Sonny Longo, who owns the company, is in Italy, and we don't know when he's returning. We talked with his kid, Joe, but didn't learn very much. He says he only works there and takes orders from his father. He just blames Strong-Anderson for supplying Partsmania with faulty parts. Right now, it's our word against his.

"The key right now is to find the people who are supplying Partsmania, and that may be like finding a needle in a haystack.

"Strong-Anderson's PI guys say they have some leads, but nothing solid at this point. They're willing to share the information with us. We have a ton of paperwork and computer records we seized in the raid, but it will take weeks to sift through it.

"In the meantime, I thought it would be prudent to get out a bulletin to law enforcement agencies across the country, asking them to be on the lookout for traffic accidents that might be caused by faulty parts. Partsmania is essentially a midwestern operation. I'm sure the bastards supplying them are putting the same parts in stores in other sections of the country. It's a long shot. Maybe we'll get a lead."

Dixon agreed and suggested that Spear draft the bulletin for his signature.

"We also need to interface more directly with U.S. Customs, let them know what we suspect and ask them to be on the lookout for importers receiving bulk shipments of auto parts," he said.

"I've already talked with the chief of operations of Customs in Washington and specifically asked them to be on the lookout for bogus tie rod ends. I'll get back to them later today and pose the question about the bulk shipments. In the meantime, what we need right now is a lucky break."

"A lucky break. It always works," said the smiling Dixon.

While the two FBI agents were discussing Partsmania, Joe Longo sent faxes to all Partsmania stores, instructing managers to pull stock on all Strong-Anderson parts numbers involved in the counterfeiting scheme.

In the faxes, Longo blamed the move on shoddy workmanship by the supplier, which he said was being phased out as a Partsmania vendor. By noon, a fleet of trucks operated by Partsmania drivers and independent carriers were on the road to pick up the parts. The last pick-up was made shortly after six in the evening.

Mark Garrettson always believed in going right to the source when he wanted to find out something. He still had connections at FBI headquarters from his NYPD days and decided to use one, Todd Lund, a supervisor in the white collar crime department in Washington, D.C.

Garrettson's title as director of midwestern operations for Commonwealth was hidden behind a front called M. D.

Garrettson, Inc., Special Investigations, which was housed in a small industrial building near Chicago's O'Hare Airport.

Though he rarely practiced the trade, Garrettson was a licensed PI, and that gave him an opportunity to use former drinking buddies like Lund in his work for Commonwealth.

When he reached Lund, he told the FBI executive he was working a product liability case, had read about the raid on Partsmania's warehouse and thought there might be a link between that act and the case on which he was working.

"Any information you can get me on what triggered the raid would be mucho appreciated," Garrettson said.

"Sounds like a harmless request, old buddy. I'll call my buddy Art Dixon in Detroit and see what he has to say."

"That would be a great help. I'll owe you one."

Lund's return call came much quicker than Garrettson expected.

"Dixon said they 'shit the bed' in the raid. Turned up a big fat zero in the parts department, but confiscated a truckload full of paperwork."

"Did he tell you what they were looking for?"

"Primarily counterfeit steering components sold under the Strong-Anderson brand. That was the whole focus of the raid. He said an accident in Pennsylvania, which killed four people, was caused by a counterfeit tie rod end purchased from Partsmania's Ann Arbor store."

"Do they suspect any other brands of counterfeit products are involved?" Garrettson asked nervously.

"Not that he said. I got the impression the investigation centers around Strong-Anderson and Partsmania."

"Your guys hit any of their stores?"

"Negative. Dixon said that any counterfeit stuff in their stores was long gone by now."

Garrettson thought the conversation produced both good and bad news. The good news was that the FBI action was apparently limited, though he was concerned with what the FBI might find in the records seized in the raid. The bad news was that while the feds had suffered a setback in the raid, he knew they would not let up. That, he feared, was not in the long-term best interests of Commonwealth, especially while Partsmania was still a customer.

He was about to call Pedro with the report on Partsmania when a wiry-looking male assistant brought in a large manila envelope, which contained background checks on key Upscale executives. Garrettson was amazed how quickly his staff, aided by private investigators and credit agencies, had done such a thorough job. One by one, he pored over the reports, noting that, with the exception of Carole Nordstrom, all were heavily leveraged with debt incurred when they participated in the LBO.

Even though she had not been privy to the scheme, he was bothered by the fact that Nordstrom, one of his two contacts at Upscale, had no financial stake in the company and made a note on the front page of her three-page dosier to question Barry Warner about it. Jeremy Todd, his other contact, had a lot to lose if the company went down. All Nordstrom had was a job, albeit at a hefty salary.

Garrettson cast the reports aside and called Pedro on a secured circuit that was filtered through Commonwealth's satellite communications network. Pedro was not surprised at the results of Garrettson's conversation with his FBI contact.

"What I want to know now is what are we going to do about that sleaze Sonny Longo and his son, Joe," Pedro demanded.

"Patience, Pedro. I have an idea on how to deal with Sonny Longo and Partsmania, but I need some help right now. Have your brother Ernesto in Bogota track down Guillermo Banzil and ask him to get in touch with me as soon as possible. I think we can use his talents."

Chapter Twenty-seven

Carole Nordstrom thought Dan Sculley's idea was simple, but brilliant: Kill Barry Warner with kindness.

In the afterglow of their first lovemaking, both agreed that their primary concern was to create an environment that would enable them to be seen together in public, without stoking Warner's hatred. Sculley's solution: Create a scenario in which he and Carole could meet officially.

Warner had not wanted to take Sculley's call when it came on Monday morning. He was still pissed from the media coverage of the bank deal and blamed Sculley and his associates with feeding off-the-record information that had Barry eating humble pie and backing down rather than lose his crumbling empire.

Realizing that Sculley was his partner, he finally told his secretary to put through Sculley's call.

Sculley was all sweetness. "Look," he said. "I've been giving this a lot of thought. We both have a lot to gain if we make this thing work . . . and a lot to lose if we don't. There's a lot to be done and we can help, beyond just providing money. We have some bright people here at the bank, just as you have at Upscale.

"Let's get this off on the right foot. I'd like to host a little reception, say Wednesday night, at my club for our senior people and yours. Strictly social. I think it can make a world of difference in the way we deal with each other in the future."

"You're on," said Barry, whose quick, positive response almost staggered Sculley. "If it works well, we'll do it on a regular basis. Next time, it's on me. How many people are you thinking about?"

"Maybe a dozen or so from each side. We'll do it in one of our private rooms at Canterbury."

"What time?"

"Let's make it about six-thirty."

"I'll fax you a list of those who are coming from Upscale."

Most of the other Upscale and bank officials were already at the club when Warner pulled into the entrance. Sculley was talking with Carole when they saw Barry enter the private dining room. The bank president interrupted their conversation, walked over to Warner and gave him a warm handshake.

"Welcome, I hope this is the first of many social gatherings between your people and ours. I think things are going very well."

"I've always been a proponent of making love, not war," Barry quipped.

"A very good philosophy. Say, why didn't you tell me you had a bright, beautiful woman like Carole Nordstrom working for you? She's been telling me how happy she is that you've solved your financial problem and is letting me in on some of the new fashion concepts Upscale may present in the future. They sound exciting."

"Now that we have enough money to get creative again, we're going to pursue a lot of things that have been on hold, and Carole will be at the center of many of them."

Sculley gave Warner a weak smile, left Carole with him and walked into the middle of the room to talk with other members of the bank's senior management team.

Barry spent about thirty minutes sipping vodka and chatting amiably with several bank officials. Then, after apologizing to Sculley for having to depart for a meeting, he left abruptly.

The last of the bankers and retail executives departed by eight-thirty, leaving Carole and Sculley in animated conversation in the corner of the room. Noticing they were alone, Sculley took her hand and led her toward the dining room.

"I'd say our little strategy couldn't have worked better," he said smiling. "Come on, let's have dinner."

Chapter Twenty-eight

With Mark Spencer out of the picture, Barry took control of all facets of the company, but focused a great deal of his attention on the new arrangement with Commonwealth. He tried to walk a very discreet line between Nordstrom and Todd, dealing in generalities with Carole and specifics with Jeremy.

The situation was tricky. Upscale bought large quantities of product directly from manufacturers. Until the financial crisis, most major suppliers were on automatic reordering. When quantities of given products dropped below a certain minimum, the Upscale computer system automatically generated an order to replenish the stock to a prescribed maximum. Some of that business had to be diverted to Commonwealth without making Carole suspicious. He assigned Jeremy the task of designing a computer program model to handle it.

Unbeknown to Carole, Jeremy installed an on-line computer terminal in his home to monitor the situation.

In his typical fashion, Todd kept fastidious notes on everything he did.

Barry was adamant that Upscale punish those suppliers who abandoned the company during the height of the financial crisis. It made it easy to justify the large initial order quantities placed with Commonwealth.

In meeting after meeting, Warner was obsessed with meting out retribution to those vendors, even though Carole repeatedly pointed out that Upscale was paying a premium for the merchandise by acquiring it through distributors. Her arguments fell on deaf ears.

True to his word, Garrettson had his trucks rolling into Upscale's warehouses in Columbus and Kansas City within a week after his initial meeting with Jeremy and Carole. The very first shipments contained the very counterfeit versions of profitable fragrances that had been in short supply—including some of the world's most popular brands: Calvin Klein's Obsession, Giorgio, Paco Rabanne, Opium and Givenchy. Commonwealth had to tap sources in Brazil for Paco Rabanne and Turkey for Givenchy 111.

A few days later, it was mass market auto parts, then athletic shoes, including knock-offs of Nike, Reebok, Converse and Adidas. Then music and tapes.

There were no glitches and the pipeline was filling fast. In his travels to Upscale stores, Barry made a point of surreptitiously inspecting the departments to which bogus products were headed. As far as packaging was concerned, he could not discern any difference between the counterfeits and the real thing, nor did anyone in the stores.

Meanwhile, relations between Warner and Sculley improved tremendously, largely because of the banker's interest in Carole Nordstrom and his determination to keep her working in the Cleveland area. With no other area retailing positions to rival hers at Upscale, Sculley realized he was between a rock and a hard place as far as Carole's career was concerned.

He punctuated his desire to neutralize Warner in the relationship by deciding that no one from the financial institution would occupy its new seats on Upscale's board. Instead, he parceled them out to retailing experts. At one point, he even considered approaching the legendary Stanley Marcus of Neiman-Marcus fame about taking a seat, but discarded the idea.

Still, Sculley had no intention of letting up on the bank's pressure for Warner to perform and meet the financial commitments contained in the agreement. The pressure had to be applied subtly.

Sonny Longo finally returned from Italy, about twenty pounds heavier from stuffing his face with pasta and about $10,000 lighter from doling out cash to an assortment of hookers in Rome, Florence and Milan.

Constantly in touch with Joe during the remainder of the trip, Sonny continually acknowledged his pleasure at the job his son had done in cleaning out the Strong-Anderson counterfeits from the warehouse and stores. The entire episode had simply disappeared.

Longo knew the FBI had reams of files, phone records and the like, but was sure that agents would find nothing incriminating in his dealings with the Strong-Anderson counterfeiters.

Joe had assured him that media coverage of the raid had been limited mostly to the Detroit area and an Associated Press wire dispatch that was picked up by several regional newspapers. The stories had no negative effect on Parts-mania's business.

Most importantly, Sonny Longo's worst fears had failed to materialize. There had been no contact from Mark Gar-rettson or the Cardiz brothers about the raid, which he interpreted to mean that no one had seen the story.

He had dodged a bullet.

Chapter Twenty-nine

The handsome, darkly tanned man behind the sunglasses who walked through the American Airlines jetway at O'Hare International Airport in Chicago looked like any typical South American businessman. His navy blue suit was crisply pressed. He was carrying a tan Burberry raincoat over his right arm. His left arm strained under the weight of a black attaché case.

The raincoat and the attaché case were prearranged clues for Mark Garrettson that the traveler was Guillermo Banzil, the multi-talented paid assassin for the Cardiz drug cartel and other worthy Colombian drug operations. Garrettson had never before seen Banzil, had never seen his picture. In fact, no one in the last twenty years had snapped a photo of the slender, articulate Colombian, whose proficiency with high explosives and high-powered rifles was said to have claimed five hundred lives in the Colombian drug wars. Today, Banzil was traveling on a Mexican passport as José Garbone from Mexico City. He had cleared Customs in Dallas and changed planes for the flight to Chicago.

Garrettson waited until most of the other passengers had left the boarding area and approached him. "Would you be José Garbone?" he asked quietly.

The visitor nodded in the affirmative.

They walked briskly up the concourse and out into the muggy early August air, then stepped into a waiting light gray Ford Taurus.

"Please stop at the Hyatt so that our guest can check in," Garrettson said to the driver, a recent immigrant from Colombia and a trainee under the ex-cop. Forty minutes later they were in shirtsleeves in Garrettson's office.

"Ernesto says you're a hard man to track down," Garrettson said. "It has taken almost a month."

"In my business one does not wish to be easily accessible to friend or foe alike," he answered softly in perfect English. Garrettson found out later that most of Banzil's schooling had taken place in the United States.

"When there is a large price on your head, you are careful about trusting anyone. Don't take that as any reflection on the Cardiz family. Ernesto and his father are my good friends. The fact of the matter is I have been doing some consulting work in Israel. The government there is a good customer."

"We have acquired the tools and the parts you requested," Garrettson said, pointing to a suitcase in a far corner of the room. "They are over there. The keys to the maroon Buick in the parking lot are on the visor. The lease and insurance papers are in the glove compartment. The car is leased to one of our obscure corporations.

"The expense money you requested is in here," Garrettson said, handing Banzil a thick white envelope and a gray business card. "Please let me know if you need any more cash or anything else. You can reach me at the number on the card in an emergency. It's to a phone in an abandoned home in South Miami. When you dial the number, it's call-forwarded to a number in Massachusetts and then directed to me here in Chicago. For the time being we have set you up in a small office in another section of this industrial park. I'd rather not have you on my block when you're playing with your toys."

"I see you take precautions, too, Mr. Garrettson."

"Yes, and right now, there's no price on my head."

"One can never be too cautious."

"I understand the compensation for your work will be handled in Bogota," Garrettson said.

"It's no big deal," Banzil replied matter-of-factly. "For the Cardiz family this job—How do you say it here?—is complimentary. I have more money now than I can ever hope to spend, and most of the time no place to spend it."

They got down to business. Garrettson explained the entire relationship between Commonwealth and Partsmania. He told Banzil how Sonny Longo had breached his agreement not to sell any other counterfeit products.

"As far as we know, Longo and his son, Joe, have no idea that we know they deceived us," Garrettson said.

"People like that can get you a long jail sentence."

"If they are alive."

Garrettson explained that Sonny and Joe were the only two people at Partsmania who knew about the Commonwealth connection. "We can't operate in a vacuum. You have to have inside people who know what's going on. Sonny and Joe were very careful. Others inside the company may know they are dealing in counterfeit parts, but I don't think anyone else at Partsmania knows about our arrangement."

"That means you want to get rid of both of them."

"And their warehouse."

"A lot of innocent people could get killed if we go for it in one big caper," Banzil said, his deep brown eyes focused squarely on Garrettson.

Garrettson liked Banzil and his candor. He was smooth and polished, totally unlike some of the professional hit men Garrettson had encountered during his days on NYPD.

"I'd like for that not to happen," the ex-cop said. "No reason any innocent people have to pay for what the Longos have done to us."

"Lots of plain folks have been killed in some of our work in Colombia and it doesn't make me happy. But it's a war and in war there are casualties, both military and civilian. I can't promise you there will be no casualties."

"We've done some homework for you and we have some experienced back-up people on standby if you need them," Garrettson said, handing the Colombian a green file folder. "This contains general information on the usual daily movements of Sonny and Joe, where they live, eat, play golf and screw. I've looked over the information and there seem to be multiple opportunities to do what needs to be done."

Banzil opened the folder and scanned a half dozen sheets of paper. "Very good. This will save a lot of time and effort."

Garrettson pulled out a large blue sheet of paper from the drawer and asked Banzil to move closer to the large mahogany desk for a look.

"This is the layout of the Partsmania distribution center, located in an industrial park in Taylor, near Detroit Metropolitan Wayne County Airport. It's about 200,000 square feet.

Garrettson explained Partsmania's stocking procedures. The warehouse was organized alphabetically by vendor. All

A-vendor products were at the front of the building, the highest letter products at the rear.

"How many devices would it take to bring this place down?" Garrettson asked, moving close to Banzil.

"From the inside or outside?"

"The inside, but activated from the outside."

"The way I build them . . . four or five strategically placed. But how would you ever get them inside the warehouse?"

"You build them. I'll plant them."

"If you can do that you ought to be in my business."

"I used to be in the business of catching guys like you."

"A cop?" Banzil asked with astonishment.

"Yes, a cop."

Garrettson took the bomber into an adjacent room, where a large wooden conference table was covered with auto parts and accessories.

"Take your pick."

"What do you mean take my pick?"

"I want you to build the devices inside these parts, so I can ship them into the warehouse with our regular shipment to Partsmania. With time-delay circuits, we can set the times by radio frequency from outside the warehouse and be miles away before the big bang takes place."

"What's the time frame?"

"There's no real deadline, but I'd like to get the job handled within two or three weeks."

"That should be no problem," Banzil said confidently. "It will take me about a week to build the devices. The challenge is to squeeze them into these odd shapes you have provided me. But before that, there must be time for research so that we can accomplish our goals. We won't get a second chance."

Chapter Thirty

Banzil was on the road early. He caught Interstate 94 in Chicago, rolled around the southern edge of Lake Michigan and headed across Michigan toward Detroit. He kept the cruise control on the maroon Buick Park Avenue at sixty-five and enjoyed the leisurely drive. There was no hurry. In his business it was a cardinal sin. You took your time and planned carefully. Then you executed with precision.

Even though he had spent four years at M.I.T. studying to be an electronics engineer, Banzil had never been in this part of the United States. In fact, since starting his career as perhaps the world's highest paid assassin, he had rarely traveled to the United States, never before on a contract. He had worked extensively for the Israelis in Europe, in the Middle East and, of course, in his native Columbia, where bombing had become a major weapon in supressing the government's continuing crackdown on the drug trade.

Banzil was the son of a prominent lawyer, whose clients included the Cardiz family, and it was at his father's urging that he built the first bomb.

It was a favor. At twenty-five, Banzil had been designing electronic components for a small Bogota company, when his father, Emilio, broached the subject. No one would get hurt, the son was assured, and someone would detonate it. The explosive device was to be used to destroy a cocaine processing plant operated by a Cardiz rival.

A week later, thirty innocent people were killed when the bomb exploded prematurely in a car in front of a market while two Cardiz henchmen were on the way to deliver it for its intended use. Banzil had to build another one, and it did the job. On Sunday afternoon, Emilio Banzil handed his son an envelope containing $25,000 in cash, a whole year's salary in his current job. He built three more devices that year and received the same amount for each.

Banzil rationalized the deaths they caused. Someone else would build them if he didn't. It might as well be him. In time he was also enlisted for one-on-one hits, mostly with high-powered rifles. Though they did not know him by name, his proficiency quickly made him a legend among Cardiz loyalists.

Somehow, the Israelis got wind of his talents and made contact through the Cardiz family. They paid him $500,000 to send the Syrian foreign minister to his eternal resting place and also built the assassin a villa near Tel Aviv, which became his second home.

There was no turning back. Every time there was a major assassination or bombing somewhere in the world, he was mentioned in the press as the possible perpetrator.

Banzil was cold, calculating and a loner, but had a charming personality when he chose to display it. He didn't hate anyone, but merely looked at himself as a business consultant providing a needed service for his clients—at an extraordinarily high hourly rate.

While his work was widely publicized, Banzil was virtually anonymous, helped by the fact there was nothing remarkable about his appearance. He frequently traveled in disguise in Europe and the Middle East, but there was no need for that in the United States.

Banzil felt comfortable in the United States. He was unknown and unwanted by the authorities and was free to act just like any businessman or tourist. At least for the moment, the research part of his assignment would be easy. Executing—getting rid of the warehouse and the two Longos at the same time—would be excrutiatingly difficult. He was not sure how—or if—he could pull it off, but a week in Michigan would probably tell the tale.

There was no need to carry a weapon at this time. That and the tools of his trade were stashed in a corner of Mark Garrettson's office.

Banzil's first stop was Southfield, just north of the Detroit city limits and one of its major commercial and residential suburbs. It was home for Sonny and Joe Longo. Banzil checked into the Plaza Hotel, a fourteen-story building located adjacent to the sprawling Northland Shopping Center, which he later learned was the first regional shopping center in the United States.

One of his phobias was height. Registering as José Garbone of Mexico City, he asked the desk clerk for a room on a lower floor, low enough so that he could jump in case of a fire. He presented an American Express Gold Card and said he would be staying five days to a week. He thought paying with cash always created suspicion.

Banzil carried his own tan Hartman hanging bag to the room on the second floor. The room was pleasant enough, but unlike many of the European hotels he had frequented, this one had very little charm. After a quick shower, he donned a pair of faded blue jeans, a yellow crew neck shirt and a navy blue blazer—just the right outfit for an afternoon of shopping.

The assassin walked to the shopping center. The first stop was the J.L. Hudson department store where he purchased two pairs of Levi Dockers, matching shirts and a pair of white Reebok walking shoes.

At a camera-electronics store he bought a palm-sized Olympus Stylus camera, four rolls of film, a Sony Handycam 8mm video camera, four tape cassettes, a camera case and a small color TV monitor. He parted with more than $2,000 in cash.

It was nearly six-thirty in the evening when he returned to the hotel. Even though he knew there would be no message, he instinctively checked the message light on the phone. It was an odd feeling. He was alone in a strange hotel in a strange city and no one in the world, except the hotel personnel, knew he was there.

Banzil called room service and ordered bottles of Cutty Sark and Absolut and a cheese and cracker appetizer, then tore open the box containing the video camera and pored over the instructions. Why, he wondered, didn't Sony just give you a videotape as an instruction guide instead of making you wade through dozens of pages of print.

After testing the camera, he hooked it to the video monitor and was surprised at the excellent picture quality. The Olympus camera was much easier to figure out, but there was no way to see the results without taking a roll of film for processing. After two vodkas and a lot of cheese and crackers, Banzil decided it was time for dinner.

Uncomfortable with the directions he received from the desk clerk, he took a cab to Sweet Lorraine's Cafe, a trendy bistro on Greenfield Road. He washed down the pecan chicken with two bottles of Heineken's, returned to the hotel by cab and was asleep by ten-thirty.

Early the next morning, Banzil handed another cab driver fifty dollars at Detroit Metropolitan Wayne County Airport and proceeded to the car rental area to pick up the vehicle he had reserved at Avis. With the camera bag slung over his shoulder, he was the perfect picture of a tourist. The Avis car was one of three or four cars he would need for the assignment.

The pretty rental agent offered a choice of several models, but he settled on a black Buick Park Avenue. The directions she gave him to Metropolitan Industrial Park on Holland, off Ecorse, were terrible. It took him forty minutes to find the place. It should have taken ten.

It was Sunday and except for a few random cars in parking lots of various buildings, the place was deserted. There were no cars at Partsmania, down the road about a half mile. A two-story office building was in front of the sprawling warehouse.

Banzil pulled into the parking lot on the left of the complex and spent about five minutes videotaping and taking still pictures, especially of the entrance to the building. After paying special attention to the parking spaces reserved for Sonny and Joe Longo, he drove to the rear of the building, got out of the car and inspected the construction, which was mostly painted cement block.

He drove around the perimeter of the parking lot, which he figured could hold 100 to 125 cars. There was a slight embankment flanked by a small wooded area almost directly across from the entrance to the building. He taped and photographed the area, then, noting the route and time it took, returned to Southfield.

Later, he cabbed from the Plaza to Hertz in downtown Detroit, picked up the third vehicle, a silver Ford Taurus, and spent the rest of the day nosing around the neighborhoods where the Longos lived.

Father and son, both divorced, resided within a few blocks of each other in the most fashionable section of Southfield, one of the most integrated communities in the Detroit metropolitan area. They had talked frequently about moving to a less integrated community, like Bloomfield Hills, but stayed in Southfield rather than expand the distance from home to work any greater than it already was.

Sonny Longo's two-story red brick home looked large and luxurious from the outside. Banzil was particularly interested in the circular drive and three-car attached garage. A powder blue Cadillac Sedan DeVille was parked in front of the doubled-doored front entry, which was topped by an arched transom window. He noted which way it was facing. With very little traffic on the street, Banzil was able to capture video footage and still frames from the Taurus without drawing any suspicion.

The son's home, while newer, was not nearly as impressive. It, too, was red brick, but access to the two-car garage was from a large concrete apron in the rear of the house. It would be difficult and very dangerous to think about planting a device under those circumstances, Banzil thought.

Back in the room, he poured a vodka and pondered what he had seen so far. Garrettson's scenario for the distribution center would be the easiest to pull off. A practical plan for getting rid of Sonny and Joe at the same time would require long and thoughtful planning. Nothing Banzil had seen in their neighborhood made it a promising locale for the hit.

Tony Longo took a deep breath when his secretary announced that Mark Garrettson was calling from Chicago. "It's Mark from Commonwealth," the senior Longo whispered to his son who was in the office for a meeting. "What do you think he wants?"

"I'd rather not think about it."

"Better take the call."

"Just called to see how one of our best customers is doing these days," said Garrettson, oozing charm.

"Joe's with me. We're doing just great. The new arrangement with you guys is working out well. Every little bit helps."

"As always, we appreciate the prompt payment. Wish all of our customers were that way."

"Thanks to you folks our cash flow is terrific. Every invoice for every vendor is discounted."

"That's nice to hear, Sonny. Say, how was your trip to Italy?"

"Wonderful. Ate too much, drank too much and screwed too much."

"Same old Sonny."

"I'm too old to change."

"I may be down your way one of these days in the near future on some other business," Garrettson said. "If it happens, I'll holler and we can all hang one on."

"We'd enjoy that. It would give us an opportunity to show you the warehouse expansion we completed in the spring."

When the conversation was over, both father and son breathed a collective sigh of relief.

Chapter Thirty-one

As the second-ranking officer at Upscale, at least in terms of title, Carole Nordstrom answered only to Barry Warner. Thus, it was no surprise to the director of accounts payable when Nordstrom called and asked for an update on the orders placed with Retail Distribution Services, Inc., Commonwealth's front organization.

An hour later, Harry Robinson, a rumpled-looking man in his mid-fifties, arrived at her office with a ten-page computer printout, listing the products purchased, the wholesale price of each and the overall total. Nordstrom was stunned that in a period of less than three weeks, Upscale had spent more than $50 million with Garrettson's distributors. Without saying why, she asked Robinson to return later in the day with an item-by-item breakdown, comparing the prices normally charged by regular manufacturing vendors with those from the distributors.

That report was much more disturbing. In every case, the distributor price was 3 to 7 percent higher than the manufacturer-vendor price—$2.5 million higher for all of the Retail Distribution Services invoices.

While she knew all along Upscale would be paying a premium to get its shelves filled quickly without paying cash in advance and to allow Barry to make a point to the wide range of vendors that cut off the firm's credit, the amount was significant and bound to go much higher if Barry continued his vendetta.

Carole reached across the desk and picked up a small, battery-powered calculator. Within a minute, the magnitude of the excess costs over a one-year period flashed on the screen. Allowing for the front-end loading that took place because of Upscale's weakened inventory position during the crisis, Carole calculated that Upscale would spend more than $400 million in a year with Garrettson. Dealing with Garrettson's company would cost Upscale an extra $20 to $25 million a year . . . a lot of money, she thought, for a company that had just been to the brink of bankruptcy.

Carole sat at the desk tapping her fingers and trying to put it all together. Why would Barry pay through the nose and still guarantee payment of the invoices, she wondered. Why was he so adamant about punishing the vendors when he knew damn well the credit cut-off was just good business practice, considering the state of Upscale's finances at the time? It didn't make a lot of sense unless there was more to it. She wrestled with the possibilities. One stood out like a sore thumb: The company Mark Garrettson represented must have had something to do with helping Barry maintain control of Upscale.

She thought about talking over the situation with Jeremy Todd, but decided against it. Instead, she turned to her computer terminal and typed out a memo to Barry, reviewing her calculations and pointing to the exceedingly high cost of dealing with the distributors.

She concluded: "I know how you feel about the vendors who cut off our credit, but at this point is it worth the additional cost?" she asked. "If you don't mind my saying so, it appears we are cutting off our nose to spite our face. My recommendation is that we bury the hatchet with the vendors and proceed with our normal suppliers."

Carole pulled a copy of the memo from her laser printer, handed it to her secretary, asked that it be delivered immediately to the chairman's office and waited for the response.

It had not been a good morning for Barry, largely because Jennifer Burns turned a cold shoulder to his sexual advances and his ex-wife had called from California and railed at him for not paying any attention at all toward the two sons he had helped bring into the world.

Barry knew she was right, but the fact was he felt no real attachment to the sixteen-year-old twins, whom he had seen only two dozen times in the ten years they had been divorced. Every minute he spent with them reminded him of the miserable marriage that had produced the offspring.

Barry rationalized that the millions he shelled out in a highly publicized settlement had set her and the boys up for life. He had met his responsibility. In his mind, end of story. However, as the boys grew older, her demands for more time from him came more often. His answer was pat: "I'm just too busy."

"You're nothing but a self-centered prick," she had screamed and slammed down the receiver.

When he arrived at the office a few minutes before noon and read Carole's memo, he went into orbit.

* * *

Nordstrom was just leaving her office for lunch when the call came to report posthaste to Warner's penthouse office. Barry was waiting for her in shirtsleeves. "Who else got a copy of this memo?" he demanded, leaping from his chair and crumbling the memo in her face in the same motion.

"Just you," she said with a smile, sensing she had touched a very raw nerve. She decided to let Warner's tirade run its course.

"Look, I run this fucking company and don't you ever forget it. I'll decide who my suppliers will be and I don't need your meddling advice, buttressed with grade school mathematics. If I want to spend $25 million to teach some ungrateful whores a lesson, I'll do it.

"I'm the guy who put up the money to save jobs for you and the rest of the people around here, and I'll spend it any damn way I want to spend it. Do I make myself clear?"

Given her relationship with Dan Sculley, Carole couldn't help but chuckle.

"Aren't you overreacting a bit? We're talking about a lot of money here. As far as I know, I'm still executive vice president of this company. And that entitles me to voice an opinion. I just did what any good manager would do. I looked at the numbers unemotionally and pointed out to you what I thought was a mistake. But you are absolutely right. Most of it's your money. If you want to piss it down the drain, God bless you. I have nothing more to say about the subject.

"I'm late for a lunch date," she said, turned and started walking out the door.

Sensing that he had come on too strong, Warner called her back. He calmly told Carole the deal with Garrettson was only a temporary arrangement, which was partially true.

In this case, temporary meant three or more years. He said once Upscale's merchandise mix stabilized again, they would take a look at the vendor situation.

"It's not as if we've cut some of the manufacturers out entirely," he said. "We've just reduced the amounts we're buying to teach them a lesson. I feel comfortable with that."

Sensing Barry's conciliatory tone was just a smoke screen, Carole ended the conversation with a wave and a smile. "As always, you cast the winning vote."

Warner was concerned. He knew Carole was inquisitive, sharp and not easily intimidated by his tirades. He also knew she would be back again soon with a new set of figures, and she would keep coming back until he gave her a rationale that bore more practical weight than emotion. Given the nature of the deal, that could never happen.

He also knew that manufacturing vendors would soon be asking questions about the reduced purchase volume, and he wasn't sure Carole was the one to respond.

He began pondering a solution to what was becoming a very prickly dilemma, and none of the options was pleasant.

At Ristorante Giovanni that night Carole broke a promise she made to herself when the Upscale financial crisis was solved—that she and Sculley would not discuss Upscale or Barry Warner. In fact, they had playfully established a dollar fine each time one or the other mentioned the name of the company or its chairman.

It had worked. Dining together almost every night, their conversations had been marvelous. Both left their businesses at the curb. They talked about the food, music, books, movies, plays and places they enjoyed, and were surprised at how much they really had in common. The evenings usually ended with Sculley spending the night at her condominium.

"You're awfully quiet. Something must be bothering you," Sculley said as Carole sipped an Absolut on the rocks and barely offered anything toward the evening's conversation.

She reached for her purse, pulled out a dollar bill and pressed it into Sculley's hand. The banker knew what it meant.

"Before I say anything, I want you to promise that, for now, this conversation will be strictly between us, and you will take no action because of it," Carole said, allowing herself a weak smile.

"All of that for a dollar?"

"All of that for a dollar."

"I promise."

In great detail she told him about the deal with Garrettson and his distributors and shared with him the memo and computer printouts she had sent to Barry.

"Your a feisty lady," Sculley said after hearing Carole describe Warner's tirade and how she responded.

"That's the only way to deal with him."

"But you're right. There's no doubt in my mind but that this deal has something to do with the last-minute decision Barry made to come up with the money," Sculley said, chewing on the end of a fingernail. "We're talking about some big money and, obviously, some big-money people behind it. The kind of cash Barry came up with just isn't hidden in someone's mattress."

After, over dinner drinks, Carole conceded that—given the bank's position in Upscale—Sculley couldn't let the situation fester for a long period of time. They agreed on a strategy that would not compromise Sculley's promise or Carole's executive position at Upscale. Carole would continue to monitor the situation, without again confronting Barry. Sculley would try privately to find out a lot more about Retail Distribution Services, Inc., and its president, Mark Garrettson.

Chapter Thirty-two

Banzil arrived back in Chicago the following Thursday and went immediately to Mark Garrettson's office. It was almost six in the evening and Garrettson suggested they chat over cocktails at a small neighborhood pub. They drove separately—Banzil in the maroon Buick Park Avenue and Garrettson in a shiny black Lexus LS400 coupe.

The bar, called Stool Pigeons, was located on busy Manheim Road, about a half mile from Garrettson's office. A half dozen patrons were seated at the bar and a dozen others were scattered at dark wooden tables in the rear. They took the last table in the back.

Banzil immediately gave the ex-cop a briefing on the Michigan research. One evening, Banzil told Garrettson, he sat two bar stools away from Sonny Longo at his favorite bar.

"He's sort of intense, isn't he?" Banzil asked.

"That's putting it mildly."

"The notes you gave me said he goes there almost every night. He was in the place the two nights I was there. Left one night with a tall, good-looking blonde of about forty.

Both nights he left about nine. We might be able to take him out there."

"How about the kid?"

"A little more unpredictable. Doesn't frequent any particular saloon, but spends a lot of time at a health club near his home. From his build, I'd say he pumps a lot of iron. I bought a membership there so I could get a close look at him and look around. Nice place. It also has some possibilities."

"Put it on your expense account. What about the warehouse?"

"You've already done the brain work on that one."

"Have any idea when?"

"Give me another week or ten days and I'll be ready to execute. I'll be in my little cubbyhole tomorrow working on the parts to the puzzle."

"Just be careful," Garrettson said. "I wouldn't want anything to happen to our industrial park."

Banzil smiled and left alone.

In some ways, Special Agent Hal Spear thought investigating white collar crime was one of the bureau's most difficult assignments. The work was tedious, and you sometimes didn't leave the office for weeks. This was how the Partsmania investigation was proceeding.

The agents had seized more than fifty cartons of records, including bank statements, checks, purchase orders, delivery statements, vendor invoices, computer tapes and just about any other record a business could keep. Records had to be cross-tabulated and cross-checked to determine if there were any trends that would suggest fraud or, in this case, unusual or unaccounted for purchases, sales and receipts.

So far, more than a month of checking by six agents, all of whom were either lawyers or accountants by education, had failed to produce anything substantive. Spear knew they could always subpoena additional records, but didn't want to go out on a limb until he had more to go on. The failure to obtain anything useful in the search for bogus parts gnawed at him.

Spear had just opened another carton containing Partsmania records when he was summoned to the telephone, the caller an official from U.S. Customs in Washington, D.C.

"Think we might have something for you regarding that auto wreck case you called about some time ago," the caller said with a slight southern drawl.

"Go ahead. We could use some good news."

"This came from our Houston regional office. About a week ago, a tractor hauling a container off-loaded in Long Beach, California, was stopped for a routine border check at Nogales on the Mexican side of the Arizona–Mexico line.

"A Mexican border patrolman noticed that the container had been sealed in Korea, and the seal was still unbroken. When he opened the container, he discovered the boxes inside were labeled "Made in the U.S.A." The boxes contained steering and brake parts under several names, including Strong-Anderson. The Mexicans detained the driver and notified us immediately."

"Pretty smart, that Mexican border patrolman. Where was the stuff headed?"

"The consignee was a Mexican auto parts broker in Hermosillo, about 120 miles south, but the parts apparently were not intended for sale in Mexico," the customs agent continued. "They were to be shipped back to the states, which is a common practice in the counterfeiting business.

Creates confusion and messes up the trail. We were just lucky on this one."

"Any idea who they were intended for in this country?"

"The Mexicans used their persuasive powers on the broker and he spilled his guts, said the parts were eventually to be delivered to a distributor in Dallas. Our people in Texas raided the distributor early this morning. I just got word they confiscated a trailerload of parts and several cartons of documents, which are being taken to Houston right now."

Spear was eager to know if there was any paperwork referring to a company called Partsmania, but was told that kind of information was premature.

"If you don't mind," Spear said, "I'm going to ask our Dallas bureau to monitor this. In the meantime, we'd appreciate any further updates. Many thanks for the info. This could be the big break we've been hoping for."

Spear grabbed his notes and barged into the agent-in-charge's office. "I've always said that I'd rather be lucky than good," he said with a huge smile on his face. Thanks to some enterprising Mexican border guard, we may be closer to putting Sonny Longo's nuts in a vise."

Chapter Thirty-three

Banzil opened the blue and white box with the red AC logo and pulled out the contents, an AC-Delco 1788CW air filter. He didn't know whether it was the real thing or not and didn't care. He carefully measured the dimensions, then pried off the black metal top and removed the fan-fold, oil-wetted paper that was sandwiched between coarse screening on the outside and fine inside screening.

He carefully molded PETN plastic explosive into half-inch thick strips about nine inches long and placed them between the two layers of screen. Undetectable by X-ray, PETN—a claylike substance—was the kind of explosive terrorists used to blow airliners from the sky. There would be no X-ray detection problem here.

Working with the skill of a watchmaker, the Colombian carefully wired the explosive to a small green circuit board connected to a tiny battery-powered two-way radio. When signaled by an RF transmitter, the bomb's radio would activate a time-delay process that would eventually cause a blasting cap to set off the explosive. Banzil set the timing device to fifteen minutes, put the altered filter back in the box and set it aside.

Next, he flushed a gallon of Prestone antifreeze down the toilet and cut the bottom off the bright yellow plastic container with an Exacto razor. After building a device inside the container, he reattached the bottom with epoxy glue. Banzil admired his handiwork. He was good and he knew it.

With no place to go, the assassin worked into the weekend and built four more similar devices to fit into an oil filter, shock absorber and brake shoe boxes. The final device went into a plastic Zerex antifreeze container.

Banzil wasn't exactly sure whether he'd use them or not, but he also crafted two more devices that could blow an automobile to smithereens and could be exploded from as far away as a quarter-mile. Both were set to go off instantly.

Saturday mornings at Upscale's corporate headquarters were casual and largely unproductive. Most middle and senior managers showed up only to appease Barry, who made attendance on Saturday almost a fetish. His general function on that day was to walk the halls and take mental attendance of who was and who wasn't there. His secretary always provided him a list of those executives who were traveling.

Barry had a memory like a trap and when it came to reviewing all corporate managers, which he did personally, he never failed to use Saturday attendance as a partial yardstick on how much additional compensation to award his executives. It was his own little game and most resented it. And when word filtered down through headquarters that the chairman would be out of town for the weekend, the place was like a morgue on Saturday morning.

After spending two days in New York, one with Sculley, Carole Nordstrom was tired and nursing a bad cold, but made the seven-minute trip to Upscale just to make an appearance. On the way to her office, she stopped at the coffee room, poured a cup of black coffee into a white ceramic cup and went to her desk. She thumbed through a stack of pink phone messages that had accumulated while she was gone and organized them in the order they would be returned on Monday. Then she attacked a pile of mail that was almost six inches thick. Midway down the stack was a beige intra-company envelope marked **Personal and Confidential**. Inside was a memo from Robert Alexander, senior buyer for fragrances, cosmetics and other related products.

"During the past two weeks," Alexander wrote, "we have had more than two hundred complaints from customers across the country concerning the quality of fragrance products purchased in our stores. They include some of the top and most expensive brand names.

"Some customers have complained that the scent of the fragrance lasts only a few hours, while others said the scent lasts too long.

"This is a unique situation. In the five years I have been in this job, the complaints have been minimal, no more than a dozen or two a year.

"In the case of the current complaints I have instructed our fragrance department managers to issue a credit, cash refund or replace the product. In one case, a customer even returned the replacement bottle. She said that after wearing the fragrance for the day, it smelled like motor oil.

"At my request, the stores have sent a number of returned fragrance packages to my attention here at headquarters.

"I think we should discuss this at your earliest possible convenience."

Carole picked up the phone and dialed Alexander's extension. There was no answer. He apparently felt exempt from Saturday's command performance. She put his memo in the center of her desk as a reminder to call him first thing Monday morning.

At eight-thirty Monday morning, Alexander, a small wiry man with black curly hair, was ushered into Carole's office. He was carrying a small corrugated carton filled with fragrance boxes.

Carole shut the door and led him to a corner sitting area, where two love seats flanked a large cherry coffee table at right angles. Alexander opened the box and carton and spread boxes of Poison, Luscious and Chanel No. 5 on the table.

Nordstrom opened a vial of Chanel No. 5 and put a dab on her left hand. Then she did the same with Luscious, the hot new fragrance introduced just a year ago.

"If I keep this up I'll smell like a cheap French whore before the day's over," she chuckled. "What do you make of this?"

"If it was one brand I'd say the manufacturer had a quality problem. But with multiple brands, I think we're dealing with something far more serious. I think these bottles contain counterfeit perfume."

"Who else is aware of this besides the store personnel?" she wanted to know urgently.

"My secretary has seen the product come back and that's about all here. I wanted to talk with you before I sent this stuff back to the manufacturers and distributors for credit."

"At this point, I assume we don't know where the stuff is originating."

"Right now, there are only two possibilities: the manufacturers or the new distribution firm that has been supplying part of our needs."

"For the moment, let's keep this between us. If this gets out on the street, it could be a disaster in the marketplace. It could seriously damage one of the major and most profitable segments of our business overnight. After what we've been through we don't need that now."

"But don't you think we ought to advise Mr. Warner?"

"Let's wait until we get all of the facts together and determine whether these fragrances are indeed counterfeit. In the meantime, get me a breakdown on all fragrances we buy from manufacturers and distributors and how much of each we sell."

"That shouldn't be too difficult."

"When Saks Fifth Avenue opens at Beachwood Place—about ten, I think—head over there and purchase one package of each of the top ten fragrances we sell," she said. "If you need a cash advance, Missy can get it for you. Otherwise, just expense it."

"I'll just put it on my VISA card."

"A couple more things. I know there's a trade association that represents cosmetic and fragrance manufacturers. Get me the phone number and the name of someone I can talk with there. And find out if U.S. Customs has a lab nearby where we can send this stuff for analysis. I'll see you at three o'clock."

* * *

The waitress brought a bottle of Grgich Hills Chardonnay, vintage 1988, which Dan Sculley said was California's best. They touched each other's glasses, then sipped the wine, which Carole agreed was wonderful.

Carole told Sculley in precise detail about Alexander's memo and their follow-up meetings. The banker was riveted to every word she spoke.

"What's the annual fragrance volume at Upscale?" he wanted to know after she completed a long monologue.

"It has always been one of the hot categories for the chain. If I remember correctly, our volume last year was in excess of 6.5 percent of total volume. That would put it in excess of $420 million. I might add it's also very profitable. In fact, it's one of our most profitable categories, one of the few in which we don't take any markdowns."

"You're wise to keep this matter close to the vest, at least for now," Sculley said. "I have a hunch that this, combined with the information you gave me about the cost of doing business with distributors, might turn out to be a lot bigger than either of us could imagine."

Chapter Thirty-four

The elegant brownstone on West 53rd Street in New York City was hardly the type of building one would expect to house a commercial testing laboratory. Bob Alexander was expecting something more industrial looking.

Marcel Deausalt, the top marketing man for Luscious, was already in the reception area when he arrived. "The chief chemist will be a few minutes late," Deausalt said after the two exchanged pleasantries. "The receptionist is brewing coffee."

"I've already had three cups."

"How many samples did you bring?"

"Aside from Luscious, four others. Snowburst, Crystal, Poison and Chanel No. 5. Manufacturers of the other four have promised to have control samples delivered here by about nine-thirty."

"Good. I have the control sample of Luscious in my attaché case."

Blaming his tardiness on a faulty alarm clock, Martin Rubin, chief chemist and part owner of the laboratory, finally showed up at eight-thirty and disappeared down a long gray corridor. He returned a few minutes later in a crisp white lab coat and led the two to a large laboratory on the second floor.

"Mr. Alexander is the fragrance buyer for Upscale, a major discount department store," Deausalt told Rubin. He says the chain has received an unusual number of customer complaints about the quality of some of the fragrances sold in his stores, including our Luscious.

"This is a control sample of Luscious," he said, handing an unopened silver box to the chemist.

Alexander passed Rubin an opened box containing a vial of the fragrance. "This is one of the packages returned by a customer, who said the fragrance odor disappeared after about four hours. I have four more fragrances for testing, but we're waiting for the control samples to be delivered by the manufacturers."

"Give me two to three hours and we'll have a definitive answer on Luscious," said Rubin, a short, slender man with a gray beard and piercing blue eyes. "You're welcome to stay and observe the process."

Rubin moved quickly across the room to a towering, slender metal-clad cylinder, which he said was part of a gas chromatograph system. "With a one microliter sample of the fragrance—that's one millionth of a liter—we can obtain a precise qualitative and quantitative analysis of whatever we put in the system. In this case, it's the fragrance."

"That's incredible," Alexander said.

"The average fragrance is a complex mixture consisting of forty, fifty to sixty compounds," the chemist continued in a monotone. "When the test is completed you'll see a precise reading on the graph of every compound it contains.

"First, we'll run the control sample, then the suspect. Finally, we'll match the peaks on the two graphs. Missing peaks indicate a lack of one or more compounds."

"But if the system can actually tell you what is in a fragrance, what's to stop counterfeiters from using the same device to formulate their knock-offs?" Alexander asked impatiently.

"The more sophisticated counterfeiters do just that—actually copy the formula," Deausalt said. "Where they fall down is in the packaging. That's usually a dead giveaway to the trained eye.

"In most cases where we spot a counterfeit, we'll see as many as two, three or four compounds missing from the mixture. While the fragrance may smell like the original, the missing compounds usually affect the length of time the smell lasts."

Rubin went about his job meticulously. Running the gas chromatograph on the control sample took just over an hour; the suspected mixture took fifteen minutes longer.

"No question about it," said Rubin, pointing to four missing peaks on the graph from the suspected counterfeit, "this one is plainly a phony."

Alexander rushed into an adjoining office, called Upscale and had Missy interrupt Carole Nordstrom who had just convened a meeting with senior marketing department managers. Carole left the others in her office and took the call at her assistant's desk.

She was not really surprised when Alexander told her the Luscious product was phony.

"Thanks," she said calmly. "Call me as soon as you get the rest of the results. If you can't get me here, try my unlisted number at home." She gave him the number and hung up.

Returning to the lab, he found Rubin already injecting a microliter of Crystal into the testing system. After the pair watched the chemist for another half hour, Deausalt suggested lunch.

Over corned beef sandwiches at Charlie O's at Rockefeller Center, the two spent an hour discussing the ramifications of Rubin's test and the potential impact on Upscale.

"The only thing I can suggest is to develop a profile of the counterfeit packaging and check each box against it," the marketing man said.

"With our inventory in 650 stores that could be a nightmare."

"I suspect it might."

Things finally began coming together for Special Agent Hal Spear. The long and tedious search through the records seized at Partsmania revealed a definite pattern of deceit. Agents found no invoices for large quantities of Strong-Anderson parts, though there were documents showing shipment of the parts from the warehouse to individual stores. Likewise, there were no checks issued to cover the cost of the bogus parts.

Spear surmised that either the Longos had a separate checking account to handle the transactions or they dealt in cash. Sonny and Joe were paid very large salaries for a company of Partsmania's size, and it was Spear's assumption that part of the compensation was to cover both the purchase and the profits on the counterfeit merchandise.

But the most promising news came in the aftermath of the raid on the Dallas distributor fingered by the Mexican parts broker. Prompted with information from Spear, FBI agents in Dallas had put the fear of God into Lee Ling, the transplanted Korean who was supplying Partsmania with the phony Strong-Anderson parts.

Ling's tongue began to loosen when agents confronted him with the possibility he might be charged with complicity in the Pennsylvania accident that killed Dr. Freeman and the rest of his young family. The frightened Ling spilled it all. He told agents how the parts were manufactured by his brothers and other suppliers in Korea and generally shipped to the United States and Mexico in bulk for repackaging. He admitted supplying Sonny Longo for about two years, but said he understood he was only one of the counterfeit suppliers to the Michigan firm.

On the same Tuesday that Robert Alexander was in New York with the phony perfume samples, Spear and an assistant U.S. attorney were in Dallas to confer about the case with agents in that city.

They were told that in return for a government recommendation of leniency and payment of a significant fine, Lee Ling had agreed to testify against Sonny and Joe Longo and provide additional documentation not found during the raid of his establishment.

"My guess is that with Ling's testimony you have an air-tight case against Longo and his son," one agent said.

"I have another wrinkle to the Upscale situation," Dan Sculley said to Rod Benson, the bank's vice president of security, who previously had been asked to check on Retail Distribution Services.

"We still have nothing definitive on the last assignment," said the tall, angular Benson, a former FBI agent. "The only thing we know is that the company occupies about 2,500 square feet in a small industrial park near

O'Hare Airport in Chicago. My contact in Chicago estimates that from the traffic in and out of the office a dozen or more people work in the place. He has no idea what they do."

"Keep working on it, but this takes the highest priority and I want it done on the Q.T.," Sculley said, carefully explaining Carole's information on the Upscale fragrances, including the news he had received moments before from Carole confirming that the Luscious package was a counterfeit.

"See what you can find out about the new fragrance distributor and its link to Retail Distribution Services, and check out your buddies at the FBI for an update on what's happening in the world of counterfeit fragrances and other products," Sculley said.

By day's end, Rubin the chemist confirmed that the four other packages contained counterfeit fragrances, news that Alexander passed on to Carole just before she left the office for the day.

"If all five products you took to New York are counterfeit, there are probably other phony brands, too," Carole said with a note of concern.

"The only way we can tell is to pull random packages from our shelves and send them off for testing," the buyer replied. "I'll organize that when I return tomorrow."

"Good. I think we'll just sit on this thing until we get all of the information, then take the next step. No need for you to rush back tonight. Enjoy yourself in the Big Apple. We have lots of work to do when you return."

Alphonse Spindler, a huge black security guard, leaned out of the small metal and glass cubical at the entrance to the warehouse grounds, saw Mark Garrettson and waved him through. "Evening Alphonse. The guy behind me is okay, too."

"Right on, Mr. Garrettson."

They parked side by side in a small executive area near the entrance to the building. Garrettson carried a black Tumi attaché case. Banzil opened the back door of his rental car and pulled out a large brown trash bag containing his handiwork. Standing about eight feet away, Garrettson admitted he was uneasy about being around explosives.

"Nothing to worry about without the trigger," Banzil assured him.

Garrettson led him into a reception area, disarmed the alarm system and motioned Banzil to follow him into the warehouse.

"The Partsmania order should be assembled at the last bay," Garrettson said. Banzil counted eight bays.

Garrettson told the assassin the Partsmania order was organized alphabetically according to brand name and was loaded into the truck that way. That arrangement facilitated put-aways at Partsmania's distribution center.

Garrettson took off his dark blue suit jacket and draped it over a chair beside a large gray metal desk, then wheeled a small portable cart containing a power tape dispenser to the Bay 8 staging area.

"Let's see what you have?" he asked.

Banzil slowly lifted an assortment of items from the trash bag and gently put them on the floor.

Using a razor knife, Garrettson carefully opened a case of AC-Delco air filters, removed one of the filters and replaced it with Banzil's altered version, then resealed the carton. He did the same with the other bombs, the last one being the Zerex antifreeze container.

Garrettson placed the items taken out of the cartons into the plastic trash bag, pushed the tape cart back to its original position and led Banzil out of the building.

"You sure this will do the job?" the ex-cop asked.

"Trust me."

Chapter Thirty-five

"Sixty to $80 billion a year. I had no idea the counterfeit business was that big," said Dan Sculley, obviously flabbergasted at the contents of the five-page memo prepared by his security chief. "This is no mom-and-pop business."

"On the contrary, it can be," replied Benson, seated on the other side of Sculley's large mahogany desk. "A great deal of the counterfeiting is done by small unorganized groups and much of their bogus stuff winds up in flea markets and on the streets of New York and other major cities. While there have been some rumors of Mafia involvement in the business, my source at U.S. Customs says there doesn't appear to be one dominant player in the counterfeit arena."

Benson told his boss that a former colleague in Washington had steered him to a high-ranking official at Customs, who spent an hour bringing him up to date on the current state of product counterfeiting in the United States and around the world. Fragrances represented one of the hottest areas for counterfeiters, but virtually anything he could imagine was the purview for knock-off artists.

"Let me throw something at you," Sculley said leaning forward on his elbows. "You said there doesn't appear to be any broad-based organization controlling many facets of counterfeiting."

"That came right from the guy I talked to at Customs."

"But suppose there was, and Customs didn't know about it? What if there is a well-hidden group with very deep pockets that could infiltrate a chain like Upscale with counterfeit products? They wouldn't have to supply enormous quantities of any one product. Listen! Upscale sells over $400 million a year in fragrances alone. Ten percent of that is $40 million. What would it be worth to get a foothold in a chain with 650 stores?"

"What are you trying to say?" Benson asked quizzically.

"I'm trying to say this thing may go right to the top of the company."

"Somehow, I don't think you're kidding."

Barry Warner was on a tour of Upscale stores, and it was turning out to be a cross-country orgy for the Upscale chairman. The hastily arranged visit to stores began in southern California, where Warner took off the afternoon to service Brenda Goodman, regional vice president for store operations.

The Canadair landed in Denver just before midnight Tuesday. An hour later, Warner was stashed in his suite with Betty Lou Firman, manager of the Upscale store in Boulder. Over a room service breakfast the next morning, the chairman told her he was sorry but would not have time to visit her store this time around.

"I know our associates will be unhappy," she said feigning disappointment. "They've been looking forward to seeing you again."

"Cut the bullshit, Betty Lou," Warner said with a scowl. "You know they wet their pants every time I show up."

"Oh, that's not true."

"Seriously, how are we doing in Boulder?"

"Things are great. As I'm sure you know, we've had solid increases every week since that financial thing was settled. And we're rarely out of stock on any item."

"Any problem areas I should know about?"

"Well, I don't know if it's a problem, but we've had an unusual number of returns in our fragrance department, when we usually don't have any."

"What's the complaint?"

"Most of it centers around the staying power of the fragrance."

"Have you talked with anyone at corporate about it?"

"I've had a conversation about it with Bob Alexander, the fragrance buyer, and have Fed-Exed some of the returns to him. He says my store is not alone in this situation."

"I'll check it out when I get back."

Warner tried to telephone Bob Alexander from 35,000 feet on the flight from Denver to Des Moines, but was told he was out of town. In the rest of a whirlwind day, he visited stores in Des Moines, Louisville and Cincinnati and then headed for New York City and a rendezvous with a New York regular, Marci Simon.

In bed with her at the condo, Barry couldn't get the fragrance quality problem out of his mind. There was something ominous about it. But that didn't stop him from performing admirably for his senior apparel buyer.

"You're still the greatest," she gasped while limping to the bathroom after two hours in which Warner tried vainly to get his rocks off.

"That's what they tell me," he said, then immediately fell off to sleep.

Banzil waited until it was well after dark before leaving the hotel. Wearing a navy blue jogging outfit with a loose-fitting jacket to hide the devices taped to his belly, the bomber walked down three flights of stairs and exited in the parking lot. The black Chevy Caprice he had rented was just a few steps from the exit door.

He drove slowly past Tony Longo's red brick home. A gas post light at the entrance to the driveway was burning. The only other illumination came from two brass lantern lights on either side of the double front entry doors. Banzil saw no lights burning inside the house, Longo's powder blue Cadillac was parked in front of the three-car garage, but barely visible from the street.

Wanting one more look at the scene, the assassin drove to the end of the darkened street, backed out and passed Sonny Longo's house again. He parked three blocks from Longo's street, slid out from behind the steering wheel and began jogging.

When he reached the far end of Longo's property, Banzil edged off the sidewalk and hugged a long row of high hedges that stretched to the back of the lot. He dropped to his knees about halfway to the attached garage and crawled until finding an opening at the bottom of the hedge. He squeezed through about twenty feet from the Cadillac.

Having observed Longo's car on at least two other occasions in the parking lot of his favorite bar, Banzil knew that the vehicle was equipped with a security system, which he assumed was armed. Any slight jarring motion could set off the alarm.

With the beam from a tiny penlight, Banzil found the spot on the lower fire wall where he would affix the device. He gripped the penlight between his teeth, peeled a thin plastic layer off the pressure-sensitive material on one side of the device and pressed the bomb firmly against the fire wall. Then he gripped the device between his thumb and forefinger and tried to remove it. It was solidly in place.

Twenty minutes later he was cruising past the home of Joe Longo, with the same mission in mind. It was almost midnight and he was in luck. Joe's white Acura Legend was parked in the front portion of the driveway, meaning he would not have to penetrate the area near the rear garage.

Father and son had one thing in common, he thought. They didn't garage their cars. He was thankful for that.

Banzil had just turned the car around and was leaving the street when a Southfield police cruiser turned into the street. It was a good sign, Banzil thought. The cruiser made a quick trip up the street and probably would not be back for quite a while. Banzil needed only five minutes.

About a dozen cars were parked halfway up the short block when Banzil returned to plant the device. He parked the car about five hundred feet from Joe Longo's home and started jogging toward it. The sounds of laughter and country music from a party across the street filled the air.

He stopped at the entrance to Longo's driveway and bent down to tie his shoe. Sure no one was looking, Banzil crawled along a five-foot-high row of evergreens along the edge of the driveway until he reached the car. It took him less than ninety seconds to crawl under the vehicle and affix the second bomb.

On the way back to the Plaza Hotel, Banzil marveled at how smoothly things had gone. He had allowed an extra day as a contingency, but tonight it all fell into place. He could relax for the next thirty hours, finish the job on Friday night and be on his way out of the country sometime Saturday. That is, unless Mark Garrettson had more work for him.

Chapter Thirty-six

Bob Alexander, the chief fragrance buyer, was about to leave for a meeting with Carole when Barry Warner's secretary called and summoned him to an immediate meeting with the chairman. Alexander tried Carole's number to tell her about his change in plans, but the line was busy and he had to relay the message through her secretary.

There could be only one reason for Warner's call, Alexander thought, as he walked nervously from a far corner of the headquarters building to the front staircase leading to the chairman's penthouse, a private enclave that was generally off-limits to all but senior officers. Somehow, Warner must have gotten wind of the fragrance quality problem. Alexander assumed Carole would be in the meeting, too.

Alexander had never been in Warner's office. In fact, in seven years he had never been involved in a one-on-one meeting with the chairman, despite the fact the products his department purchased accounted for better than 10 percent of Upscale's total volume and an even greater percentage of profits.

Warner, in shirtsleeves, was talking on the phone when his secretary ushered the buyer into the office. He motioned Alexander to a seat, covered the phone with one hand and told the secretary to find out what Alexander wanted to drink. The buyer opted for Diet Coke.

There were no pleasantries when Warner hung up the phone, and it was obvious to Alexander that Carole Nordstrom wasn't coming.

"I just came off the road from a cross-country tour of stores," he said coldly. "Betty Lou Firman, manager in Boulder, informed me there had been an unusual number of returns in her fragrance department. She said she discussed the matter with you and was told it was not an isolated incident."

"It was not," Alexander said huskily.

"Suppose you tell me about it."

Gaining confidence with every word, Alexander did just that, including the latest information received from the laboratory in New York. The chairman's worst fears were realized when Alexander told him the details about the trip and about laboratory confirmation that five of the chain's best-selling fragrance brands were counterfeit.

"Did it ever occur to you that you might have come directly to me with this situation?" Warner wanted to know.

"You know better than me that's not the way we do things around here, Mr. Warner," Alexander said smugly. "You made the rules about following the chain of command. I expressed my concern to Carole Nordstrom and suggested it might be appropriate to notify you. She said we would wait until we got more information, including the lab reports."

Warner's throat went dry. "You did the right thing, but so far I've heard nothing from Carole on the subject."

Alexander shrugged his shoulders, as if it was not his problem.

Warner wanted to ask the senior buyer whether he had an inkling into how the counterfeit brands got into Upscale stores, but decided to end the meeting.

"I'll get together with Carole as soon as possible," Warner said. "I'm sure we'll be needing your valuable insight in the future."

After Alexander left the office, Warner sat behind the desk with his arms folded for a long time, pondering the situation. When he finally looked at his watch it was a few minutes before five. He picked up the phone, dialed Jeremy Todd's number and got his voice mail message, that he would be out of the office until Monday.

The next call was on his private phone to Pedro Cardiz in New York. The Colombian was shocked when Warner told him that the quality of the counterfeit fragrances had put the entire deal in jeopardy. Pedro was especially distressed at the news that Carole Nordstrom was spearheading the investigation into their origin. He asked Barry to stand by at home for a conference call later in the evening with Ramon and Mark Garrettson.

On her way downtown to meet with Dan Sculley, Carole phoned her office to ask if Warner had called. She knew before leaving the office earlier than usual that Alexander had been summoned to Barry's office, and she was sure it was related to the fragrance problem because Barry didn't usually meet with the corporate peons. She expected that Barry would be madder than hell after talking with Alexander and finding out she took matters into her own hands without informing him. She was surprised to learn he had not yet called.

The hasty trip to Sculley's office was in response to a message he left on her home answering machine, which she now checked remotely every hour or so. Carole did not like to call the banker at his office, but made an exception in this case because of the urgent nature of his call.

"Bring me something to read," he said, a cryptic reference to the laboratory report on the perfume.

"Only if you promise to take me to Sammy's for dinner."

"I'll have my secretary make a reservation right now."

Sculley and Rod Benson, his security chief, were seated at a small conference table across the room from the bank CEO's desk when Carole entered the office, escorted by Sculley's well-endowed secretary.

"Anything new today?" Sculley wanted to know after introducing her to Benson.

"Barry's back in town after touring stores from coast to coast. I assume he heard something about the quality problem from a manager or two because he had Bob Alexander, the chief fragrance buyer, in his office a few minutes after arriving this afternoon. By the way, here are copies of the lab reports you requested. No word yet from other fragrance vendors."

Sculley passed the reports to Benson, who, without reading them, tucked the documents into a manila file.

"Rod's come up with some information on the source of the fragrances being supplied through Retail Distribution Services," Sculley said.

"The fragrances are coming from The Distribution Company in Wilkes-Barre," Benson said in a dry monotone voice. "It's owned by a company called Sans Souci, Ltd., based in London. We haven't been able to pin down the ownership, but we're working on that.

"The Distribution Company also owns a chain of seventy-five perfume boutiques, called La Fragrance, which operate in New York, Chicago, Philadelphia and other major cities. Our sources tell us the founder and owner of the chain, a man named Rudy Dorfman, was forced to sell out when he got into deep debt to the distributor. With seventy-five stores, La Fragrance is a major player in the U.S. fragrance retailing business and handles most major brands."

"And I suspect counterfeits of most major brands," Sculley interjected.

"My hunch is that these guys may have the best of both worlds. They buy legitimate fragrances for their retail stores in large quantities and get the lowest price. Then they mix the real stuff with the counterfeits, which cost them next to nothing, and make a killing selling the mixture through their own stores and to customers like Upscale. The poor consumer is rolling the dice and doesn't know whether she's getting the real thing or not."

"How do we prove that's the case at Upscale?" Carole asked.

"That's a good question," Sculley said, "but it's only part of the puzzle we have to solve."

Chapter Thirty-seven

The weather forecast called for thundershowers, but at seven o'clock on a warm and humid Friday evening there was barely a cloud in the sky. Banzil, dressed in blue jeans and a pale yellow oxford cloth shirt with a button-down collar, turned off the air conditioner in the black Caprice, opened the driver's side window and breathed in the rushing air. On the seat next to him was a black object that looked like a TV set remote, only about twice as thick. It was the powerful radio frequency transmitter that when activated would level the Partsmania distribution center and send Sonny Longo and his son, Joe, into orbit. It was effective up to a half mile, plenty of distance for what Banzil had to do.

Execution of his plan called for split-second timing and a little bit of luck, which mainly pertained to Sonny and Joe following their usual daily patterns. First, he would pull the trigger at the distribution center, then in rapid succession, get father and son. Even if he missed one of them this time, Banzil knew he would eventually prevail. Both of their cars were moving time bombs. He controlled the time. All he had to do was get within 2,640 feet.

He reached the entrance to Metropolitan Industrial Park in less than thirty minutes. Under normal circumstances he would have waited until darkness before exploding the devices. If the warehouse was his only target, he would have done it that way.

Banzil drove the Caprice past the Partsmania offices and distribution center. The parking lot was empty, which pleased him. There would be no unnecessary casualties. He swung the car around in an empty lot up Holland and headed back the other way. There was no traffic on the street. Approaching the distribution center, he picked up the transmitter in his right hand, lifted it to the level of the passenger car window, aimed it at the building and pressed the "send" key slowly a half dozen times. A tiny red light blinked each time, indicating a valid transmission. The bomber drove the car slowly out of the complex. There was no hurry. The first bomb was set to explode in fifteen minutes, the rest at ten-second intervals.

He was easing along Ecorse about a mile from Partsmania when he heard the first blast, followed by five more tremendous explosions, just as he had planned. In fact, the blasts were so intense, personnel at the FAA's air traffic control tower at the nearby airport thought a plane had crashed on take-off or landing.

It took controllers several minutes to ascertain that the blasts, which quickly erupted into a raging fire and billowing smoke that darkened the sky for miles around, were not aircraft related.

Banzil, pleased with the precision nature of his efforts, lingered in the area until he heard the sounds of sirens, then drove to Interstate 94 and headed for Southfield.

Arriving at The Blue Fox, Banzil was elated to see Sonny Longo's Cadillac parked in its customary spot in front of the building, meaning he was inside. He drove the Caprice up to a window-level pay telephone in the parking lot of a 7-Eleven diagonally across the street from The Blue Fox and made the call.

"Is Sonny Longo there?" Banzil asked the bartender who answered.

"Hang on a minute . . . Sonny it's for you."

Banzil could hear Longo's bellowing voice.

"Find out who it is."

"Who's calling?" the bartender asked gruffly.

"This is Rick Major. I come in there often. Tell him I just heard a bulletin on the radio. His Partsmania's burning out of control."

The bartender relayed the message.

"What is this some fuckin' crank call?" Longo shouted as he jumped from the bar seat and grabbed the phone. There was no one on the other end. A call to the local fire department changed his tone.

"I'll settle up with you later," Longo said to the bartender and bolted out the door. Longo ran about fifteen steps to his car, started it and peeled rubber. Banzil waited until the Cadillac had traveled about five hundred feet and pushed the "send" button on the transmitter. Watching from the 7-Eleven, he saw a tremendous ball of orange fire and the blue car lift off the pavement, then sink back to the ground, a crumbled mess of smoking, twisted metal. There was no sign of Sonny Longo, who a second ago had filled the driver's seat. The blast shattered the windows of The Blue Fox and sent patrons scurrying into the street. No one paid any attention to the black Caprice rolling slowly out of the 7-Eleven parking lot.

"Two down and one to go," Banzil whispered as he headed for the Olympic Health Club, a mile and a half away.

It was eight o'clock. Joe Longo should be getting out of the shower.

He drove into the parking lot of the health club, but saw no sign of Longo's white Acura Legend. The thought crossed his mind that Joe might have switched cars with someone else. But a phone call to the club confirmed that Joe Longo was not there and, in fact, had not been there all day.

One of the club attendants said it was the first time in more than a month that Joe had missed a workout.

Banzil drove to Longo's home, but the Legend was not there, either. The assassin knew that Longo would eventually come home. Time was still on his side.

The beeping sound of the remote pager on the nightstand aroused Joe from a wine-induced sleep. It was almost 10:00 P.M. He had been in Gina Riggero's bed since four o'clock when the two returned from an elegant birthday lunch at The Golden Mushroom, complete with two bottles of expensive Chardonnay.

"Who the hell is calling me at this hour?"

"At least you know it isn't me," Gina said, giving him a playful rub on his thigh, which instantly aroused him again.

Longo picked up the pager and looked at the digital read-out. **Urgent. Call Marty Rubio. 344-5567.**

Rubio, Longo's first cousin and best friend, was Partsmania's treasurer. He was one of the few, besides father and son, who knew the company was dealing in counterfeit products. Rubio was intimately involved in the deal with Lee Ling, but had not been introduced to details of the Commonwealth deal or its participants.

"Thank God you're okay," Rubio blurted when he heard Joe's voice.

"Why? Shouldn't I be?"

Rubio was silent for a moment, then told his cousin the awful news. Sonny Longo was dead, the victim of a car bombing. The corporate office and warehouse was still burning out of control.

"Oh my God," Joe moaned as he slumped back onto the pillow. "Who? . . . How did it happen?"

"People in the area near the distribution center said they heard a series of explosions, then saw the sky filling with black smoke. About forty-five minutes later, someone called The Blue Fox and asked to speak to Sonny. When your Dad didn't hurry to the phone, the guy left a message about the fire. Your Dad called the fire department, verified the place was burning and took off. About five hundred feet from The Blue Fox, a bomb blew the car to smithereens. The cops said the bomb apparently was set off by remote control. It's amazing. They knew just where to find him."

"I'll call you right back," Longo said, almost overcome by a wave of fear.

He quickly told Gina about the conversation.

"Your poor father," she cried, then started sobbing uncontrollably.

Joe picked up the phone again and dialed the health club.

"Olympic Health Club. This is Mario."

"Mario, this is Joe Longo. Did anyone call me there this evening?"

"Yeah, a couple of hours ago. Didn't identify himself, but I told him you hadn't been here all day. First day you missed in a long time."

"Thanks, Mario."

"Thank God today was your birthday and we decided to have some fun," he said hugging the dark-haired Gina. "You saved my life."

"Same guys who got the old man are gunning for me," he said in the return call to Marty Rubio.

"How do you know?"

"I know."

"What are you going to do now?"

"I'll tell you one thing I'm not going to do, that's drive the Legend. Pick me up at Gina's. We need to talk."

Banzil drove past Longo's home three more times, then gave up and went to bed at midnight. He was back at seven, but the white Legend still was not there. Banzil was sure now he had lost his edge.

On the way back to the hotel, he stopped at a pay phone and called Mark Garrettson, who drowsily answered the phone.

"I'm afraid we ran into a little snag," the bomber said apologetically. "The warehouse is gone and so is Sonny Longo. The kid slipped the noose . . . didn't show up where he was supposed to be. He hasn't surfaced at all. I'll spare you the details."

"Hey, listen, it was an almost impossible task, given the timing," Garrettson said philosophically. "I wouldn't worry about the kid right now. Let's take the heat off him. He's probably scared shitless and out of town by now. Let's chalk him up as unfinished business for the moment."

"I have plane tickets out of Chicago tomorrow."

"Not so fast, my friend. Something's come up and we may have some other business in Cleveland. I'll be in touch at the hotel."

242

Chapter Thirty-eight

The bombing death of Sonny Longo and the destruction of the Partsmania distribution center rated a banner headline in the Saturday morning *Detroit Free Press*. Police were trying to find Longo's oldest son, Joe, the story said, but as of press time he had not been located. The authorities said they had no clues.

One sidebar described Sonny Longo's business career: how he had expanded from one tiny service garage and parts department in Southfield into a 100-store chain with mega-millions in sales. Another, about four paragraphs, related scant details of the FBI raid weeks ago, but made the point that federal agents found no evidence of counterfeit products in the distribution center.

Hal Spear, wearing a white terrycloth robe and slippers, was eating breakfast at the kitchen table when his wife brought him the morning paper. The agent almost choked on the rye toast when he saw the headline. He carefully read and reread the stories, then called the special agent in charge of the Detroit office with the news.

"I remember Lee Ling saying in Dallas that he thought Longo was dealing with other counterfeiters," Spear told his boss. "My hunch is that the bombings have something to do with another outfit peddling bogus parts. Maybe Sonny Longo wasn't paying his bills. At any rate, the locals don't seem to have much to go on."

The SAC told Spear to muster up any additional help he required immediately and to report back to him later in the day.

Spear called agent John Crenshaw, one of the agents who had been working the case, and assigned him to check out the distribution center bombing.

"I'll look in on the Southfield police. Maybe I can get a lead to the whereabouts of Joe Longo. My guess is that whoever deep-sixed his father also has a bomb ticketed for Joe. The kid's probably walking around town with brown underwear, if you know what I mean.

"We can touch base in mid-afternoon, compare notes and then offer whatever help the bureau can provide in the way of scientific support for the locals. I'll call the U.S. Attorney's office and alert them. Looks like there'll be no grand jury session next week."

Southfield detectives were surprised when Spear arrived at mid-morning and provided details of the federal counterfeiting investigation. Spear told the detectives he did not believe the two bombings were related to a case that was supposed to go to the grand jury the following week. More than likely, he said, the bombings were an off-shoot of another counterfeiting activity.

"It was all done in a very sophisticated and professional manner," said one detective who identified himself as the team leader on the case. "From what I've read," he said, "the way in which Sonny Longo was dispatched is a fairly typical mode for foreign terrorists. So far our investigation shows that the bomb was attached to the fire wall of his Cadillac and apparently was detonated by a remote device at some distance."

"Did you find any parts of the car bomb?" Spear wanted to know.

"Not yet. It was a pretty powerful blast. The area is still cordoned off and we have guys on their hands and knees trying to find the slightest clue. It's pretty messy and like finding a needle in a haystack."

"If you come up with anything, we'll have our guys in Washington take a look. What about the oldest kid?"

"No sign of him, but we received a call about an hour and a half ago, telling us where we could find his white Accura Legend. The caller claimed he was Longo's cousin and said he wouldn't doubt it if we found a bomb hidden somewhere."

"We've asked the Detroit PD bomb squad for help, and they've already towed the car. I'm expecting a call momentarily."

That call came just as Spear was ready to leave for home. The lead detective listened to the caller for several minutes, then ended his silence.

"The FBI's in on this now," he told the caller. "I'm sure they'll want to look at the device and the car. An agent named Spear is here. I'll give him your number."

"I guess Joe Longo dodged a bullet," Spear said.

"He dodged more than a bullet. They found a powerful bomb attached to the fire wall of his car, rigged to be detonated instantly by a radio frequency transmitter. Apparently, the bomber missed connections with Joe Longo or they'd be having a double funeral."

* * *

It was mid-afternoon when Crenshaw and Spear made connections. "The distribution center's history," the other agent told his supervisor. "There are six pretty good craters spread across the length of the building. How they apparently got six bombs inside the building may be the mystery of the year. Whoever pulled this off was no amateur. The only thing left standing is the office wing and that's badly damaged."

Spear told his associate about the unexploded bomb found in the Accura.

"I'd be surprised if Joe Longo's hanging around Michigan waiting for the killers to try again," Spear said of the survivor. "I'm not sure he'd be anxious to talk with us, either. I know he'll show up eventually, but I hope it's not in a wooden box."

Joe Longo was shaken, but alive and very tired, when he arrived with Gina on a chartered jet in Hilton Head, South Carolina. It had been a very long night. First, Joe and Marty Rubio visited the smoldering ruins of the corporate headquarters and distribution center. Neither got out of the car. Then, back at Gina's, Joe told Rubio all of the details about the Commonwealth connection and the deal his father had made concerning exclusivity.

"I was against the whole arrangement from the beginning, but we needed the money to save the company and he was the boss. Obviously, the Cardiz brothers found out about the FBI raid and put two and two together, but they never let us know what they knew. In fact, Dad got a call from their midwestern honcho, a guy named Mark Garrettson, shortly after he returned from Italy. He said the conversation was very cordial."

"What do you think they'll do next?" asked Rubio as he poured a large tumbler full of Scotch.

"I don't think they'll rest until they find me. As far as they know, my Dad and I were the only ones in the deal from our side who knew about Commonwealth. Now you know."

"Have you thought about going to the feds?"

"Frankly, it's a two-edged sword. On the one hand it could land me in the can. On the other hand, I can probably trade information for protection. It's something I'm actively considering."

The cousins sipped tumblers of Scotch and mapped a strategy to keep the company in business while Joe figured out how to stay alive. For the time being, Rubio was put in charge of the operation.

They agreed to communicate only over cellular phones, which were virtually impossible to tap, or via pay telephones. But never the same one twice in succession.

No one was to know Joe's whereabouts.

Joe's condo overlooked the island's largest deep-water yacht basin and a fifteen-acre marina with 170 slips. The suite at Shelter Cover Harbor was located in a four-story cream-colored low-rise building with a red tile roof. Part of an attractive development that included several condo buildings and a collection of quaint shops and restaurants, the complex was patterned after the sunny portside villages of the Mediterranean.

It was directly across from the main entrance to Palmetto Dunes, one of the largest plantations on the island. Joe had purchased the three bedroom suite two years ago and spent a fortune redecorating it, including the cost of three expensive Leroy Neiman prints. His next investment was going to be a sleek powerboat.

An avid golfer with a three handicap, Longo loved the relaxing atmosphere at Hilton Head. He had made a dozen trips to the hideaway during the past year, mainly two- and three-day affairs devoted to testing the island's formidable array of magnificent golf courses.

Driving toward Shelter Cove on crowded Route 278, Gina and Joe realized simultaneously that neither had eaten anything in nearly twenty-four hours. They pulled into Fuddruckers and devoured large burgers and fries. Joe piled his burger with a mountain of raw onions, and washed it down with two Miller Lites. Suddenly, he felt an overwhelming desire to sleep.

"I'm exhausted," he told Gina when they arrived at the condo. "After a little nap, we'll go over to the mall and get whatever you need." In the haste to leave Southfield, neither had packed. In Joe's case it was no problem. He kept a separate wardrobe at the condo.

Even though it was sultry ninety degrees outside, Longo opened the sliding bedroom balcony door facing Broad Creek so he could get a dose of fresh air. He stripped to a pair of tight-fitting Jockey shorts, collapsed on the navy blue down comforter and quickly fell asleep. Gina lay down next to him and gently rubbed his back.

The sharp ring of the cellular phone on the nightstand jarred him awake. It was Marty Rubio.

"You were right. The cops found a bomb attached to the fire wall of your car."

Joe tried to put the events of the past twenty-four hours out of his mind as he squired Gina around Hilton Head, but it was difficult. The toughest thing to take was the fact that his father was dead and he wouldn't be home to bury him.

They killed time by shopping at various malls, an effort that left Joe $3,000 lighter. They had an elegant dinner at Alexander's at Palmetto Dunes, which Joe said was the island's best.

Wherever they went, Joe sized up every male in the vicinity. At Alexander's he took a seat with his back to the wall so that he could survey anyone coming into the dining room. If the guy who killed his father was searching for him, he surely knew what Joe Longo looked like. Unfortunately, Joe did not have that advantage when it came to identifying a potential killer. Gina continually urged him to relax, but he couldn't.

By the end of the weekend, Joe was convinced that every step he took might be his last. He knew he couldn't spend many more days living in mortal fear.

Chapter Thirty-nine

The three other men seated around a small mahogany table in the forward cabin of the corporate jet were grim-faced as Barry Warner raised his voice two octaves and derided the others for the shoddy merchandise that threatened to wreck the entire counterfeiting scheme and, perhaps, Upscale itself.

Ramon and Pedro, who flew in the jet from New York, and Mark Garrettson, who arrived in another aircraft from Chicago, sat with their arms folded, waiting for the diatribe to end, but the words kept flowing out of Barry's mouth.

When Barry threatened to keep the $250 million advanced by Commonwealth and throw the bogus merchandise out of the stores, Mark Garrettson, the designated intimidator, had heard enough. He reached across the table, grabbed Warner by the collar of his Fila warm-up suit and pulled him forward.

"I think we've heard quite enough," he said coldly, then shoved the retailer back into his chair.

"We're all upset about the fragrance quality problem," Ramon said softly. "Believe me, it was not done purposely. We have taken immediate steps to correct the situation, and

I assure you it won't happen again. All of your ranting, raving and threatening are not going to make things any better.

"What we're here today to discuss is how we can limit the damage and proceed with our arrangement with a minimum of inconvenience. Remember, we're all in this for the long haul."

In response to a question from Pedro concerning additional information about Carole Nordstrom and her role in the investigation, Warner reviewed his conversation with Bob Alexander. He told the others he had not yet discussed the situation directly with Carole, having preferred to await the outcome of the morning meeting. He assured them that only Alexander and Nordstrom of corporate staff knew that counterfeit fragrances had been found in the stores. Even Jeremy Todd was unaware of the situation, he said, and word had not filtered down to the store level.

Pedro wanted to know if there was any way to neutralize Nordstrom's role and get her sidetracked onto something else. Warner said that, given her determined nature, it might be difficult.

"She's already upset that we're buying a lot of product from your distributors instead of giving all of the business to our regular manufacturing vendors," Warner said. "I told her it was only a temporary thing."

"What would happen if you told her you were personally taking charge of the fragrance situation and would be working directly with this Alexander fellow?" Ramon asked.

"She might accept that, but she'd be all over my ass to find out the results . . . and quickly."

"My suggestion is that you try that tact so that we can buy some time and get our act together, then begin formulating a long-term solution to the problem. In the meantime, Mark is going to stay here for the next several days so that we can find out a little bit more about your Carole Nord-strom.

Two hours later, Warner was pacing his office waiting for Nordstrom to arrive. He had decided boldness and a blustery, indignant approach was the best way to unnerve and untrack her.

Carole knew what was coming, but she was determined not to be intimidated. She told Sculley the night before she wasn't about to take a lot of crap from Warner over the issue of taking charge.

If he didn't like it, she had said, he could fire her and then she'd take the whole thing public. She would tell him that, too.

She was as cool as a cucumber when she walked into the penthouse office and took a seat, directly across from him. Barry sensed her arrogance, but it did not deter him from climbing all over her for failing to inform him about the suspected counterfeit perfume.

The conversation was almost a replay of his response when she suggested they end the silly game of punishing the vendors who had cut off Upscale's credit.

Surprised at her belligerent attitude, Warner sensed that Nordstrom felt she had him by the balls and he decided to back off.

"Look," he said. "I appreciate your concern. Obviously, this is a very serious matter. What I'm talking about is a lack of communication. I didn't appreciate the fact I learned about the problem from a store manager."

"It's a lot deeper than that, Barry. For some reason, you've instructed us to deal with these new vendors. All of a sudden, counterfeit perfume shows up in our stores. What's going on here?"

"That's what I'm trying to find out. I have a helluva lot more at stake here than you have, like more than a half billion dollars. Do you think I want to jeopardize twenty years of hard work? I'm going to dig into this myself and make sure I get to the bottom of it.

"In the meantime, I'll notify Mark Garrettson of Retail Distribution Systems that we are suspending fragrance purchases from him. You can instruct Bob Alexander that all future orders go to our regular vendors. It goes without saying that we want to keep a tight lid on this situation. A leak could be devastating."

"What you've said makes a lot of sense," Carole told him.

Barry smiled, too, when she left the office. Garrettson and the Cardiz brothers wouldn't appreciate losing the fragrance business, but he had bought the time they requested and, hopefully, saved the deal.

Hal Spear spent Monday morning with three bomb experts flown to Michigan from FBI headquarters in Washington. They rummaged through the flattened Partsmania distribution center, looking for clues to the series of bombings that destroyed the building and $20 million in auto parts as well. The experts marveled at the total destruction.

"The only way this could have been done was with help on the inside," said one of the experts. "From the location and size of the craters, it appears the bombs were strategically placed inside various cartons of parts. Someone had to have a fairly thorough knowledge of the physical set-up and operational procedures."

"We haven't been able to question any of the employees as yet," Spear offered. "Most of them are attending Sonny Longo's funeral."

They went from the distribution center to Southfield police headquarters to inspect what was left of Sonny Longo's car and the defused bomb that had been removed from Joe Longo's Acura.

"I'd say this was designed with a bit of overkill," another of the experts said as he looked over the hunk of plastic explosive that had been detached from the electronic detonating equipment. "This amount of explosive would have destroyed an over-the-highway tractor-trailer rig."

"There are only a handful of bomb builders in the world who could construct this device," the third scientist said after carefully examining the electronics. "Two of them are Libyan-trained terrorists. A third may be a Colombian who reportedly is under contract to the Israelis, a very mysterious guy named Banzil. His name keeps surfacing, but no one knows what he looks like."

"Do you think one of the three or some other foreigner was imported for this job?" Spear wanted to know.

"It's possible, but my guess is there's no way either of the two Libyans could get into this country. Banzil is another story. I don't think any law enforcement organization in the world has a photograph of him, which means he can travel the world at will and dispense his own particular brand of terrorism."

Considering the circumstances, Joe Longo thought his score of seventy-nine for the tough George Fazio course was more than respectable. The long fairways, an ample array of water holes and tough greens had provided a mental challenge that served—at least partially—to take his mind off his flight for life.

It was just after three when he got back to the condo, where he joined Gina for lunch on the balcony overlooking the busy Shelter Cove Marina. While she was doing the dishes, Longo got the phone number of the Detroit FBI office from information and placed a call to Special Agent Hal Spear, whose name he had remembered from the raid.

Spear was just wrapping up with the bomb experts when the operator transferred the call. When Longo identified himself, Spear motioned to one of the bomb experts to pick up another telephone extension to monitor the call.

"Where the hell are you?" Spear asked.

"I'll get to that later. We need to talk."

"There's nothing I'd like better."

"I assume by now you are aware of what happened."

"I know what a lucky guy you are. I'm sitting here with some of our bomb types from Washington, looking at a device that had your name on it. It's pretty awesome."

"I can assume that whoever built that bomb and the one that killed my father is still on my tail."

"That seems like a logical conclusion."

"Listen, if you guys can help me, I think I can help you."

"I'm sure we can work out something, but first you have to tell me where and when."

"I'm in Hilton Head, South Carolina. There's a connection through Raleigh-Durham that will get you in just about noon tomorrow. Check into the Hyatt Regency at Palmetto Dunes. I'll call your room about three and tell you where we'll meet."

"How many people know you're down there?"

"Counting you, four. And one of them is me. I'd like to keep it that way. As you can understand, it's a matter of life and death."

The silver Lincoln Towncar pulled up in front of the Embassy Suites precisely at noon. A tall, bulky man with a fleshy face and very little hair got out of the driver's side and greeted Mark Garrettson like a long lost brother.

"It's been a long time, Pal," Max Goldfarb said. "About five years I reckon."

"Too long."

"Get in and we'll get rolling."

"I have a half dozen other PIs on standby if we need them," Goldfarb said as he pulled out from under the canopy and out onto Park East Drive. "They're just a plane trip away."

In the world of private investigators, Max Goldfarb was the guy you called when you had the toughest jobs. A former New York cop who for a time had been Garrettson's patrol car partner, Goldfarb had been a star in the NYPD plainclothes unit for a dozen years before opting for early retirement.

Every crook in Manhattan had shuddered when the crafty Jewish dick was assigned to a case.

When he cashed in, he was out of police work for exactly twenty-four hours. The day after fellow officers gave him a gold watch, a lawyer friend called and offered $5,000 to get the goods on the wife of a client who was shacking up with his partner. The money was too good to pass up. Five years later, he had one of the biggest PI firms in New York, with two dozen ex-cops under his wing. His clients ranged from

Ross Perot to the Cardiz brothers and Mafia Don John Gotti.

"How are things going?" Garrettson asked his long-time friend.

"Too much administrative bullshit to deal with. That's why it's nice to get on the road into something meaty. Speaking of meat, I'm famished. All they gave me on the plane was a bag of peanuts and a cup of coffee."

Goldfarb pulled off Chagrin Boulevard into the take-out lane at Burger King, ordered two whoppers, an order of fries for himself and one whopper for Garrettson.

Back on the street, Goldfarb guided the Lincoln with one hand and stuffed the whoppers into his mouth with the other, washing them down with giant gulps of Coke.

Between bites on his own sandwich, Garrettson outlined the assignment without telling Goldfarb the reason—check out key executives of Upscale, particularly Carole Nordstrom, the executive vice president.

They spent the better part of the afternoon consulting local maps and driving by the residences of the subjects. Goldfarb made notes on a small wire ring pad he pulled from a pocket inside his gray jacket.

The final stop was along George Zeiger Drive to the entrance of The Village, where Nordstrom resided. Goldfarb shrugged his shoulders when he noticed the security gate at the entranceway, which Garrettson said had caused him some concern.

After inspecting the perimeter of the property from the car, Goldfarb assured his client that keeping tabs on her would be no problem, especially since the back security gate was unmanned and there was no meaningful fence around much of the development.

Back at the Embassy Suites, Goldfarb told Garrettson that it would take a small army to monitor the lives of all the people on the list.

"As a matter of fact, I've been giving it some thought. For now, let's just concentrate on Carole Nordstom. Then we'll go from there."

"How serious do you want to get?"

"Twenty-four hours serious."

"That will take a couple of wiretaps and some reinforcements."

"Whatever it takes. I want to know where she goes, who she talks with and what she says. We're talking about a $250-million deal here. Obviously, cost is of no significance."

Chapter Forty

Joe Longo and Gina were seated at the bar in San Miguel's, a trendy Mexican cafe at Shelter Cove, when Hal Spear and the resident FBI agent from Hilton Head walked through the front door. Had he not recognized Spear from the raid, Joe would have known the pair must have been from the FBI. On a ninety-degree day, they were the only ones in the place wearing business attire.

Longo motioned for the agents to join them. After the introductions, the four moved to a table in the corner of the outside patio. The two agents ordered Diet Cokes, Joe and Gina two more margaritas. Joe asked for a bowl of salsa and more chips.

Spear opened the conversation by informing Longo that he and Partsmania were subjects of a federal investigation and started to read him his rights.

"Look," Longo interrupted angrily, "I called you. Let's cut out the formal bullshit and have a conversation. If formal statements are in order in the future, we'll deal with that later. Right now, my primary concern is self-preservation, which I am willing to trade for some information that could make you a hero."

259

"Okay, we'll have a conversation and see where it goes from here."

Joe, wearing faded blue jeans and a loose-fitting yellow polo shirt, started from the beginning. He told the agents how his father had started the business as a small service station handling minor car repairs, how he anticipated the boom in do-it-yourself car repairs and added a small parts department.

"It took off from there. He got out of service and concentrated on consumer parts. Later, he began supplying auto repair centers and offered around-the-clock service. By the time I got out of college, he had twenty-five outlets throughout Michigan and was ready to expand into other states.

"He was obsessed with the business and making money. It was not unusual for Dad to work sixteen- to twenty-hour days. He rarely had time for fun. Then my mother was stricken with brain cancer and died. About six months after Mom died a drastic change came over my father. He met a lady from Southfield who showed him there was more to life than working the auto parts business. She introduced him to Las Vegas and that's when the trouble began. He couldn't keep away from the tables."

Joe said that between the heavy gambling debts and the cost of opening and stocking new stores, the cash flow trickled to the point where Partsmania was months behind in paying its bills. The banks froze the company's line of credit, and most vendors put Partsmania on a cash-only basis.

"We were on the brink of going bankrupt when an outfit in New York, Commonwealth Investment Services, contacted my father out of the blue and offered to bail out the company. We went to New York and met a couple of brothers from Colombia, named Ramon and Pedro Cardiz. To make a long story short, they offered us $25 million at 12 percent in return for our stocking counterfeit auto parts in the stores. There were two stipulations: We were forbidden to purchase counterfeit parts from any other source and my father had to stay away from the tables.

"I was shocked that my father would even consider it, but he owned all of the stock in the company and made all of the major decisions. You did not argue successfully with him very often. He said it was our only chance for survival and leaped at the opportunity."

Joe told the agents how Partsmania started by taking a million and a half dollars a month in counterfeit parts, paid off the loan in four years and struck a new deal with Commonwealth.

"I'll say this about them. We had fewer customer complaints on their bogus stuff than we had from many of our regular vendors."

Spear wanted to know more about Pedro and Ramon, but Joe said that could come later, after he finished his story.

"Unfortunately, my father wasn't satisfied buying only from Commonwealth, as terms of the agreement stated. He felt their line had some holes in it, especially when it came to brake and steering components. We made twice as much money on the counterfeit stuff as we did with the legitimate merchandise. He felt it was worth the gamble. Again, against my advice, he cut a deal with an outfit in Denver to supply us with parts under the Strong-Anderson name.

"I warned him time and again that you didn't fuck with the Cardiz brothers, but he wouldn't listen."

Joe's throat was dry and he ordered another margarita. "Then you guys raided us and apparently they found out about it, but never let us know they knew. One of their executives was very cordial the last time my father talked with him. But I think it was all a charade to make us feel good.

There's no doubt in my mind but that they killed my father, tried to kill me and blew up the distribution center as revenge and to be sure that neither of us would ever talk to the police."

Spear probed about the Cardiz brothers. Joe told him he only met them once. Describing them as polished, professional and polite, he said there was no doubt in his mind they were cold as steel.

"Most of our dealings were with a man named Mark Garrettson, a former New York cop who runs their midwest operations out of Chicago. I don't know where the parts originate from, but most of what we get comes from a distribution center there."

They talked for almost four hours. Joe provided precise details about the types and brands of products, the method of payment, the kinds of trucks in which the parts arrived.

When they zeroed in on the distribution center bombing, Longo provided the probable answer as to how it was done.

"They had an intimate knowledge of our distribution center operation and how we handled and stocked the parts and products we sell," he said. "It's obvious to me that the bombs were shipped into the warehouse during a regular shipment and routinely put away into their alphabetical storage location."

Satisfied that he had learned as much as he would about the Commonwealth connection, Spear delved into the Strong-Anderson counterfeiting situation. Longo confirmed much the agent already knew from interrogating Lee Ling.

At seven o'clock, they finally got around to talking about protection for Joe Longo. The agents agreed that for the moment Hilton Head was a safe haven. The resident agent offered to have U.S. Marshalls from Charleston keep

Longo under twenty-four-hour surveillance, an offer he gladly accepted.

Elated at his forthrightness, Spear told Joe Longo that his cooperation in cracking the Commonwealth case would certainly mitigate any future charges relating to the Strong-Anderson case.

"Once I discuss this with my boss and the U.S. Attorney's office in Detroit and we develop a plan of action, we'll want you back in town to be closer to the action, and that should be pretty quick," Spear said. "In the meantime, we'll make sure your okay here. I don't think you realize how valuable you really are."

Chapter Forty-one

Hal Spear, delayed for three hours by bad weather at Raleigh-Durham, arrived back in Detroit just in time for the start of a strategy conference call at four in the afternoon. The group surrounding the speakerphone included representatives from the U.S. Attorney's office, Spear's boss and several agents from the white collar crime unit.

The FBI conference operator tied the Detroit group together on secured lines with bureaus in Chicago and New York and with Thaddeus Burden, an assistant FBI director in Washington.

Working from three-by-five cards meticulously prepared on the flight back to Detroit, Spear carefully covered details of his four-hour-long conversation with Joe Longo in Hilton Head. When he finished, he realized he had spoken uninterrupted for nearly thirty minutes.

Burden commended Spear for the completeness of his presentation. "I think everyone realizes that thanks to Joe Longo's luck in surviving the assassin's bombing attempt, we may have something very big on our hands," he said. "What we don't know at this point is whether Commonwealth is dealing in anything but counterfeit auto parts. We need to determine that, and we need to be patient enough to find out the identities of other customers.

After listening to the assistant director rattle off a series of strategic steps, Spear knew why Burden had made a name for himself tracking down white collar criminals.

"The first thing we must do is get Joe Longo back to Detroit and protect his ass," Burden said. "Aside from the information he has provided us, I think we can use him to our advantage in the investigation. Get a charter and bring him back pronto."

He ordered the Chicago office to put Commonwealth's distribution operations and Mark Garrettson under surveillance and to arrange for phone taps, if possible.

"We want to find out the origin of every truck visiting the distribution center and the destination of every truck leaving," Burden said. "If you don't have enough men for around-the-clock surveillance, let me know and we'll pull them from other offices. If we need to involve other offices in the investigation, you have carte blanche."

New York was instructed to track down the location of Commonwealth's headquarters and to put the Cardiz brothers under around-the-clock surveillance.

"Let's quietly canvas your contacts at New York–area banks. We need to find out what kind of cash flow these guys have and where it's coming from. We'll work with the IRS down here to determine if they've filed tax returns, and we'll plug in U.S. Customs to see what they know.

"We need to move swiftly, but quietly. Let's not wake these guys up to what's happening . . . yet. My hunch is there are some other big fish at the end of this pole."

* * *

At six-thirty that same evening, Rod Benson, vice president of security for Sculley's bank, was having cocktails at Morton's in Tower City with his friend, Harvey McGuire, agent in charge of the Cleveland FBI office. The two had worked together years before in San Francisco and resumed their friendship when McGuire moved to Cleveland two years ago. A string of bank robberies, including several involving Benson's institution, had kept the two in frequent communication. But tonight Benson wasn't meeting with McGuire to talk about bank robberies.

Speaking with Dan Sculley's permission and asking that the conversation be off the record for the present, Benson told the agent about the counterfeit perfume situation at Upscale.

"My boss is concerned because the bank owns a large position in Upscale, and we're also the lead lender for a major coalition of banks," Benson explained. He refreshed McGuire's memory about the highly publicized situation between Warner and Dan Sculley earlier in the year.

"I remember it was all over the business pages for a couple of weeks," McGuire said.

"Barry Warner, who controls Upscale, came up with $250 million at the last minute to help bail out the company."

"I can't remember the details but I know there were some big numbers being thrown around. Warner's a heavy roller . . . worth about a half billion, as I recall."

"But not liquid enough to dip into his own pocket for 250 mil. And that's what concerns my boss. We've checked every banking source we have in the country, and the list is enormous, but can't pin down a loan of that size. Dan Sculley has a hunch there might be a connection between the per-fume and the money."

"It sounds like a job for the FBI," McGuire said smiling broadly.

"Right now, a quiet job. The bank's ass is hanging out to dry on this one. Sales at Upscale are starting to turn around, and there's some hope we may eventually get our money back. Dan Sculley doesn't want anything to happen that will rock the boat."

"I guess what you're asking me to do is mount a discreet inquiry to see if we can find out if anyone advanced Barry Warner $250 million in June."

"Discreet is the operative word."

"Give me a week. I'll see what we can find out."

Chapter Forty-two

The surprise and shock of hearing Joe Longo was evident in Mark Garrettson's voice when he took the call made from Longo's Southfield home, where Joe was ensconced with live-in FBI agents after the chartered jet trip from Hilton Head, compliments of Uncle Sam. Although anxious, Joe relished the thought of talking with Garrettson from the security of his home and with agents monitoring the call. Unbeknown to Longo and the agents, the call from Southfield to Chicago had been rerouted to Garrettson's room at the Embassy Suites in Beachwood.

"We've been trying to get in touch with you," Garrettson lied in a voice that sounded hollow. "Sorry to hear about Sonny."

"Yeah. I guess you've heard about the distribution center, too? Our phones have been out of order."

"I understand everything's gone."

"Not much left but the offices, and they're badly damaged."

"Any idea who might be responsible for this?"

Longo paused for a moment to contain his anger.

"The police think it was gambling related. Dad was hitting the tables pretty hard again and losing big time. He also had a new passion—betting on baseball. His gambling debts were sky-high."

"The guys he was dealing with really play hardball."

"Tell me about it."

Longo explained that Partsmania was trying to regroup and had acquired a new temporary warehouse facility near the old one.

"We lucked out. It was used by a packaged goods company that went belly-up. It was made to order for us. With a few modifications we might make it a permanent arrangement. At any rate, they're installing the phones today and we should be operational by the first of the week. That's why I called. We need merchandise and we need it in a hurry. For the time being, most of our vendors are shipping directly to our stores. In your case, I don't think that would be a good idea."

"You're right about that."

"Marty Rubio is running the restocking, and I'm trying to help where I can. He asked that you double whatever you sent us last week and then double that next week, so we can build up inventory as quickly as possible. He wants to know how soon we can get merchandise."

The ever-cautious Garrettson decided to talk with Pedro and Ramon before making a commitment. Commonwealth was in the process of taking physical inventory, and he didn't know when it would resume shipments, he explained.

Longo gave Garrettson the address and telephone number of the new facility and asked him to do what he could to expedite shipment. "We're kind of desperate for merchandise, and we need your help. Let me hear from you as soon as possible."

As soon as he hung up with Longo, Garrettson was on the phone to Pedro and Ramon in New York, telling them about the phone conversation with Joe Longo.

"I don't like it one bit," Ramon said. "Don't ship him anything."

Pedro agreed and said, "Let's get someone over to Michigan to quietly check out what's going on."

FBI agents assigned to surveillance of the Commonwealth auto parts distribution center near O'Hare Airport found the perfect command post in the vacant fifth floor suite of a mid-rise office building across the street from the warehouse.

When they told the manager of the building the purpose of the investigation was to crack a nationwide auto theft ring, he was only too happy to make the suite available—without charge.

Three teams of two agents each were assigned eight-hour rotations around the clock. The suite was equipped with regular and night-sighting binoculars and a professional video camera with the 16-1 zoom lens to record the comings and goings.

Other teams of agents were dispatched to different sections in the area surrounding the warehouse. Two teams cruised constantly in rented cars that in no way looked like the plain vanilla vehicles issued to federal agents. Another pair was assigned to drive rented trucks around the area. Two more agents were in a fancy conversion van parked in the office building parking lot directly across from the distribution center, giving the occupants a prime location for checking the license plates of vehicles entering and departing the well-secured warehouse grounds. Special one-way glass prevented anyone from seeing into the vehicle.

A helicopter crew and two more agents were on alert at O'Hare Airport to join the surveillance of trucks leaving the center.

The previous day, one agent accompanied a local fire marshall on what was billed as a routine fire prevention inspection of the warehouse. The agent later prepared a sketch of the interior, showing the receiving and shipping sides of the building and the rack placement

By noon of the first day of surveillance, seven semi-trailer rigs had arrived and backed in front of the overhead doors on the shipping side of the building. All of the trucks were stark white with a diagonal royal blue stripe across the length of the trailer. There was no company identification on any of the trucks, just the mandated federal and state permit numbers required for the over-the-highway vehicles.

An on-line check of the national license plate data base revealed the trucks all were registered to Mammouth Trucking Company in St. Louis, which triggered an immediate call to agents in St. Louis for a check on the company.

A summer cold front was sweeping through the Chicago area late in the afternoon when four of the white trucks cleared the security gatehouse. The surveillance net was ready. Traveling together, the trucks navigated through the heavy traffic near O'Hare Airport, moved onto the Northwest Expressway and headed south on Interstate 294. Near Gary, Indiana, they shifted to I-65 and continued south toward Indianapolis.

Following a four-truck caravan on an interstate highway was a piece of cake for the agents. A pair of bureau cars from the Indianapolis office joined the surveillance as the trucks skirted north of the city and then headed west on Interstate

70. By the time the convoy reached the outskirts of Dayton, the surveillance units included one original car from Chicago and a new one from Dayton.

Less than an hour later the chase was over. Just north of Columbus, the four white trucks exited, made a series of turns and disappeared into a sprawling fenced-in industrial complex. The black and gold sign in front identified the facility as the Upscale Columbus Distribution Center.

One of the reasons Thaddeus Burden reached the top level of bureaucracy in the FBI was his firm belief in never putting off until tomorrow what you can do right now. He often ignored the time-honored bureau chain of command, picked up the phone and went right to the source.

A tall, well-built man with a ruddy complexion, Burden tossed his suit coat onto a chair in front of his desk, informed his secretary to cancel his five o'clock meeting on Capitol Hill, dialed the Detroit office and asked to speak to Hal Spear.

Spear, still at the desk in his small gray office, was surprised, but flattered, that one of the bureau's most senior officials had called directly, especially since he knew that the agent in charge was still in the office.

Burden wanted Spear to be the first to know that agents had tailed the four trucks from Chicago to the Upscale facility in Columbus and that the next step was to determine if the chain was, in fact, selling bogus merchandise and what types of counterfeit products were on the shelves.

"Can I assume Joe Longo is still in a cooperative mood?" Burden asked.

"He ought to be. We're living with him."

"Tell Joe Longo we need samples of as many counterfeit products as he can lay his hands on. Tell him we're also going to need his help in sorting out the real from the fake when we get some product samples from Upscale stores."

"Joe will probably have to get the counterfeits out of his stores. There's not much left of the warehouse."

"We'll also need a list of the types and brand names of the most common counterfeit auto parts and products sold in his stores."

"I already have much of that information from my Hilton Head interview."

Thirty minutes later, Burden and three supervisors were reviewing a list faxed by Hal Spear. Before the evening was over, agents in six cities, including Columbus, received instructions to visit Upscale stores, purchase selected auto parts and products and ship them overnight to Hal Spear in Detroit.

At midnight Burden awoke Hal Spear from a deep sleep, apologized for the hour, then rattled off a series of instructions that the drowsy agent jotted down on a legal pad kept at bedside. After twenty minutes in which Spear did not utter a single word, Burden told Spear to go back to sleep. "I'll see you Friday morning. I don't think I've ever spent a weekend in Detroit."

Chapter Forty-three

The favor Harvey McGuire said he would do for the bank security vice president turned out to be far from a discreet inquiry. McGuire kept his promise not to mention the bogus perfume being sold at Upscale, but needed a pretext to get the New York white collar crime boys involved. Stretching a point, he told a supervisor in the Manhattan unit that laundered Mafia money might have been the source of the money Barry Warner used to bail out Upscale. It was all the supervisor needed to hear.

In corporate and banking matters, transferring money the old fashioned way—with checks—was obsolete. The era of Electronic Data Interchange, or EDI as the pros called it, now allowed banks and corporations to transfer funds electronically anywhere in the world. Two resident FBI experts in money laundering assumed that a $250 million transaction would be handled electronically and proceeded on that basis. They decided to check electronic funds transfer logs at New York's biggest banks first and work their way down, which turned out to be a good move.

Since CitiBank, the largest, initiated the transfer for Commonwealth, the agents scored immediately. The fact they had Warner's name and a short time frame speeded the process.

The logs showed that over a three-week period in June, CitiBank had transferred a total of $250 million, in two equal installments, from the accounts of Commonwealth to Continental Bank in Chicago, care of the Warfund account, of which Barry Warner was the signatory. The money was then transferred into another account controlled by Warner and subsequently was dispersed in two $125 million transfers to Upscale.

In a rather cursory check, the agents could not find out anything negative about Commonwealth. They learned the company regularly had liquid assets ranging up to a billion dollars. The firm had never borrowed a penny from Citi-Bank, and no one they questioned could ever remember meeting the principals.

In Washington, D.C., agents from headquarters, in contact with the Drug Enforcement Agency, were shedding more light on Pedro and Ramon Cardiz, including the fact that they were indeed the sons of a Colombian drug lord.

Preliminary data passed up to Thaddeus Burden pointed out that the sons had never been tied directly or indirectly to drug trafficking. Investigating agents could not confirm with any degree of certainty that laundered drug money had been used by the Cardiz brothers in their business interests around the world, but assumed that somewhere along the line the sons received some well-placed help from their father.

Word on the street, agents wrote, was that, regardless of the origin of their start-up nest egg, Pedro and Ramon were shrewd, American-educated businessmen with no hint of criminal behavior . . . until now.

"We've found the source of the money, but not much else," Harvey McGuire confided to Rod Benson over cocktails at Morton's. The Cleveland SAC then proceeded to tell the bank security chief details of the money swaps between Commonwealth, Warner and Upscale.

"The guys in New York who checked it out didn't have much to say about Commonwealth, except that the company apparently has substantial real estate and manufacturing holdings around the world. They have a lot of money in the bank, but no apparent ties with the mob."

"That information will make me a hero with Dan Sculley," Burden said beaming. "Even with his wide-ranging banking connections, he couldn't come up with this."

Harvey McGuire found himself smack in the middle of a counterfeit trafficking investigation the next morning, when Thaddeus Burden telephoned from Washington to brief him on the Upscale case and suggest he be in Detroit on Friday to discuss the role McGuire's office would play in the investigation.

"Hold on to your chair, sir," McGuire said. "This will blow you away."

"What are you talking about?"

"This. Several days ago, the director of security for a bank here—a former FBI guy—asked me to confidentially check out the source of the money one Barry Warner, the chairman of Upscale, received in June when the banks threatened to take over the company.

"The bank guy told me that Upscale management was currently investigating the source of counterfeit perfume that turned up in some of its stores. His boss, the chairman of the bank, thought the source of the money might have something to do with the counterfeit scheme."

"That's fucking unbelievable."

"There's more. I asked white collar in New York for help tracking the money. They traced the $250 million from Commonwealth Investment Service's account at CitiBank to Warner's account at Continental Bank in Chicago and then into Upscale."

"Why is the bank so interested?"

"It's the lead lender in a consortium that supplied a major portion of the funding for Warner when he acquired control in a leveraged buy-out a couple of years ago.

"By the way, the bank guy asked that I keep the perfume information confidential. His boss is afraid that word leaking out about Upscale dealing in counterfeit merchandise could destroy the company and put the bank's investment in jeopardy."

"Fuck confidentiality. This is a criminal investigation. Keep your bank buddy out of the loop for now. When he eventually finds out what we're up to, he'll understand. Right now, this thing is starting to move like a runaway roller coaster."

When the day began, Dan Sculley and Carole Nordstrom were on different sides of the continent. Sculley was in New York for a series of meetings; Carole had rushed to the West Coast to meet with designers creating new boutique fashions for Upscale stores. Both were due back in Cleveland at about nine-thirty in the evening.

Since Carole had cabbed it to the airport, Sculley suggested they meet at the American Airlines Admirals Club, then head for the east side and a late dinner.

Sculley's plane was delayed for nearly two hours on the runway at LaGuardia and it was nearly eight-thirty when he finally got a chance to check his phone mail. There were nearly a dozen messages, but only the one from Rod Benson carried an urgent tone, asking the chairman to call him at the office, in his car or at home.

Sculley was pleased with the information Benson had acquired from his FBI sources, but disappointed that no direct link had been developed between the source of the money and the counterfeit perfume.

"There has to be some connection," Sculley said. "No one comes leaping out of the blue with $250 million in cash, unless there's a big pay-off."

They were just closing the Admirals Club when Carole walked through the door and virtually into the arms of a surprised Sculley, who had decided to head for the gate assigned to her slightly delayed flight. After a long, warm embrace, which embarrassed the club attendant, Sculley grabbed Carole's tan Hartman hanging bag and ushered her out of the terminal and into the VIP parking area.

Once on I-480 heading east, Sculley telephoned the maitre d' at Ristorante Giovanni and told him they would be arriving in less than twenty-five minutes. Then he settled down to tell Carole about what he had learned from Rod Benson.

"I just know there's still more to it," Sculley said in frustration. "Why did Commonwealth lend him the money?

What were the terms? I'm still convinced it has something to do with the counterfeit fragrances."

"What makes you so sure?"

"I just have this hunch and I'm going to play it. I've instructed Rod Benson to put the country's best private investigators on this thing. I don't care what it costs."

It was well after midnight when Sculley drove his black Mercedes 450 through the gate at The Village, pulled into the driveway of Carole's condominium, grabbed her hanging bag from the trunk and ushered her inside.

Twenty minutes later the condo was dark and one of Max Goldfarb's PI's went to work. Having seen the arrival of the car at the condo from his perch on Richmond Road, the investigator eased through the landscape barrier, approached the car and took out a small notebook on which to jot down the license number of the Mercedes.

The letters **DS** on the tag were so simple, he put the pad back in his pocket and drifted off into the night.

Chapter Forty-four

The hastily assembled area where legitimate and counterfeit products were gathered had the appearance of a giant garage sale. Rented gray and brown metal tables were set up randomly in three large empty offices on the seventh floor of the Detroit Federal Building. The institutional gray offices, in need of a good coat of paint, had been set for redecorating, but that was put on hold until the end of the current exercise.

White tags with handwritten notations done with red, blue and black felt tip pens identified the real products provided by automobile and parts manufacturers. Yellow tags were used for the counterfeits sent along by Joe Longo. Gray tags were affixed to products picked up at Upscale stores. Thaddeus Burden arrived at ten along with an entourage of technicians from Washington and immediately began wandering between the three rooms, expressing pleasure to no one in particular at the selection of the products assembled in such a short time.

When agents from Detroit, Chicago and Cleveland joined the assistant director at a well-worn slate-gray metal table, Burden asked briskly for specifics on the plan for determining whether parts purchased at Upscale were real or phony.

"We have some experts from manufacturers standing by, but for the purpose of this review, Joe Longo may be all the expert witness we need," Hal Spear said. "Partsmania sold millions of dollars worth of counterfeit products over the past several years, including just about everything represented by the products we have assembled."

"I'll buy that," Burden said. "If we can pin that down we'll know we have a case against Upscale and its management."

Awaiting the arrival of Joe Longo, Burden brought the group up to date on other aspects of the investigation. It had been clearly established, he said, that Mammouth Trucking was a wholly-owned subsidiary of Commonwealth, which was, in fact, its only customer.

In addition to its headquarters operation in St. Louis, Mammouth had major depots in San Francisco, Los Angeles, Norfolk and Wilkes-Barre.

"The coastal operations probably handle incoming counterfeit products from overseas," Burden continued. "St. Louis and Wilkes-Barre are undoubtedly used to service manufacturers in the midwest and east. It's a very tidy operation."

As Burden was telling the group about a second quartet of trucks that was tailed to Upscale's Kansas City distribution center, a young FBI agent leaned inside the doorway with Joe Longo in tow. Burden waved them in.

In a room full of men in discreet-looking business suits, no one would have mistaken Joe Longo for a fed. He was wearing a pair of tight-fitting stone-washed blue jeans and a navy blue T-shirt, which accentuated his muscular arms. He had a five day's growth of whiskers.

"Pardon my appearance," Longo said with a smile during the introductions, but I'm trying to change my identity. Thought maybe a beard would help."

Hal Spear led Longo into the largest of the three rooms, explaining along the way how the merchandise was organized. He started at one end of a row of tables and carefully inspected a stack of air filters.

"Definitely phony," he said. "Get me the real thing."

Spear handed him an air filter he knew was the genuine article.

"The packaging is almost identical," Longo said to Burden. "Look at the workmanship . . . the finish between the two. The consumer wouldn't know it, but when you've dealt with this stuff the way I have it's easy to spot the difference."

In thirty minutes, Longo identified more than two dozen counterfeit products, including shock absorbers, brake shoes, ignition kits, coolant, rotors, floor mats, engine additives, fan belts and more.

"I suspect that if you check the auto service centers at the Upscale stores, you'll find a lot more, including suspension, brake and steering components," Longo said. "Those special products are a lot more profitable, but you don't generally find them on the retail floor of a discount store."

Over a lunch of thick deli sandwiches at the conference table, Longo attempted to give the agents an insight into how the products moved in Partsmania's stores.

"Gentlemen, I can say positively that no one ever marketed an entirely counterfeit automobile," Longo said with a smile. "On the other hand, I know it's entirely possible to purchase a counterfeit version of virtually every replacement part. I suppose you could then assemble those parts into a finished automobile. It's an enormous business."

Burden wanted to know where the bulk of the counterfeit products were manufactured.

"We didn't ask. The stuff we sold came from all over the place. But it's my understanding that about two-thirds of the counterfeit auto parts sold in the world are produced right here in the United States. It's a multi-billion-dollar-a-year business."

"It's coming together," Thaddeus Burden said to the others after Joe Longo was sent back on his way to Southfield. "But, as I've said before, we have to be very, very careful not to tip our hands too soon. I'm not so much worried about the case against Barry Warner. He's not going anywhere. It's the Colombians that worry me. One hint of suspicion and they'll fold their tents like bedouins in the night, then re-erect them when the heat's off. I want to crack their entire operation in one fell swoop. Put them out of business.

Barry Warner did not appreciate Pedro's late Friday summons to be in New York on Saturday morning to discuss the fragrance situation again, but knew it would make no sense to press the issue. Barry could just have easily suggested they meet on Tuesday, when he was scheduled to be in New York anyway, but the Cardiz brothers were in control for now and he accepted it. He sensed they were very nervous.

He invited Jennifer Brooks along for a rare trip to the Big Apple with him, told her to pick a Broadway show she wanted to see and spend the day shopping to her heart's content. Cost, he teased, was no object. All she had to do was perform at night.

Barry's corporate jet arrived at Teterboro Airport across the Hudson in New Jersey about ten in the morning. Since Barry's regular driver was vacationing, Upscale's travel department made arrangements with a local livery service to provide a car and driver during the stay. The driver dropped Jennifer at Trump Tower to begin her shopping orgy and took Barry to the condo. He decided to walk to Commonwealth and dismissed the driver until mid-afternoon.

When a security guard delivered Barry to Ramon's office, Barry found the brothers attired in navy blue blazers and open-necked polo shirts. He hoped the meeting was as informal.

Mark Garrettson arrived an hour late, explaining that air traffic control had held up incoming and outgoing traffic for forty-five minutes while clearing the area for the arrival of the president, who was giving an evening speech in New York.

Pedro apologized to the pair for bringing them to New York on Saturday, but said he felt that—given security considerations—Commonwealth's offices prompted his decision.

Pedro assured Barry that the fragrance problem was now well under control, but wanted to know whether there were reports of any other poor quality merchandise from Commonwealth. Barry said the problem was restricted to the perfume.

Ramon asked if Warner had further conversations about the matter with Carole Nordstrom. Barry said she had been out of town for a few days, and there had been no contact at all.

"We're very concerned about her, Barry. More so, based on what we've heard earlier this morning. Mark, why don't you bring us up to date on Carole Nordstrom," Ramon said. "I'm sure Barry would like to know what you've uncovered."

"Since our trip to Beachwood, we've had Ms. Nordstrom under surveillance. We've tried to put a tap on her home phone, but she lives in a condo development called The Village, where the security is tight. So far, we've been unable to arrange it.

"But, fortunately, her condo is visible from a main road that flanks the property, and we've been able to use that as a good spot to keep an eye on her home. Keeping tabs on her comings and goings at Upscale are no problem."

"Just what are you looking for?" Barry asked with a touch of irritation in his voice.

"Does the name Dan Sculley mean anything to you?" Garrettson asked, knowing full well that it did.

"What kind of a game is this? You know goddamn well who he is and what he means to me. He's chairman of the bank that had us by the balls until you guys came along and put your hands on my nuts, too."

Ramon said, "That does not sound too appreciative for a guy who came within an eyelash of losing his company."

Barry just smiled weakly.

"I assume you know that your Carole Nordstrom and Dan Sculley are seeing a lot of each other," Garrettson said. "In fact, I just found this out before I left Cleveland, and I telephoned the information to Pedro from the plane. Sculley spent all of last night at Carole Nordstrom's condo. I believe his license tags bear the letters **DS**."

Barry felt a chill as he digested the implications of Garrettson's statement.

"I knew they had dinner a few times, but really didn't think much about it because Sculley has also dined with other senior managers of the company. Sculley said the bank had a major stake in the company and he wanted to get to know the people responsible for protecting that stake. I said I had no problem with that."

"Let's face it," Ramon said with a razor sharp edge on his voice, "I can't imagine the two spending that much time together under the covers and her not confiding in him about the fragrance problem."

"Frankly, I can't argue the point," Barry said passively, still shaken by the news. "But, if he knows about it, why hasn't Sculley approached me about it? That's not his style. He's the most aggressive prick I've ever encountered. I know he'd do anything to embarrass me."

"The silence may be something to worry about," Garrettson interjected.

"I just don't think we can stand by and wonder if they've discussed it and what they plan to do about it," Pedro said. "I don't handle surprises very well."

"That makes two of us," Ramon said.

"What do you propose to do about it?" Barry inquired. He was sorry he asked because Pedro threw the ball back to him, asking what the retailer's course of action might be.

"Frankly, I'm not in that line of work," Warner said sourly.

"Then, I assume we have your blessing to handle things our own way, but, of course, we may need your help," Ramon said. "By the way, a question: How well do you get along with the guy who's second in command at the bank?"

Mark Garrettson's late Saturday afternoon message to Max Goldfarb was patently clear: Get bugs planted at Carole Nordstrom's condo and Dan Sculley's home pronto or he would find someone else to do it.

Goldfarb and his chief electronics specialist knew the precise location of the condo and the junction box that fed phone lines into her home. All of that had been determined earlier in the week, when Goldfarb, posing as an out-of-town buyer, contacted a real estate firm and asked to see properties in The Village.

Saying he wanted to take some photographs to show his wife back in New York, the PI strolled unmolested along the handsomely landscaped street and snapped pictures with a pocket-sized Olympus camera. He got a perfect shot of the junction box, a long green cylinder about two feet high, which was served by underground cables. The box, shrouded by evergreens and foliage, was in the center of an island across from the Nordstrom condo.

Goldfarb spread the pictures out on the floor along with a handwritten diagram of the area around and including Nordstrom's condo and carefully went over every detail with Clyde Barnes, the small, bald-headed electronics whiz imported from New York.

It was just after 2:00 A.M. when Goldfarb dropped off Barnes in front of a small wooded lot on Richmond Road on the western edge of the village. Barnes, dressed in blue jeans and a navy blue cotton sweater, had little trouble finding Nordstrom's home and the junction box serving her condo and those of four neighbors. He quickly disappeared behind the protective shrubbery.

A former telephone repairman turned snooper, Barnes quickly opened the junction box. Using a tiny flashlight gripped between his teeth, he located the cable leading to

Nordstrom's phones. He carefully snipped the cable and connected a tiny coin-shaped device about the size of a quarter between the two ends of the severed cable. The device was a high-tech remote-controlled phone interceptor, a combination receiver and low-power transmitter that utilized the voltage off the phone line. The entire operation took about ninety seconds. Every phone in Nordstrom's home was now a microphone, regardless of whether she was talking on the phone or just having a conversation in the room.

Hugging shrubbery wherever he found it, Barnes returned to Richmond Road, crossed it and headed down a residential side street. His nerves were shattered when an EMS vehicle, siren blaring, pulled out of the Beachwood fire department garage just up the road, followed by a patrol car.

Barnes's heart was still pounding when Goldfarb picked him up a moment later.

They drove in silence for a few minutes until Barnes spotted a deeply wooded area about a half mile from The Village. Barnes instructed Goldfarb to stop the car, got out and tossed a softball-sized repeater with a one-foot antenna into the brush. The interceptor planted at Nordstrom's had a range of less than a mile, but when the signal was picked up by the repeater, it could be retransmitted distances up to thirty miles. In this case, it would only travel about three miles to the Embassy Suites.

By 3:00 A.M., Barnes had navigated a steep hill behind Sculley's wooded property, edged his way to a junction box and performed the same surgery. Barnes was tempted to plant another repeater in the woods at a nearby country club, but decided that a golfer chasing an errant ball might find it. He settled for a deeply wooded spot near a private school.

Back at the Embassy Suites, Barnes set up a transceiver on the living room desk and tested the two plants. Both responded positively.

Finally, Goldfarb dialed Garrettson's private home number in Chicago. When Garrettson fumbled with the phone and answered, the PI had a simple message. "We got it done, you prick." Then he hung up the phone.

Mark Garrettson arrived back in Beachwood late Sunday afternoon with two dark-haired, well-muscled associates in tow and checked them into the Embassy Suites. After praising Goldfarb and Barnes for their early morning efforts, the ex-cop asked the electronics expert to demonstrate the bugging system. Barnes went over the procedures in painstaking detail for Garrettson and his two friends, whom he failed to introduce, then handed Garrettson handwritten instructions for accessing the Sculley and Nordstrom phones and recording the conversations.

"You can turn the interceptors on and off like a light switch," Barnes said. "At times when you know that no one is home, you disengage the interceptors by flicking these two switches. No use listening to silence. It's deafening."

One of the strangers wanted to know the possibility of someone with the proper equipment discovering their place was bugged.

"It can be done, but the interceptor must be in the 'on' position when the sweep is being done for it to register positively."

"We'll take over the monitoring from now on," Garrettson told his friend Goldfarb. It was his way of letting the PI know he had learned all he was going to learn about the nature of this particular assignment.

Goldfarb liked the money, but was glad to be finished. He did not like the looks of the two gentlemen with Garrettson and was happy his only involvement was planting a couple of bugs.

"You may want to move this apparatus to another room," he said coldly. "We're checking out."

Chapter Forty-five

Harvey McGuire, the SAC of the Cleveland office, started the conversation by stressing the confidentiality of what he was about to tell Dan Sculley and Rod Benson. Any leak of information could jeopardize a major investigation and certainly endanger the lives of other participants. If it was necessary to involve others, they would do so on a need-to-know basis.

Benson and Sculley, sitting grim-faced with the FBI agent in Sculley's thirtieth-floor office on Sunday evening, agreed to the request.

With full permission from Thaddeus Burden, the agent confirmed all of Sculley's suspicions: Barry Warner had indeed traded the sales floors of Upscale's stores for the cash that enabled him to bail out the company; counterfeit fragrances were just part of the story.

"We need help on the inside of Upscale," McGuire said. "That was one of the primary reasons for asking you to come down tonight . . . to determine if there is someone who can be trusted to work with us."

Sculley said he had just the person—Carole Nordstrom, executive vice president of the company.

"Can she be trusted?" McGuire wanted to know.

"She can be trusted. She originally launched the in-house investigation into the perfume situation, which made Barry Warner very unhappy."

"I'm assuming the people who are supplying Upscale with the counterfeit merchandise are already aware of her role, which might put her at some risk."

"What do you mean, some risk?"

"We are not dealing with nice people here," McGuire said, not wanting to tell the banker about the fate of Sonny Longo.

"When can we meet with her? It's very important."

"I'm supposed to have dinner with her tonight when we're finished here. That would be as good a time as any."

They agreed to meet in an hour at a small Mexican restaurant near Sculley's home.

Sculley tried to reach Carole on his car phone as he headed east, but got no answer. Based on McGuire's comment about possibly being in jeopardy, his mind raced wildy. Had he made a mistake volunteering her so readily, he wondered. The twenty-five-minute ride to The Village was total agony. When he saw Carole standing outside the tennis court watching neighbors play doubles, he breathed a sign of relief.

The Sunday evening rush was over at the Mexican restaurant and Sculley and Nordstrom, the first to arrive, asked for a table in the far right corner, two tables from the nearest other party. Benson arrived next, followed in a few minutes by the SAC and a junior agent McGuire brought along to take notes.

They ordered quickly and got down to business. McGuire gave Carole an abbreviated version of what he had told Benson and Sculley. The banker had already given her the highlights, which gave her a sick feeling in the stomach.

Carole reviewed her involvement in the fragrance investigation from the moment she received Bob Alexander's note about the quality problem through the lab tests in New York and Barry's anger that she had not involved him in the situation. She covered his insistence—after the financial settlement—on punishing the vendors who had cut off Upscale's credit by diminishing their purchases. Auto parts and fragrance vendors were in that group, she said.

McGuire wondered whether she suspected others in Upscale of being involved. She pointed out that she was not a major shareholder and not a part of the LBO. Therefore, she was not really an inside part of management.

Then she remembered the meeting at the gazebo, the meeting to which she was not invited, the meeting about which Jeremy Todd had been so noncommittal.

"Shortly after that meeting, Mark Spencer, our president, resigned," she remembered. "Of course, I didn't think much about it at the time. The pressure had been tremendous and he looked awful. I think everyone took Barry at his word when he said Mark was quitting for health reasons. Now, I wonder."

McGuire wanted to know what other executives at Upscale knew about the fragrances being counterfeit. Bob Alexander, Barry and herself, she said—unless Barry had spread the word, which she doubted.

"Look, we'll be talking again in the near future," McGuire said, looking directly at Nordstrom. "I don't want to alarm you, but I'd exercise some caution until we get to the bottom of this thing. We know the people behind this can be dangerous. Handing her his card, he asked her to call if she remembered anything else or was unduly concerned with her safety.

"In an emergency, don't hesitate to call 911," McGuire said to Nordstrom as they left the restaurant.

"Look, I have a bad feeling about all of this right now," Sculley said as they drove toward The Village. "Until we sort this out and work out some security arrangements, which I will do with Rod Benson tomorrow, it's best you change your lifestyle patterns. That means tonight we're not staying at your place or mine."

Ten minutes later they checked into the Marriott Hotel in Beachwood.

Mark Garrettson and his two hired Chicago associates, Vito Ferrante and Albert Furry, were frustrated. They had taken turns monitoring the bugs planted at the homes of Sculley and Nordstrom. The only thing they heard was Nordstrom talking to her cats when she came home to feed them."

"Why don't we just go in and take them out," suggested Ferrante, the taller of the two. "Listening to this shit is boring me to death."

"That would get my vote," said Furry, who looked more like a dark-haired businessman than a hit man.

"Look, it's just not that easy," Garrettson cautioned the two experienced killers he had selected when deciding that Banzil was not the man for this assignment and sent him on his way to Israel.

"The suburban cops are tough out here. They shoot first and ask questions later, if you know what I mean."

Garrettson explained he had ended personal surveillance of Nordstrom in favor of the bugs; then added Sculley when he showed up as her lover. He said the bugging would eventually help implement the plan to kidnap Sculley and Nordstrom and dump them in Lake Erie. They would demand a multi-million-dollar ransom for the banker, but it would all be a ruse.

"There's a right time to do this," he said. "We'll probably only get one chance; it has to work."

Mark Spencer, wearing a loose-fitting Fila warm-up suit, greeted Harvey McGuire and another agent at the door to his large English tudor home on a street of very large homes in Cleveland Heights. He led them through a huge living room with a cathedral ceiling into an adjacent sun room.

In a way, he was not surprised when McGuire called to set up the appointment. Ever since he took a walk from Upscale, he knew no good could come from the scheme Barry embraced to save the company. Spencer always felt it was only a matter of time before the thing unraveled. Though McGuire did not specify the topic he wanted to discuss when he called, Spencer knew it could only involve one matter.

The seasoned retail executive had decided a long time ago that if ever questioned about the counterfeit scheme, he would simply tell the truth, and he planned to do that this morning. It had nothing to do with the fact that from the day he gave up the presidency of Upscale and a seat on the board, he had heard only once from Barry Warner and then to quickly answer a financial question. He assumed that his one-time boss was still brooding over Spencer's refusal to join the others in endorsing the counterfeit plan.

With nothing to hide, Spencer felt totally relaxed when McGuire began the questioning. Spencer readily acknowledged that he was at a meeting at the gazebo in June, which involved selected members of the LBO team. When asked the subject of the meeting, he readily volunteered what Barry had proposed. He was the only one to speak out against the plan, Spencer said firmly. The others easily acquiesced when Warner stressed the possibility each faced for losing his investment in the LBO.

Finally, he related the anxiety and sleeplessness and his decision to tell Warner he could not go along with the deal and would leave the company.

McGuire had what he wanted. As they prepared to leave, the SAC asked Spencer to keep their visit confidential. At another time and place, Spencer would have automatically picked up the phone and called his long-time friend, Barry Warner. But not this time. Barry had made his bed and would have to sleep in it.

"What will happen?" Spencer asked the agents as he walked them down the long driveway.

"I honestly am not in a position to speculate at this time," McGuire answered. "But I can tell you one thing: This is big. That's why we appreciate your cooperation and hope you will keep your word about not divulging anything about our visit."

Garrettson, Ferrante and Furry packed the monitoring gear into two large attaché cases and took it with them, insurance against it being discovered by some snoopy hotel employee while they were out of the hotel.

With Garrettson driving, they cruised slowly past Sculley's home and collectively decided that though the property was relatively secluded it was not the place to grab the bank chairman and his lady friend. Garrettson had already ruled out Nordstrom's place because of the security.

Knowing the fearless nature of Ferrante and Furry, Garrettson was less concerned about how they were snatched than with disposing of the bodies in Lake Erie and making sure they never surfaced. They decided to take one thing at a time and concentrate on purchasing a pleasure boat on which to take Nordstrom and Sculley on a one-way cruise to the bottom of the lake.

They drove east along Lake Erie and found a small marina in a beachfront community called Mentor-on-the-Lake. Garrettson left the others in the rented Buick Park Avenue and located the proprietor, a burly, bearded man who was painting the side of a cabin cruiser that had been pulled out of the water.

Garrettson told the proprietor he wanted to spend about $10,000 for something that could be used primarily for fishing. The owner showed him a 1987 fiberglass Wellcraft with a 165hp engine and canvas top. Garrettson bought it for $9,500 in cash, including six months of free docking.

With that part of the puzzle solved, they headed back along the lake looking for a suitable place to pull ashore and load the bodies. They settled on a small secluded stretch of beach about a mile from the marina, shrouded by pines and heavy grass.

Satisfied with their selection, the trio stopped for a leisurely lunch and headed back to the hotel for another session of monitoring, hopefully one of the last.

Chapter Forty-six

Carole Nordstrom and her two chaperones arrived in the bank building lobby on Wednesday afternoon at precisely the same time Benson and Sculley emerged from an escalator leading from the parking garage. The bank chairman brushed a light kiss on her cheek and asked how her day had gone so far.

"Nothing earthshaking," she replied nervously . . . "until I found out I was going to have company wherever I travel for the foreseeable future."

"I'm afraid I'm in for the same kind of treatment," Sculley said. "That's what happens when you associate with a beautiful woman who's in great demand."

"Why you, too?"

"I have no idea, but Rod said that's what the FBI wants to do. I'm sure we'll find out more about it upstairs."

Harvey McGuire, two assistant AICs and three other agents were in the executive floor waiting room when Sculley, Benson and Nordstrom alighted from the elevator. Sculley led them to his office overlooking the lakefront, tossed his coat on a couch and headed for a small cherry wall cabinet.

"I don't know about anyone else, but I'm having a drink," he said. "Can I get something for anyone else?"

Carole asked for Scotch; Benson and the agents settled for 7-Up.

"We'll be more comfortable in here," Sculley said as he swung open a pair of French doors leading into a small, but elegantly furnished, executive conference room. He motioned McGuire to take the chair at the head of the table. "At our place, whoever calls the meeting sits here. That's you," Sculley said smiling.

"Mark, I think you'd better start by telling Mr. Sculley and Miss Nordstrom why the sudden twenty-four-hour security," Benson said.

"Let me start by saying we're not one hundred percent positive about anything, but we have strong reasons to suspect that you both may be in significant danger," McGuire said. "We can only assume that the people behind the counterfeit scheme are aware of Miss Nordstrom's role in uncovering the counterfeit perfume. We also have to assume they know the two of you spend a great deal of time together. Putting two and two together, they could come to a logical conclusion that Miss Nordstrom has shared the information with you. As a major investor in Upscale, Mr. Sculley, you might rightly be concerned and expected to take some action that could be detrimental to the operation.

Concealing an unconfirmed tip received from the Chicago FBI office that a pair of hit men had been sent to Cleveland for an unspecified assignment, McGuire suggested that for the time being the two spend as little time as possible around their respective residences. He also raised the possibility that both residences might be bugged and asked the pair to restrict their conversations to social chit chat.

"With your cooperation, we'll sweep both residences for electronic eavesdropping within the next twenty-four hours," McGuire said. "In the meantime, we've taken the liberty of reserving a suite for tonight at Stouffer's Tower City Hotel and a couple of adjoining rooms for your chaperones."

"I'll need to go home this evening and in the morning to feed my cats," she said.

"That's no problem as long as our agents are with you. As a matter of fact, we'll use one of your visits as an opportunity to test for bugs."

"How long do you think this will last?" Sculley asked.

"Right now, your guess is as good as mine," the AIC responded. "But, hopefully, not too long."

"Now, there's something else we need to discuss, Miss Nordstrom," the SAC said. "Your hunch about Mark Spencer was right. He resigned because he was unwilling to go along with Barry's grand plan. Unfortunately, he was the only executive present at that meeting who would not go along with the scheme.

"The rest just went along with Barry, even though they knew what they approved was a blatant criminal act," said McGuire, ticking off a list of others at the meeting.

Nordstrom kept biting her lower lip and shaking her head in disbelief.

"I guess that sort of sews up the case," Rod Benson said. "Where do you go from here?"

McGuire told the group that Upscale was only part of the story; the ultimate goal was to smash the counterfeit ring and put it out of business.

"Based on what we already know, we could probably arrest Barry Warner and the others right now, but we want to use Warner as leverage in getting to the people behind the ring," McGuire said. "To do that we need your help, Miss Nordstrom."

"My help?"

"We want to confront Warner with some of the information we have . . . just enough to make him run scared to the people who gave him the $250 million. We'd like you to confront him. Be direct, aggressive, inflammatory—anything to make him lose his cool. We'll be listening."

"Believe me, this is one role I won't have to rehearse."

Chapter Forty-seven

Rod Benson was already seated at a booth for two when Carole arrived at Pizzeria Uno, part of a large chain that originated in Chicago and specializes in deep dish pizza. She was wearing a gray pinstripe Donna Karen suit with a white silk blouse. Benson thought she looked smashing and envied his boss' good taste in women.

Considering what she was about to do, Nordstrom told Benson she felt remarkably calm. In fact, she was famished and suggested they order immediately so she would have enough time to eat and then get wired.

They decided to split a four cheese deep dish pizza—a blend of mozzarella, feta, romano and muenster, Benson ordered a small Caesar salad. Nordstrom opted for the house salad served with red wine vinegar dressing.

The service was exceptionally fast. By one o'clock, Benson was tapping on the door to room 224 at the Holiday Inn, where the restaurant was located, to let the agents know they were ready. McGuire was there to supervise the operation along with two of his local agents and an electronics specialist flown in from Washington, D.C. Two more agents were in an electronics van in the hotel parking lot. It would move closer to Upscale once Nordstrom left for her office.

"I had a tough time deciding what to wear today," Nordstrom said smiling.

"You did fine," McGuire said.

"It's perfect," said the electronics specialist. "We can hide the microphone under the lapel. It should work like a charm. But first, we need your help with this." He handed her a garterlike elastic band with a small two-inch pocket attached to it.

The pocket contained a tiny gold-colored receiver/transmitter designed to capture the sound from the lapel microphone and retransmit it to a more powerful receiver in the van, where Carole's conversation with Barry would be monitored and taperecorded.

Carole went into the bathroom and slipped the elastic strap and its contents over her knee and tugged it up to the lower part of her thigh. Heeding the specialist's warning that she might be wearing it for some time, she adjusted the strap until it was comfortable.

Back in the room, the specialist used a super-thin two-way tape to attach the dime-sized microphone/transmitter under the right lapel.

"Excellent. Now take a walk down the hall and hum a little tune for us," the specialist said. Using a walkie-talkie, he notified agents in the van he was commencing a test.

"We're reading you in stereo," one of the van operators quipped when he heard Carole sing a few bars of "The Party's Over."

"Quite apropos, don't you think?" she said of the song.

Arriving at her office at Upscale, Carole tested the system again by calling Warner's secretary to determine whether he would be on time for the three o'clock meeting.

She was assured he would be in at the appointed hour for the meeting. McGuire, the specialist and the two men in the van heard her loud and clear.

Carole was nonfunctional for the next hour. For most of the time she sat frozen at her desk, fueling the outright contempt she felt for Barry Warner. She had no misgivings at all about her role and hoped for only one thing: Warner would wind up behind bars.

Barry could tell by the frosty look on Carole's face and the fact she walked into the office empty-handed that the meeting had nothing to do with new fashions, which had been the pretext for meeting with him. Sitting directly across from him, she made sure he knew it from the outset.

"More than two weeks ago we had a conversation about counterfeit fragrances being sold in Upscale stores," she started. "At that time you told me in no uncertain terms to back out of the situation; you would handle it. To my knowledge, nothing has changed. I think I know why."

"I beg to differ with you," Warner shot back leaning forward in his chair. "We've had very few complaints concerning our fragrances. I've personally monitored it. I think what we had was an isolated incident or two."

"That's a crock. I've talked with a dozen store managers over the past ten days," she lied. "Without exception every one has said something about the quality of some of the fragrances we've been selling."

"I think I remember telling you to keep your nose out of this thing," Barry said, his voice rising. "Was there something about that order you didn't understand?"

"I'll tell you why I think you've stonewalled on this thing. It's because your ass is in this thing, along with a bunch of other people at Upscale."

"That's a pretty slanderous statement, young lady, one that can get you into plenty of trouble."

"You don't scare me, Barry. Here's what I think: You made book with the counterfeiters to stock fragrances and other products in our stores in return for a hefty loan or gift, whatever, which you used to meet the bank's demands for cash."

"Listen, I don't have to take this crap from you and I don't intend to. Get the fuck out of here. And, I mean permanently," he said as he rose out of the chair and moved toward her.

Carole folded her arms and looked straight into his eyes. She was pretty sure he wouldn't hit her, not with his secretary in the outer office. "I'll get out of here when I'm good and ready and not a second before."

Warner backed off.

"You're a disgrace to this business and to the legitimate people who work here. You sold Upscale to the counterfeiters to save your overblown ego, and that's exactly what I intend to tell the police."

"I don't know what you've been smoking, but you're hallucinating," he said and started laughing. "You and your Dan Sculley must have made this up while you were smoking a few joints."

"Dan Sculley had nothing to do with this," Carole said, not surprised in the least that Warner had finally brought up his name.

"I'd be very careful about coming to conclusions and running your mouth," Warner said, showing her to the door.

"When I get finished with you, you'll never get another job in this business. That I can promise you."

"Marvelous performance," said Harvey McGuire, who had been in the back of the van monitoring the conversation. "If my guess is right, the next thing he'll do is make a long distance phone call."

Warner was trembling with anger and concern when he telephoned Upscale's director of human relations a few minutes later. "Carole Nordstrom doesn't work here anymore, as of this minute. I want her out of here now. And don't process a dime of her severance package until you've discussed it with me."

Carole was one step ahead of Warner. She stopped long enough in her office to grab her Rolodex and a few personal belongings from the top drawer of her desk.

"I'm out of here. Fired," she told her assistant, Missy, on the way out the door. "I'll explain it to you later."

Carole was sure she was coming back.

Barry knew Pedro and Ramon would not be pleased with his news. He also suspected that word Carole Nordstrom had threatened to go to the police would certainly speed up whatever they had planned for his former executive vice president.

He made the call from a drive-up pay phone less than a mile away. He was told the brothers were in a meeting and could not be disturbed. He persisted. She asked for the number and said someone would get back to him within the next ten minutes.

FBI agents monitoring Commonwealth's satellite phone network picked up Warner's incoming call and waited patiently for one of the Cardiz brothers to return it. They never did.

Pedro instructed his secretary to page Mark Garrettson on his digital pager and relay Barry's phone number.

Expecting one of the brothers, Warner was surprised when the caller turned out to be the ex-cop.

"Where are you?" Garrettson wanted to know.

"At a drive-up pay phone at the corner of South Woodland and Richmond, less than a mile from the office."

"Stay there. I'll join you in a few minutes."

Warner was shocked. He did not know Garrettson was still in the area.

Less than ten minutes later, Garrettson, traveling alone, cruised around the corner of the intersection and motioned Warner to follow. Garrettson's Buick and Barry's white Mercedes traveled in tandem for more than a mile until Garrettson pulled into the parking lot of a strip shopping center, turned off the ignition and joined Barry in the front seat of the convertible. Neither noticed the gray Mercury Sable that pulled in behind them.

"I didn't know you were here," Barry said.

"Not many people do."

"I was surprised. I thought either Pedro or Ramon would call."

"They have other clients, too. What's the problem?"

Barry gushed out the details about the confrontation with Carole.

"Doesn't surprise me. What did you tell her?"

"I threatened her with a slander suit and fired the bitch."

"Sounds like a sound management decision," Garrett-son said sarcastically.

"What the fuck did you want me to do, admit it?"

"Calm down pal. I'm on your side."

"I'm sure she's in this with Sculley and that really complicates the issue."

"I know, we're working on it," said Garrettson, turning and walking toward his car. "Don't panic. I'll be in touch."

Back at the hotel, Garrettson discussed the urgency now associated with the Nordstrom-Sculley situation. But all agreed, they were not yet prepared to make the final move."

Harvey McGuire was ecstatic when he returned to his office in the Federal Building late in the afternoon. Agents tailing Warner from Upscale to the pay phone and then to Landerwood Plaza had struck pay dirt. With a high-powered telephoto lens they had captured a photo of Warner and the man who met him at the pay phone. McGuire guessed it might be Mark Garrettson.

An hour later the SAC was in Dan Sculley's office for a meeting requested through Rod Benson. Sculley laid it on the line. He needed twenty-four to thirty-six hours before the agents closed in on Warner. Sculley wanted to do a little housecleaning at Upscale and take public relations steps that would help mitigate the negative publicity that would surely arise when the media got hold of the story.

"I have no desire to jeopardize your investigation," Sculley said with the aura of a bank officer. "But at the same time we have hundreds of millions of dollars at stake. I've got to protect the bank's investment and, hopefully, the future of Upscale."

Sculley told the SAC that his major purpose was to force Warner and other insiders to resign and to replace them with new executives who would be recruited in the future.

"That means telling Warner you have proof he's involved in this thing up to his eyeballs," Sculley said.

"Personally, I don't have a problem with it, but I'll check with Washington and get back to Rod with an answer by noon tomorrow."

Nordstrom and Sculley spent the night at the downtown hotel, which again frustrated Garrettson and his friends. Garrettson lamented that bugging the phones had added zero to their ability to track Nordstrom and Sculley. He was sorry now he had dismissed Goldfarb and his associates from their surveillance duties so hastily. Another day of this and he would call them back into service.

Chapter Forty-eight

The telephone call from Pete Cosgrove of First Union Trust left Jeff Weinstein virtually speechless.

"I'm sorry, but effective immediately we're shutting down your line of credit," Cosgrove told Upscale's chief financial officer.

"You can't do that. We have an agreement."

"I don't make policy around here," the bank's executive vice president said sharply. "I do what I'm told to do. Our chairman says no more line of credit. Until I hear otherwise from him that means no more line of credit. Period."

"But I don't understand."

"I just follow orders."

Barry was on his way to a meeting in downtown Cleveland when Weinstein reached him on the cellular phone with the news. In a way, nothing surprised Warner. Sculley was making his move. Combined with yesterday's session with Carole, it meant things would probably get ugly. While he had an inherent dislike for the banker, Warner never misjudged Sculley's ability as a street fighter.

Feigning a calm demeanor, Barry thanked Weinstein for the call and asked him to prepare an analysis of Upscale's cash flow projections—how long the company could survive without First Union's credit line.

"Not very long," blurted the CFO.

Warner dismissed his editorializing and bluntly instructed him to put the numbers on paper so they could discuss the situation intelligently when he returned to the office in the early afternoon.

Feeling pressed to move ahead with his own plan to protect the bank's investment, Sculley decided to move ahead with his plan, even if it meant pissing off the feds.

His first stop in the morning was at the home of Mark Spencer, whom he had called late the previous evening. Apologizing for the hour, Sculley had asked for an early morning meeting to discuss a subject of mutual interest. Spencer told him that if the matter involved Upscale, he was wasting his time. Aside from receiving a handsome $25,000 a month pension, he had no connection with the company.

"What I want to talk about concerns assuring that you will always receive your pension check," the banker had said. That got Spencer's undivided attention

"There are two things I want to talk about this morning," Sculley said, sipping a cup of black coffee poured by Spencer's wife. "One is about a meeting you attended with other Upscale executives at Barry Warner's home last June shortly before you resigned. I know the subject of that meeting concerned trading the sale of counterfeit products for the bail-out money Barry needed. I know what was discussed in minute detail. I also know that you were the only person to speak aggressively against the plan. By the way, Barry does not know I have this information."

"What you say is correct," Spencer said without emotion, but wondering how Sculley got the information.

"You resigned a few days later, presumably because of that situation."

"Right again."

"I admire your integrity."

"If you don't have that you don't have anything."

"Barry has no inkling of this, but there are going to be some significant changes at Upscale in the very near future—almost an entirely new management team. You are a seasoned hand with a lot of good years left in this business. I'd like you to be a part of it. I'm not asking for a commitment right now, just that you think about it. The job would be as chairman and chief operating officer."

"Who would be CEO?"

"I would rather not answer that right now, except to say it will be a seasoned pro in the business . . . someone you could work well with."

"I've had a love affair with retailing all of my life," Spencer said in a husky voice, a tear forming in his eye. "It broke my heart when I left Upscale, but I could not remain under the circumstances. I've put too much of my life and reputation in this business to let greed ruin it. Do I want to come back now? Part of me probably says 'yes.' The other part says 'no.' But I will think about it."

Sculley scribbled his private phone number on the back of an embossed First Union business card and handed it to Spencer and said, "Please keep this meeting confidential and let me hear from you soon."

By now, Sculley thought as he got into his Mercedes, Pete Cosgrove had already delivered the bad news to Jeff Weinstein. The next step would be a showdown with Barry. This would be the time to deliver the knockout punch.

Rod Benson got the okay for Sculley's plan from McGuire just before noon and was able to pass it along to his boss during a brief conversation in the bank's executive dining room. At the same time, Benson told Sculley that the bureau wanted to do a bug sweep at his residence and that of Carole's early in the evening.

About the same time, Harvey McGuire and two of his agents were lunching at the Marriott, five hundred feet down Park East Road from the Embassy Suites. The two agents were part of a six-man team that had checked into the Embassy in the morning, less than an hour after the FBI in New York confirmed that the man photographed in the parking lot with Barry Warner was Mark Garrettson. McGuire had faxed the photograph of Garrettson to key offices across the country, asking if anyone could identify the subject. An agent in New York quickly identified him as a former New York cop who had taken early retirement and disappeared into the world of executive security.

It was early afternoon and none of McGuire's agents had reported seeing anyone resembling Garrettson or one or more men who could be professional killers. They did report finding Garrettson's rented Buick in the parking lot. Mc-Guire said he would arrange for his electronics specialist to bug it that evening.

On discreet inquiry, the front desk said it had no one by the name Garrettson registered. McGuire said the ex-cop had probably registered under an assumed name.

One of the two agents at the table said it would not be hard to get a room number if and when Garrettson was spotted leaving a suite. The five-story building had a floor-to-ceiling atrium and virtually all of the room doors were visible from the lobby floor.

The SAC said once Garrettson and whomever he was with were spotted that they be kept under tight surveillance. Now that Carole Nordstrom had threatened Barry with exposure, the counterfeiters would probably accelerate whatever plans they had for her.

"We don't want to lose them for one minute, not one minute," McGuire said.

When he returned from the downtown meeting, Warner went directly to Jeff Weinstein's third-floor office. The news he received was not as bad as he thought it would be. Weinstein produced a two-page summary that showed the company's cash position in the best shape it had been for more than a year.

"We might have to stretch our payables cycle a bit— from thirty to forty-five days," Weinstein said. "Assuming business remains as strong as it has been, we won't be under any immediate pressure for the short term. Long term is another story. I don't think we can make it over the long pull without a major line of credit, but for now we still have most for the $250 million you put up intact."

"That's good news," Warner responded. "That means we don't have to go crawling on our knees to that cocksucker

Sculley. We'll proceed with business as usual. That ought to surprise the bastard."

Barry made another decision. He decided not to pass along word of the bank's action to Pedro and Ramon. The less they knew now the better. It would keep them from panicking.

The electronics specialist imported from Washington had succinct instructions for Carole when he met her and the tailing agents outside her condominium. "Ignore the fact I'm with you. Just do the things you do when you come home—talk to your cats, whatever. Meanwhile, I'll be as quiet as a mouse."

He explained that the electronic sweeping device, which looked to Carole like a bathroom scale, could only detect a bug if active. In all probability, the specialist said, anyone bugging her home would use interceptors planted in a ground-level junction box that could be turned on or off from a remote location. She really didn't have to say a word, he explained. If the system was turned on, the needle on the sweeping device would indicate it immediately.

Carole walked through the front door and greeted Nippon and Claiborne enthusiastically. The technician was on her heels and followed her into the kitchen. He moved toward an ivory-colored wall phone. The needle on the sweeping device sprung to the right. The place was live.

She led him to the rest of the phones in the two-story condo. The result was the same. The interceptor planted in the junction box outside had turned all of her phones into live microphones.

The specialist carefully placed the sweeping device on a living room couch, took out a pad and penned a note to Carole.

Feed the cats and tell them you'll see them later tonight. Then, let's get out of here.

The specialist went through the same scenario with Dan Sculley twenty minutes later . . . with the same result.

Dial Miss Nordstrom's number and leave a message on her answering machine, the technician wrote in a note to the banker. **Tell her you're going shopping and will call her at home later.**

Ferrante, munching on the remnants of a club sandwich and a bag of potato chips from room service, was monitoring two receivers in the living room of the mini-suite he shared with Furry and heard both conversations.

Ferrante's call to Garrettson awakened him from a nap. "Looks like our friends are in the neighborhood tonight," he said.

"I'll be right over there."

Harvey McGuire, the SAC, was not surprised when he learned shortly after seven that his hunch about the bugging was correct and passed the information along to Thaddeus Burden, who was waiting in his Washington, D.C., office for results of the sweep.

"Splendid," the high-ranking FBI executive said enthusiastically. "This puts us in control. We're now in a beautiful position to spring a trap. But for the time being, we must control the movements of Sculley and Nordstrom and what they say. I'll see you in Cleveland tomorrow."

* * *

FBI agents on the surveillance team got their first look at Garrettson in the hotel room when he alighted from the elevator alone, walked briskly out the front door and left the premises in the rented Buick. It was shortly after 9:00 P.M.

Agents on top of the office building noted the movement and radioed the two cars that were positioned to follow the vehicle. Garrettson turned left out of the hotel parking lot onto Hotel Road, turned right on Richmond and headed north. Fifteen minutes later he pulled into the parking lot of Cuyahoga County Airport, got out of the car and walked swiftly to a slender white corporate jet parked on the tarmac. Pedro Cardiz came down the steps to greet him.

They conversed for a minute, then climbed the stairs to the jet. Seconds later, another figure moved out of the darkness near the small airport terminal and went up the stairs and into the aircraft. The stairs retracted and a white door slid down to seal the cabin. Two agents parked in the lot heard the whine of the jet engines, saw the craft taxi to the end of the runway and lift into the sky.

When the sleek aircraft leveled off, Pedro unlatched his seat belt, edged toward the galley and asked what the others wanted to drink. Ramon and Garrettson asked for Scotch. The second man to board the aircraft wanted vodka on the rocks. Pedro poured their drinks and a gin and tonic for himself. He popped open a can of cashews, took a few nuts for himself and handed the can to Garrettson.

The seats were positioned so Pedro and Ramon were facing Garrettson and the other man.

"We appreciate your meeting with us on such short notice," Ramon said to casually attired Tony Hartley, Barry Warner's tennis-playing buddy, confidant and traveling companion. "We're just going to take a little joy ride, then return quickly. We'll have you back in an hour. It's much easier to have a private conversation up here."

"Pretty expensive security, I'd say," Hartley remarked and took a sip of his Scotch.

"Since you were with Barry at the inception of this, we thought we might call upon you for some extracurricular help, for which, may I add, you will be handsomely rewarded."

Ramon reached into his attaché case and took out a large manila envelope that was bulging in the middle.

"This is for you as a token of our sincerity," Ramon said.

Hartley opened the clasp and peered into the envelope and pulled out a stack of bills with a $100 wrapper on it.

"There are nine others like that in the envelope," Pedro said. "And there's more where that came from."

"And what evil deeds do I have to do for this money?" Hartley asked with a smile.

"Nothing evil at all," Pedro said softly. "Sometimes we get the feeling that we are not getting all of the information we need from Barry to make major decisions. He often seems preoccupied."

"Barry's my best friend. He's always been a straight shooter, but he's a very busy man."

"And very honorable," Ramon added. "The kind of guy you can deal with on a handshake."

"Look, let's get to the bottom line," Pedro said. "We just need someone on the inside for Mark to talk with to get a sense of what's going on at Upscale."

"Obviously, Barry has no idea you're talking to me."

"That's right," Ramon said flatly. "And we'd like it to stay that way. We're not asking you to do anything illegal or immoral, but we know how close you are to Barry. We'd like you to be our eyes and ears inside the company. We're willing to pay dearly for that."

Hartley looked at the bulging envelope and the decision was easy. He had never been as close to $50,000 in cash in his life. He certainly never came close to winning anything like that when he was a struggling pro on the satellite pro-tennis circuit. Whatever wealth he had largely had been the result of Barry's generosity and was primarily in Upscale stock.

Barry paid him well for his role as his tennis buddy and traveling companion, but Hartley basically lived from paycheck to paycheck. He was intrigued with the potential to milk the brothers for even more cash.

"I'll try it," he said, not trying to sound too eager. "I guess there's nothing to lose."

Not knowing how much Barry confided in Hartley about the counterfeit perfume situation, Ramon probed the tennis player about Barry's relationship with Carole Nordstrom.

"Oh, you don't have to worry about her," Hartley blurted. "Barry fired her."

"We didn't know that," Ramon said, trying to conceal his surprise. "Is there anything else you think we should know about Upscale?"

"I assume Barry's told you that the bank has cut off our line of credit as of right now. Barry's steaming about it."

Chapter Forty-nine

Dan Sculley thought the showdown with Barry Warner should be on neutral ground and selected a private dining room at the Clevelander Club, atop one of the city's tallest office buildings.

When Barry walked into the room alone at one, Sculley was flanked by Pete Cosgrove, executive vice president, and Howard Dunsmore, a rotund figure who was the bank's senior vice president and legal counsel. They quickly ended an animated conversation and were unsmiling when Warner approached the table and took a seat directly facing Sculley.

"I don't like the odds here," Warner quipped.

You won't like what we have to say to you either, Sculley thought to himself.

"I've taken the liberty of ordering for us. That way we can have the utmost in privacy," Sculley said. Almost on cue, a chubby, dark-haired waitress arrived with mulligatawney soup, chicken salad plates and a pot of steaming coffee.

Warner could never remember a meeting where the tension was so thick. He decided to break the ice.

"Jeff Weinstein has informed me that you have severed our line of credit, which is in direct violation of the agreement we reached back in June when the refinancing package was negotiated," Warner said, trying to remain calm. "You can't do that just on a whim."

"As you recall," Cosgrove jumped in, "that agreement gave us the right to abrogate it in the event of extraordinary circumstances jeopardizing the bank's investment."

"But we're doing very well. Our balance sheet is much improved and I'd say your investment is in a whole lot better shape than it was a few months ago."

"No argument," Sculley responded coldly. "You and your people are to be commended for turning this situation around, but that's not the issue. This is," he said handing Warner a typed two-page document.

Warner studied the document that had been prepared by Carole Nordstrom. It was a tight bill of particulars documenting the counterfeit products-for-money scheme from beginning to end.

"This is pure bullshit," he said, raising his voice several octaves. "It's pure fiction, probably written by that whore you're sleeping with, who—by the way—no longer works for Upscale."

Without warning, Sculley leaned forward and grabbed the retailer by his tie and yanked him forward, tugging on the tie until Warner's face became flushed.

"I'd be very careful about calling anyone a whore, you motherfucker. You're the whore, a dishonest whore at that. You can call it fiction, but we know it's fact. Combined with other information we have gathered, we know you are up to your ass in counterfeiting.

"I think that gives us the right to cut off your credit line and demand that you resign immediately as chairman and chief executive officer of Upscale. By selling bogus merchandise, you've put the reputation, the future of the company and our investment in grave danger."

"You'll have a helluva time proving it," Warner gasped as the banker loosened his grip on the tie.

"I don't think so. We'll start with Mark Spencer, who had the integrity to quit when you proposed to trade your shelf space for blood money."

Warner was devastated at the mention of Mark Spencer. Sculley did not give him a chance to respond.

"We're going to give you until tomorrow morning at nine to sign this," Sculley said, shoving a one-page document into Warner's hand. It was a letter of resignation prepared earlier in the morning by the bank's chief legal counsel. It cited "personal reasons" for leaving the company.

"And if I don't sign it?"

"If you don't sign it, you and the rest of your associates at Upscale will be telling their story to the FBI," said Sculley, knowing full well that they would be doing it whether Warner signed the letter or not.

"Good day, gentleman," said Warner walking toward the door. "You'll be hearing from my attorney. Thanks for the lunch." In the ten minutes he was in the room, Warner never touched the soup or salad.

"What do you think?" Cosgrove asked as soon as Warner closed the door.

"Frankly, I don't give a shit whether he signs it or not. Barry Warner's history."

"You must be the world's biggest schmuck," attorney Seth Garfinkel said after rushing to the gazebo to hear Warner unfold the entire story. "You're worth almost a half billion dollars. Why in God's name would you risk everything in a deal like this? Why didn't you ask for some advice?"

"Because I didn't need a lecture like I'm getting now," Warner sneered. "I rolled the dice and came up with crap. Look, Seth, I pay you for advice and action, not for moralizing. Can you help me or not?"

"First, with Mark Spencer on their side, I don't think you have any choice but to resign. You have no cards to play, but you do have an enormous investment in Upscale. By avoiding a fight with Sculley, who by the way now holds all the cards, you may help protect it.

"Secondly, my guess is that Sculley wants more than just getting you out of Upscale. He wants you behind bars. If I were you, I'd make a call to Preston O'Malley. He's the best criminal lawyer in town. You're going to need someone like him."

Shortly after 5:00 P.M., Dan Sculley's secretary brought him the good news, a faxed copy of Barry Warner's letter of resignation sent from his Hunting Valley home. A note on the transmission sheet said the original would be delivered the next morning. It asked that Sculley or one of his executives contact Seth Garfinkel immediately to discuss timing of the release.

Twenty minutes later Howard Dunsmore, the bank's chief legal counsel, told Garfinkel that the announcement would be made after noon the next day, following a special board meeting called by Dan Sculley. There would be no need for Warner to attend.

"May I remind you," Garfinkel said as he prepared to end the conversation, "that Barry Warner still is the majority stockholder in Upscale. His resignation does not change his shareholder rights."

"Right," Dunsmore said curtly and clicked the receiver.

At that same time Pete Cosgrove was contacting Jeff Weinstein, Jeremy Todd and Walter Hood, the key Upscale management executives on the Upscale board, summoning them to a seven o'clock meeting with Sculley in a private room at Canterbury Golf Club.

Deciding to confront the trio at the same time, Sculley waited until all arrived before springing his surprise, photocopies of the document Sculley had presented to Warner earlier in the day. Weinstein felt like throwing up. Todd slumped back into his upholstered chair. Only Hood, director of store operations, spoke up.

"What do you want from us?" he asked in a semibeligerent tone. "We didn't do anything illegal. This is the first I've heard about counterfeit products since that meeting in June. If Barry did it, he did it on his own."

"On the contrary," Sculley said. "You and the others authorized Warner to proceed with the plan. I'm not a lawyer, but I'd say that's complicity. I have verification of what happened at that meeting from someone else who was there."

"Who?" Hood demanded.

"Mark Spencer . . . Pete give them the letters."

Cosgrove handed each of the executives a manila folder containing an individually typed letter of resignation from his management position and the board.

"I suggest you sign these immediately," Sculley demanded. "It will make things a lot simpler."

Todd wanted to know Barry's status. Sculley said he had already received Barry's resignation. When Hood said he didn't believe it, Sculley reached into his black attaché case and produced a copy of the fax.

Weinstein wanted to know what would happen if they refused to sign.

"You'll have a tough time holding down your job and a director's position from a federal penitentiary."

Cosgrove took three black ballpoint pens from his pocket and handed one to each of the directors. They signed.

"Thank you for putting the interests of the company ahead of your own interest," Sculley said sincerely. "You have my assurance we will honor our contractural and severance obligations to you, as long as you remain publicly silent and do nothing further to harm the corporation. After all, it's in your best interests. You are all substantial stockholders in Upscale."

Sculley waited until Cosgrove and the others left and called Carole at her condominium, where she was alone, except for the two FBI agents stationed in the driveway. He wanted to blurt out the news of Barry's resignation, but quickly remembered the conversation could be bugged.

"Good news," he said cautiously.

"What? she asked eagerly."

"We'll talk about it at dinner. I've made reservations for nine at Nightown. Pick you up at quarter to nine."

Ferrante was monitoring two receivers in his mini-suite at the Embassy Suites when he intercepted the conversation. Garrettson, with two FBI agents in tow, had just left the hotel to meet with Tony Hartley at Flo and Eddie's Sports Bar and was not expected back for an hour.

325

Furry, the more experienced of the two, suggested they leave immediately to case the restaurant. Ferrante found the number in the yellow pages and called for instructions on how to get there.

Furry penned a note to Garrettson: **Gone hunting. See you later.**

Chapter Fifty

Furry and Ferrante had about forty-five minutes to survey the situation and made the most of it. They drove to the area in separate cars, parked one on a nearby street and continued the rest of the way together. Located at the top of Cedar Hill near the boundary of Cleveland Heights and Cleveland, Nightown occupied the entire ground floor of an old three-story building, which had apartments on the top two levels. A parking lot on one side accommodated about a dozen cars, but in the evening patrons used the bank parking lot across the street. A back door of the restaurant opened to a large municipally operated lot with parking meters and special permit slots.

Furry parked the car in the bank lot across the way. The two walked across busy Cedar Road and entered the restaurant with two couples who arrived at the same time. The couples were wearing casual clothes. Furry and Ferrante were wearing sport jackets to hide their weapons. The pair took the last two stools at an L-shaped bar in front of the place and ordered—Ferrante a Bud, Furry Michelob Light.

Furry—thin, wiry and slightly balding—asked the bartender for directions to the men's room. He walked through a small dining room to the rear of the restaurant and turned to the right. He could see a larger dining room with a bar that ran parallel to the one on the other side of the wall—the one at which they were seated.

On the way back, he passed through another dining room with four tables separated by wooden and glass partitions down one wall and mostly tables for two and four throughout the rest of the room. That dining room was crowded and only a few tables for two were empty. The burgundy walls were covered with paintings, photographs and old artifacts; the lighting was low and intimate.

Furry returned to the bar, chatted briefly with the muscular, dark-haired Ferrante and then turned to strike up a conversation with an attractive blonde seated next to him. She and an equally attractive female turned out to be flight attendants for Continental. Furry thought that at another time the two would have presented great possibilities.

Sculley and Nordstrom arrived through the front door at a few minutes after nine, walked to the end of the bar and were greeted by the maitre d', who gushed over them like long lost friends and promptly seated them at a partitioned table for four.

Harvey McGuire, Thaddeus Burden and two female agents were seated at a rectangular table a few feet away. Sculley acknowledged their presence with a wave of his left hand from hip level.

Two other agents were positioned at a table for two across on the opposite wall. Six others were spread throughout the remainder of the restaurant and bar.

Furry and Ferrante each had another round, paid their check and left. Two agents at the other end of the bar noted their departure, assumed they were not the pair from

Chicago and turned their attentions to watch the comings and goings of other patrons.

The two hit men drove about three miles to Shaker Boulevard and stopped in front of a large red brick home set on about an acre of land. Only a single lamp was lit in the front window. Ferrante walked down a long driveway, hugging a tall line of shrubs all the way. He walked across the back lawn and into the adjoining yard. He stopped at the nearest corner of a large English tudor home, took a pair of wire cutters from his coat pocket and snipped a thick telephone cable entering the house.

They drove back to where Ferrante had left the other rented car, a black four-door Ford Taurus. Four FBI agents stationed near the back of the restaurant did not notice the car when it pulled into the municipal lot and settled in a space about two hundred feet away.

Furry drove the other car out of the lot through a rear driveway, stopped and removed a tiny cellular phone from his pocket. He dialed the Nightown and said it was urgent he speak to Mr. Dan Sculley. The maitre d' knew just where to find him.

Sculley left the table. The right hand of every FBI agent in the dining room automatically moved to a position that would facilitate grabbing a weapon.

"We have your daughter Jennifer," the caller said in a gruff voice. "We grabbed her and a friend on the way home from a softball game."

"Who are you?"

"Never mind who I am. Just do as I say and nobody will get hurt. Cross us and you'll never see your daughter again."

"What do you want from me?"

"Pay the check now. Then you and the lady with you casually walk out the back door. There's a black Ford Taurus parked in a spot to the right in the last row of the parking lot. Go to the car and get inside. The keys are in the ignition. We'll give you further instructions when you get into the car."

"A black Taurus. I understand."

"Now, remember what I said," Furry said emphatically. Don't cross us. I'm calling on a cellular phone. One false move and I'll dial a partner who's with your daughter and friend. He's not at all bashful about killing teenagers. You got ten minutes to get into the Taurus."

Sculley hung up the phone, glanced at his Rolex and dialed his ex-wife's number. A recorded phone message reported the line out of order. Fearing that his anxiety had prompted him to dial the wrong number, he tried again. Same message. He was ashen when he returned to the table.

"What's wrong?" Carole asked. "Are you ill?"

Sculley could barely get the words out about the phone call.

"Did you call your ex-wife?"

"The phone company says the line is out of order."

Sensing there was something wrong, but not wanting to blow their cover in case the hit men were in the restaurant, Harvey McGuire strolled over to Sculley's table and shook his hand as if he were greeting a long-time friend.

"They've kidnapped my daughter," Sculley blurted at the SAC.

"Hold on. Start from the beginning."

Sculley told him about the phone call.

"Look, in all probability they are bluffing and cut the phone line to heighten your anxiety," the AIC said.

"How can you be sure?" Sculley demanded.

"I can't. What's your ex-wife's address?"

Though the banker had lived in the home for years, he strained to remember the number and finally choked it out to McGuire.

"It's about five minutes from here," Sculley said.

"I'll be back in a few minutes. You pay the check and get ready to go, but don't leave without me."

Sculley looked at his watch. It had been five minutes since he hung up the phone.

McGuire went to the men's room. Two sections of the day's *Wall Street Journal* were spread under the two urinals. He looked around, saw no one was in a stall with a door, went inside and spoke firmly into a handheld radio. He instructed two agents in the front of the restaurant to proceed directly to the address on Shaker Boulevard. They were to verify the presence of Mrs. Sculley, her daughter and son.

"Don't turn on the siren," McGuire said, "but get there as fuckin' fast as you can and report back to me immediately with an affirmative if the daughter is there, a negative if she's not. Then he selected another channel on the radio.

Acting on instinct, the SAC assumed the hit men were not in the place. "Code blue," he said. "At the back door."

Most of the agents in the restaurant left their tables and the bar and headed for the ramp leading to the back door. The two female agents and Thaddeus Burden remained in their seats.

Returning to the table, McGuire asked Nordstrom and Sculley to get up and head for the back door, but not to leave the restaurant until he gave them a signal.

"We gotta go," he said to Burden and the two female agents and quickly explained the situation on the way to the back door.

McGuire coolly briefed the agents at the back door ramp and then sent two couples into the lot with instructions to stop and converse as if they had arrived in separate cars and were chatting before saying good night. One of the male agents, wearing a navy blue blazer and light gray pants, just like Sculley, had the same build as the banker.

His blonde female companion looked a lot like Carole Nordstrom and was dressed almost identically to the retail executive in white pants suit with red blouse. McGuire and Burden had reasoned that in the darkness it would be difficult for anyone to distinguish between the real Nordstrom and Sculley and the agents posing as the couple.

The two couples went out the back door, strolled down a short walk and stopped to chat at the edge of the parking lot. One couple waited for one of the FBI cars in the lot to blink its lights, a signal to cross the lot.

Inside the restaurant, Sculley agonized and kept looking at his watch. It had been seventeen minutes since he hung up the phone.

"Don't worry," the SAC assured him. "Nobody can tell that it's not Miss Nordstrom and you in the parking lot. I'm sure whoever is out there believes you are following their directions."

Finally, McGuire's radio crackled. "Affirmative."

"Your kid's okay," McGuire said with a smile. "Go to the bar and have a good stiff drink. Don't leave until we come and get you."

Using the portable radio, McGuire calmly issued a series of commands to his units in front and behind the restaurant, then ordered the flashing headlight signal. The Sculley/Nordstrom look-alikes began walking across the lot.

Ferrante was hunched in the back seat of the Taurus with a 9mm pistol and silencer in his right hand. Furry had ducked behind a large trash bin near one of several apartment buildings flanking one side of the parking lot. The

332

screeching sound of peeling rubber startled him. Within an instant three cars had surrounded the black Taurus, a fourth blocked his view of the couple walking across the lot.

Ferrante heard the commotion, picked up his head and looked into the blinding beam of a powerful flashlight shining through the rear window. When he heard one of the agents shout "FBI," he dropped the gun on the floor and surrendered peacefully.

Furry decided to make a run for his car, parked on a side street about 100 yards from the lot. He broke from behind the trash container about the time a car with two agents pulled the wrong way into a one-way exit out of the lot.

The agent behind the wheel rammed the car into reverse, backed out onto the main street and headed toward the fleeing gunman. Furry turned, dropped to his knees and fired a volley of shots at the windshield of the beige Chevy.

Two bullets shattered the windshield, but whistled between the agents and exited the rear window. The driver jammed on the brakes and brought the car to a skidding stop about twenty-five feet from the gunman, who was still firing. The other agent opened the door, slid to the ground on his belly and fired. One bullet caught Furry in the chest, a second rocketed through the cheekbone just below the right eye. As Furry tumbled forward, the other agent put another bullet into his head for good measure. A moment later, McGuire, Burden and a dozen other agents were standing over the lifeless Furry.

Mark Garrettson was just watching the tailend of *The Tonight Show* to kill time until the two associates returned from what he hoped was a successful mission. Suddenly, a local newsman interrupted the program with a bulletin.

"FBI agents tonight thwarted the attempted kidnapping of the chairman of First Union Trust and a female companion outside a Cleveland Heights restaurant. Details are sketchy, but an FBI spokesman just confirmed that one of the assailants was captured, the other killed. Chairman Dan Sculley and the woman, identified as Carole Nordstrom, an executive with Upscale, were unharmed. Stay tuned for details."

"Fuck," Garrettson shouted at the screen, then cut the power. Using a portable cellular phone, he called his pilot in Chicago, instructed him to round up the co-pilot and to pick him up as soon as possible at Cuyahoga County Airport.

"Call me on my private cellular number as soon as you have an ETA. We'll be going to New York," he said.

Deciding to travel light, he grabbed only his attaché case, slid out the door, walked down the emergency stairs from the third floor and exited through a rear door into the parking lot. Fearing the FBI might have spotted his car, he walked behind several office building to the Marriott Hotel and checked in.

On the way out of the hotel four hours later, Garrettson grabbed a copy of the *Cleveland Plain Dealer*, tucked it under his arm and got into a waiting cab for the airport.

Airborne on the way to New York, Garrettson finally unfolded the paper and learned to his dismay that he had a double dose of bad news for Pedro and Ramon.

Chapter Fifty-one

The remnants of the Upscale board—nine out of thirteen—sat in stunned silence in the bank conference room as Dan Sculley pledged them to secrecy and painted the sordid details of Warner's counterfeit plan and the resignation of Upscale's founder and the others. Looking none the worse for the previous evening's ordeal, the banker admitted his role in chairing the meeting was unusual, given that he had no official title, no seat on the board. Describing the situation as highly unusual, he said the bank's high-risk loan position and $500 million stake in the company justified bold action. There wasn't a dissent.

Not wanting to divulge too much, Sculley told the board that the FBI had launched a preliminary investigation into the sale of counterfeit perfume, but declined to be more specific. One of the board members wanted to know whether the previous evening's attempted kidnapping plot had anything to do with the probe.

"The only thing I will say is that we are cooperating with the authorities in this entire matter," Sculley said.

The key issue now, he told the others, was to protect the reputation of the company and to develop a plan to deal with

335

any adverse action that could damage sales, if and when the counterfeit operation became public information. That, he explained, was the reason it was vital to keep the information within the confines of the boardroom.

Sculley said he was recommending two major steps to hastily rebuild company management—the immediate election of Carole Nordstrom as president and chief executive officer and the rehiring of Mark Spencer as chairman and chief operating officer, with both being elected to the board. The vote to accept the proposals was unanimous.

Sculley's secretary summoned Spencer and Nordstrom from the bank chairman's office where they had been waiting since the start of the meeting. When Spencer took a seat at the head of the table, Sculley praised him for his integrity in resigning over the counterfeit issue.

"If others involved had been as courageous, we probably wouldn't be in this mess right now," the banker said.

At the conclusion of the board meeting, Sculley read a brief four-paragraph news release announcing the resignation of Warner and the three others as well as the election of Spencer and Nordstrom to the key management positions.

Quoting Sculley, the release said the resignations resulted from a "clash in management philosophy" between executives of the firm and its principal outside shareholder and financial lender. The release stressed that Sculley and Warner would have no further comment.

By noon, the banks PR department had faxed the release to the Press Release Newswire in New York and it was disseminated to every major newspaper, wire service, broadcast news outlet and business magazine in the country. Members of the bank's PR staff personally delivered copies of the release to all local media.

As the news was being disseminated, Nordstrom and Spencer were huddling with the remaining key management personnel. The new chairman and president scheduled a meeting for all headquarters people for two o'clock and a chainwide broadcast over Upscale's satellite network for three.

Word of the four resignations and the top management changes spread through headquarters like wildfire. It made no sense to anyone.

The public relations departments of the bank and Upscale were deluged with requests for further information and the availability of key executives and Sculley for interviews. The response was the same. The four-paragraph news release said it all.

The entrance to Barry Warner's estate was so crowded with news media that Warner's security guard finally called Hunting Valley police for help in dispersing the crowd.

Barry was taking no phone calls and for good reason: He had an enormous hangover. At noon he was barely coherent.

The Cardiz brothers and Mark Garrettson were sitting in Ramon's office pondering their options when Pedro's secretary rushed into the room with the Upscale management change announcement, which had just moved across the Dow-Jones Wire.

Based on a small article contained on the business page of the newspaper picked up by Garrettson at the Marriott, they were not totally surprised. Resulting from a well-placed leak to a newspaper business reporter, the story—without going into detail—speculated that major management changes, including the resignation of Barry Warner and other directors, would be announced later in the day.

The brothers were furious that Warner had not communicated with them.

"With Barry Warner out of Upscale our deal is dead, and we're out $250 million," Pedro said.

"I can't imagine why Barry would resign and do it without talking with us," Ramon said. "He has controlling interest in the company and from our last conversation, Upscale was doing much better financially."

"Obviously, there was extreme pressure from someone, probably Sculley," Pedro responded. "My hunch is that Nordstrom went to Sculley about the perfume incident and convinced him that Barry was part of it. That started the ball rolling. Sculley threatened Warner with going to the cops, Warner panicked and resigned."

"That goddamned botched kidnapping didn't help matters much, either," Ramon said. "We'd have been much better off if the feds got both of your friends. Do you think the survivor will talk?"

"First of all, he has no idea who hired him, except me," Garrettson said. "Secondly, guys like that wouldn't give you the time of day."

"At least that's encouraging," Pedro said.

"Look, the bottom line right here is this," Ramon interjected. "If push comes to shove, I think we can trust Barry to remain silent. As far as I know he's the only one living who can link Upscale to us."

"I don't agree with you," said Pedro, rising from his seat and pacing. "Right now, I wouldn't trust Barry Warner for a minute. He's out for only one person: Barry Warner.

Frankly, I think we have to do something about him and quickly."

"I'll buy that, but right now my concern is getting back a good portion of the $250 million we gave Warner to save his company."

"We have his stock as collateral," Pedro said.

"What do we do—go to Sculley and tell them we want to sell the stock back to the company. You and I know it's worth shit without Warner running the show. I think we make it very clear to Mr. Warner that we want a refund. Now."

"Hey," Pedro said, "if he had the ability to come up with $250 million in cash, he wouldn't have needed us in the first place."

"I don't think you understand, Pedro," Ramon said sarcastically. "In that instance, we were talking about money to save his company. This time, we're talking about $250 million to save his ass. He'll come up with it. Then we'll close out this deal."

Chapter Fifty-two

The security guard at the entrance to Barry Warner's estate shoved aside the orange barricade that had blocked the media from entering the grounds and directed two FBI cars up the red brick drive to the house. Warner, dressed in pale yellow slacks, a brown polo shirt and sandals, greeted Harvey McGuire, Thaddeus Burden and a third agent, a special assistant to Burden. He led them to the gazebo, where his housekeeper had set up a tray of soft drinks and iced tea. The agents helped themselves to iced tea.

When they were seated on white wicker chairs in one corner of the octagon-shaped, open-air structure, McGuire officially informed the retailer that he was the subject of a federal investigation that involved trafficking in counterfeit merchandise and, possibly, aiding and abetting the kidnap attempt of Dan Sculley and Carole Nordstrom.

McGuire read him his rights.

Warner's throat went dry and he could barely speak. His head was still throbbing from an overdose of vodka.

"I suppose I should have my lawyer here with me," Warner said. In fact, he *had* tried to reach Seth Garfinkel, but his personal and corporate attorney was in court.

340

Warner had not gotten around to contacting the criminal lawyer Garfinkel had recommended. Barry decided to wing it.

"Now that we have gone through the formalities, Mr. Warner, maybe we can be of some help to each other," said Burden, who identified himself as one of the bureau's top officials.

"Frankly, it's my opinion that we have enough evidence to charge you right now on several counterfeiting counts," Burden continued. "As our investigation into the kidnapping attempt develops we'll address the possibility of additional counts."

"Let's get one thing straight right now," Warner said sharply. "I had nothing... nothing... to do with the attempted kidnapping of Carole Nordstrom and her lover."

"If that's the way it shakes out you have nothing to fear in that regard," McGuire said.

"As I said when we started, we may both be able to help each other, Mr. Warner," Burden said in a conciliatory way. "Hostility may win you a lot of points in the retail arena, but it's going to get you nowhere here. Let me put it to you in a nutshell. Because of your excellent reputation as a businessman and no previous record, you may get away with minimal punishment for counterfeit sales.

"Not an awful lot of people have gone to jail for that crime. We had a case recently in which several people were convicted of running a $100-million-a-year counterfeit athletic shoe ring. No one went to jail. Judges tend to take into consideration the defendant's cooperation with the authorities.

"If we can tie you to the kidnapping attempt, that's a horse of a different color."

341

"Look," the exasperated Warner said, "I don't know what I have to say to convince you of the fact, I had nothing to do with the kidnapping. I didn't know about it until I read the newspaper this afternoon."

Burden took off his gray suit jacket, tossed it on the back of an empty chair and poured another glass of iced tea. He turned his back to Warner and started pacing back and forth.

"Let me tell you what else we know, Mr. Warner. We know that funds were transferred from Commonwealth Investment Services to your bank accounts in Chicago the day you and the lending banks worked out your differences.

"We also know a lot about your partners in this scheme, probably more than you do. Ramon and Pedro Cardiz are the sons of one of the world's most evil men, Raul Cardiz, a multi-billionaire drug czar in Colombia. Raul Cardiz has been responsible for hundreds of deaths around the world, including this country.

"We are convinced that money from that drug empire was used to start this counterfeit operation and remains a method for laundering substantial amounts of money on a continuing basis."

Warner sat silently, taking it all in, wondering how Burden and his men had assembled all of the information without tipping their hand.

"Yours is not the first company that Commonwealth has infiltrated with its shelf-space-for-cash ploy," Burden continued. "We are trying to make it the last. It may also interest you to know that it was nothing you or anyone in your company did that sent us looking at Upscale. It was a totally unrelated situation, involving a large auto parts retailer in the midwest. By the way, the owner of that chain was blown to bits because he crossed Pedro and Ramon Cardiz.

"These are extraordinarily dangerous people to whom human life means absolutely nothing. Frankly, with you out of the Upscale picture and armed with knowledge of the Commonwealth principals, I wouldn't take any bets on your long-term chances for survival."

Warner swallowed hard, digesting what the high-powered FBI executive had to say. The counterfeit products case was pretty solid. The mention of potential kidnapping charges scared him to death.

"Over my working lifetime, I've made hundreds of deals," Warner said, breaking a long silence. "Most of them have been done on gut reaction. Then I sent in the lawyers to tidy things up. I feel that way about this situation. What do you want me to do and what's in it for me?"

"I'll answer the second part of your question first," Burden said. "In the final analysis, we'll limit your exposure in this case to the counterfeit operations. There will be no more mention of the kidnapping charges."

"Fair enough," said Warner who knew a good deal when he saw it.

"Now," McGuire stepped in, "we want to know everything about the Commonwealth operation and your involvement, from the first moment you contacted them or they contacted you."

Warner got up, poured a vodka and tonic and started talking. By eight o'clock, he was famished and suggested they take a dinner break. Burden agreed. Warner telephoned the kitchen and asked his housekeeper to grill four steaks and prepare a salad.

Warner disappeared into the house and returned in a kelly green bathing suit and dived into the swimming pool.

"Just clearing the cobwebs," he said when he emerged and slipped into a white terrycloth robe that had been left on a chaise lounge.

The four dined on strip steaks, a Greek salad and fresh cut French fries and talked. It was mostly a monologue. McGuire, Burden and his assistant occasionally interrupted with a question. The assistant took notes on three-by-five cards, building a stack on a nearby table that reached almost three inches high.

McGuire wanted to know how Warner expected to get away with the scheme.

"It's the technology," Barry answered. "With barcodes, point-of-sale registers and automated warehouses, product identification has been reduced to a few vertical lines and some numbers. Entire truckloads of merchandise virtually come and go without being touched by human hands. They are directed through the warehouses by scanners and computers."

The FBI agents were impressed.

As the questions came to a close around midnight, Burden wanted to know how much of the $250 million Warner still owed the Cardiz brothers. Warner said the deal was so short-lived there had been no accounting as yet. He guessed the counterfeit product purchases by Upscale had made a minimal impact on the debt.

"You did say they had $250 million in your Upscale stock as collateral?" Burden asked.

"I'd say it would be very difficult at this time for them to cash in on it. We're essentially a privately held company. With Sculley running things, I'd say damn near impossible."

"I'm sure they realize that," Burden said. "Which means that very soon they'll probably be asking you for the money that's due them. I promise you they'll be very persuasive."

"As long as the Cardiz brothers think they have a chance to collect what you owe them, we don't believe you are in any immediate danger," McGuire added. "We must be notified the second you are contacted by someone from Commonwealth. Then we'll deal with the second part of our plan."

"In the meantime, you are extraordinarily important to this case, and we don't want to take any chances," Burden said. "We want to put taps on your phones and begin twenty-four-hour surveillance as soon as possible. We assume you have room in the house for a team of agents."

Warner laughed. "How many rooms do you want?"

Chapter Fifty-three

Thaddeus Burden was right. Pedro and Ramon wanted their money back in a hurry. Wary about contacting Warner directly, they used his good friend Tony Hartley as an intermediary. In a detailed phone conversation from an East 57th Street pay phone to Hartley's condo in Beachwood, Pedro was charming, but firm. Hartley took notes on a yellow legal pad.

Pedro told Hartley the obvious—with Barry out of Upscale, their deal was dead. Commonwealth was entitled to a complete refund of the money it had advanced to Warner. The brothers set a one-week deadline for return of the funds—the method to be determined later.

Tony interrupted Pedro to suggest that given the problem Barry had raising the money in June, a week might not be enough time. Hartley said he knew the entire sum had long since been transferred into Upscale's accounts and was out of his friends hands.

"I'm sure if you stress the urgency of the matter, Barry can find a way to do it," Pedro said, not saying what would happen if Warner failed to meet the deadline.

"Obviously, I can't speak for Barry," Hartley said, "I know he'll want to speak with you directly."

"When he's ready, get in touch with me and we'll make some secure kind of arrangements to communicate."

The conversation between Barry Warner, calling from a tapped pay phone at Cleveland-Hopkins International Airport, and Pedro at another pay phone in Manhattan took place at noon on Saturday. Pedro was low key. He said the brothers were sorry the way things had worked out, but— given the circumstances—it was best the two sides wound up their affairs quickly.

Pedro wanted to know why Warner left the company so abruptly. Warner said Sculley, aware of the bogus perfume and, like Nordstrom, convinced that Warner had sold shelf space for the right to place counterfeit products in Upscale, had threatened to go to the police with Nordstrom, unless Barry resigned.

"I was just trying to protect us all," he said.

Barry agreed wholeheartedly that it was time to put the counterfeiting deal to bed. He said returning most of the $250 million would be no problem because as part of the resignation settlement, Sculley had agreed to compensate Warner for a good part of the money he put into the company in June.

Warner said he was expecting a bank check for a still unspecified amount on Monday and would endorse it over to Commonwealth. In return, of course, he wanted possession of the Upscale stock certificates held by the brothers.

Given the circumstances, including the botched kidnapping of Sculley and Nordstrom, which he assumed was the work of Mark Garrettson, Warner said the endorsed check made more sense to him than depositing the money in his account and then transferring it back to Commonwealth. Besides, Warner told him, a portion of the money would be in cash he had skimmed from the business over the years."

"Look," Warner said, "Tony Hartley and I are heading south to my place in Palm Beach next week to play some tennis and enjoy the new boat I purchased a year ago. Fortunately, I still have some of the trappings of power. I personally bought the Canadair Challenger airplane and leased it back to the company. It's mine and I intend to use it.

"I have two suggestions. One we could wrap this thing up and play some tennis in Palm Beach. Or we can meet you and Ramon somewhere enroute. I'll trade the check for the stock certificates."

"I like the idea of meeting somewhere enroute," Pedro said. "As it turns out, Ramon and I will be in North Carolina on Wednesday. That might be a good day. I'll get back to you with the precise details through Tony."

"I think he bought into the whole deal," Thaddeus Burden said when Warner hung up the phone. Burden had been monitoring the call in a small nearby office provided by airport officials. Another agent brought Warner into the room.

"Well done," Burden said. "Now comes the tough part."

"How's that?" Warner wanted to know.

"Making sure that nothing happens to you and Tony Hartley. We can't really do anything about that until we know where you're going. Secondly, we have to dummy up a check in such a way that we don't jeopardize Uncle Sam's money and come up with a couple of million in hundred dollar bills."

The Challenger took off just after nine on Wednesday morning for a rendezvous two hours later with Commonwealth's Boeing 737 at Kinston Regional Airport in Kinston, North Carolina, about thirty miles from Greenville. Warner and Hartley were not alone. Four agents from the Cleveland FBI office were riding with the two and a special cargo—two million in cash—stashed in a navy blue athletic bag.

Hartley did not know the agents were going along. On advice from Burden, Warner didn't mention the purpose of the trip to Hartley, other than it was a fun trip.

It was only when the one-time tennis pro arrived at the airport fifteen minutes before take-off that he learned there was a stop on the way to West Palm Beach; Barry was going to meet with Pedro and Ramon to collect his stock certificates. The agents were along to make sure nothing happened to Warner and Hartley, he said.

Thaddeus Burden was already in Kinston along with a small army of agents, including expert marksmen from headquarters and a dozen more from North Carolina. A half dozen agents were on or near the tarmac, posing as ramp workers and workmen putting down a new roof on the small general aviation terminal.

Warner's jet was on the ground with the stairs retracted and the cabin door still closed when Commonwealth's 737 landed and taxied toward the terminal. Warner recognized it as the same plane the brothers had used for their tour months ago. The larger jet taxied to within seventy-five feet of the Canadair. The engines went silent. A moment later

Warner saw Pedro in the doorway beckoning him to come to the plane.

Tony Hartley came down the stairs first, followed by Warner, who was struggling to get the blue athletic bag filled with money down the stairs. He almost fell forward once, but quickly grabbed the handrail.

As Warner started up the stairs of the 737, two FBI marksmen disguised as roofers crawled into positions behind several rolls of roofing material. The scope on one of the agent's high-powered rifles was focused on the front tires of the 737. The other was aimed at the open doorway of the plane. Pedro and Ramon had warm greetings for Hartley and Warner when they reached the cabin.

Thaddeus Burden, sitting in a small room in the terminal, heard every word of their conversation. Warner was wired with a sophisticated remote microphone rigged by an FBI electronics specialist.

Warner, seated at a table facing the brothers, opened his attaché case and pulled out a small letter-sized envelope. He removed four yellow bank checks drawn on Continental Bank of Illinois, each in the amount of $55 million. He turned them over and endorsed each with a thick black Mont Blanc pen.

"Here's $220 million," he said. "There's another two million in cash in the bag I brought with me. That's all you're getting. I'm keeping the rest for the aggravation you cost me, to say nothing about the job."

"Fair enough," Ramon said.

"This whole thing has been one fuck-up after another," Warner said. "When we made this deal, you promised we would get nothing but quality merchandise; then you deliver garbage and get my executive vice president so bent out of shape she threatens to go to the cops, and then almost gets herself killed by your goons."

"We're sorry about the perfume, but there's nothing we can do about it now," Ramon said.

The co-pilot came out of the cockpit to take a drink order. "It's a little early, but why not," Barry said, ordering a vodka on the rocks. Hartley ordered the same, the brothers Scotch on the rocks.

When the drinks were served, Barry raised his glass. "Cheers. Here's to a great deal that got royally fucked up. And you guys had the nerve to ask for your money back. I'm glad it's over."

"Relax, Barry, you're not going anywhere, except with us," said Mark Garrettson as he stepped through a small door to another compartment at the rear of the aircraft. He was pointing a 9mm revolver at Warner. A second man entered the cabin and aimed a gun at Hartley.

"What's all the artillery for?" Hartley said jokingly.

"You're taking a trip with us," Garrettson said.

Pedro picked up the intercom phone. "Close the door, start the engines and let's get out of here," he commanded.

"Okay, guys, let's do it," Burden shouted into his hand-held radio and bolted out of terminal door.

Before the pilot could close the door, an FBI marksman on the roof fired a smoke grenade into the cabin, instantly filling it with thick, choking smoke. The second marksman punctured the tires.

The gunman standing next to Garrettson, a Colombian imported from Cali especially for the trip, panicked and fired his weapon wildly. One shot tore into Tony Hartley's right shoulder; the second pierced his heart. Warner, choking from the smoke, heard the shots, dived to the floor and landed with his face on Hartley's bleeding chest.

"Stop shooting, Guillermo, you'll kill us all," Garrettson screamed as the smoke engulfed the entire cabin.

"This is the FBI. Don't move," Burden shouted through a power megaphone. "Don't move."

A half dozen gun-toting agents wearing gas masks stormed the aircraft. There was no resistance, only the sounds of wheezing and coughing as the brothers, Garrettson and the Colombian gunman groped for the doorway. Barry Warner silently hugged the floor.

At the same moment, hundreds of agents across the country were raiding Commonwealth's headquarters in New York, its various distribution entities across the country and Mammouth Trucking Company's main office in St. Louis.

By the time the smoke cleared in the plane, agents had dragged Garrettson, his bosses and the gunman down the stairs and forced them to lie face down on the tarmac, surrounded by a dozen agents wearing black vinyl jackets with the yellow letters FBI emblazened on the back.

Warner, his face and clothes stained with Tony Hartley's blood, took one last look at his dead friend and staggered down the stairs, followed by an agent carrying the navy blue athletic bag containing the cash.

Burden ordered the Columbians and Garrettson to their feet and watched as agents cuffed them.

"You're under arrest," he said.

"For what? Pedro gasped."

"Let's start with murder and kidnapping, then for good measure we'll throw in trafficking in counterfeit merchandise. Any more questions?"

Chapter Fifty-four

The Cardiz brothers went on trial in U.S. District Court in New York in early January, but the trial lasted only three weeks. The government had the deck stacked.

Mark Garrettson testified against the Colombians in return for a reduced sentence and government protection, if and when he was ever released from prison alive. Warner and Joe Longo each were on the stand for three days.

Sensing that the brothers were in a hopeless situation, the expensive legal team assembled to defend them offered to plea bargain in mid-trial. Wanting to get the entire story before the American people, government prosecutors refused.

For nearly three weeks, the story received top media billing across the country, shell shocking consumers into the fact that many of the products they purchase in their favorite stores might not be the real thing.

When the trial was over, the jury convicted the brothers on every count, 250 in all, ranging from ordering the murder of Sonny Longo and the kidnap attempt of Sculley and Nordstrom to multiple instances of trafficking in counterfeit goods.

After denouncing them as the kingpins of the $200-billion-dollar-a-year international counterfeiting business, Federal Judge George Heard threw the book at them. Each got a thirty-five-year sentence

In Cali, Colombia, Raul Cardiz offered to fold up his U.S. drug operations in return for the freeing of his two sons. U.S. Attorney Mortimer Alvarez, the chief prosecutor, called the proposed deal a "joke" and laughed at him at a news conference.

Joe Longo's cooperation won him a total reprieve from prosecution. He was already on the road to legitimately rebuilding the regional retail auto parts chain prostituted by his father.

Under the leadership of Carole Nordstrom and Mark Spencer, Upscale quickly put the counterfeiting problem to rest and, with funds provided by Dan Sculley's bank, moved aggressively to remodel existing stores and move into new markets. A new fashion line introduced by Upscale won Nordstrom accolades throughout the industry and won her an award as "retail executive of the year" from a major magazine.

The romance between Carole Nordstrom and Dan Sculley flourished. On the anniversary of their first meeting, they were married at a small ceremony at Canterbury Golf Club.

Thaddeus Burden kept his end of the deal with Barry Warner. The U.S. Attorney's office allowed the disgraced retailer to plead guilty to one count of trafficking in counterfeit merchandise. Federal Judge Herbert Brown, rejecting the pleas of dozens of friends, civic leaders and others for leniency, fined him $250,000 and sentenced him to three years in jail and one thousand hours of community service when he was released. He served eighteen months at a minimum security prison in Michigan.

Ironically, the day he walked out of prison was the first day of an initial public offering of Upscale stock. His $500 million investment more than doubled overnight. As much as he hated Dan Sculley, he could thank the banker for that.

On an unusually warm fall day, FBI Agent Hal Spear sat in the Birmingham, Michigan, office of Dr. Gerard Freeman. In contrast to the bitterness Spear had encountered months before when he called for information on his son, Robert, the doctor was warm and friendly. Time had a way of healing, Spear thought. A picture of the son, his wife and two children who had perished in the I-90 accident was in a gold frame on the edge of the mahogony desk.

For more than an hour, Spear described to Dr. Freeman how that tragic, but isolated, traffic accident on the highway near Erie, Pennsylvania, had been the spark that eventually brought down one of the world's largest counterfeiting operations.